THE AWKWARD SQUAD

Sophie Hénaff

THE AWKWARD SQUAD

Translated from the French by
Sam Gordon

MacLehose Press
New York • London

MacLehose Press
An imprint of Quercus
New York • London

Copyright © Editions Albin Michel—Paris 2015
English translation copyright © 2017 by Sam Gordon
First published in the United States by Quercus in 2018

ISBN 978-1-68144-003-3

Library of Congress Cataloging-in-Publication Data

Names: Hénaff, Sophie, author.
Title: The awkward squad / Sophie Hénaff.
Other titles: Poulets grillés. English
Description: First edition. | New York : MacLehose Press, [2018]
Identifiers: LCCN 2017045299 (print) | LCCN 2017053710 (ebook) | ISBN 9781681440019 (ebook) | ISBN 9781681440002 (library ebook) | ISBN 9781681440033 (hardcover) | ISBN 9781681440026 (softcover)
Subjects: LCSH: Policewomen—Fiction. | Cold cases (Criminal investigation)—Fiction. | BISAC: FICTION / Mystery & Detective / Police Procedural. | FICTION / Mystery & Detective / Women Sleuths. | GSAFD: Mystery fiction.
Classification: LCC PQ2708.E53 (ebook) | LCC PQ2708.E53 P6813 2018 (print) | DDC 843/.92—dc23
LC record available at https://lccn.loc.gov/2017045299

Distributed in the United States and Canada by
Hachette Book Group
1290 Avenue of the Americas
New York, NY 10104

Manufactured in the United States

10 9 8 7 6 5 4 3 2 1

www.quercus.com

To my own little gang,
and my parents too.

Glossary

36, quai des Orfèvres—the iconic headquarters of the *police judiciare* in Paris; division often referred to by its address alone

brigade criminelle—the murder squad; combines elements of the American homicide division and major crimes unit; responsible for investigating murders, kidnappings, and assassinations; referred to colloquially as *la crim*

brigades centrales—the division of the six central brigades within the *police judiciare*, including the *brigade criminelle*

brigade de protection de mineurs—brigade dealing with the protection of children: kidnappings, distressed families, abuse

brigade de répression du banditisme (BRB)—the antigang squad

brigade mondaine—the vice squad

capitaine—captain; senior to *lieutenant* and junior to *commandant*

brigadier—sergeant

commandant—chief of detectives

commissaire—police commissioner, a rank just below that of *divisionnaire*; has both administrative and investigative roles plus full police powers

commissariat de police—the police station serving as the *commissaire*'s headquarters

divisionnaire (commissaire divisionnaire)—chief of police, one rank up from *commissaire*; has both administrative and investigative roles, plus full police powers *juge d'instruction*—"investigating judge"; responsible for determining if a case should go to trial; a role somewhat similar to that of an American district attorney

IGS (inspection générale des services)—French police monitoring service; equivalent to the internal affairs division of an American law enforcement agency

lieutenant—the first rank of the French police officer's scale

police judiciaire—the criminal investigation division of the *police nationale*; equivalent to the American Federal Bureau of Investigation (FBI)

RAID (recherche, assistance, intervention, dissuasion): the elite law enforcement unit of the French police; deals with counterterrorism and surveillance of high-profile criminals

1

Paris, August 9, 2012

Anne Capestan was standing at her kitchen window waiting for dawn to arrive. She drained her mug in one gulp and set it down on the shiny green tablecloth. She had just drunk her last coffee as a police officer. Or had she?

The brilliant Commissaire Capestan—the star of her generation, undisputed career-ladder-climbing champion—had fired one bullet too many. As a result, she had been dragged before an Inspection *générale des services* disciplinary hearing, received several reprimands, and been handed a six-month suspension. Then radio silence, right up until the telephone call from Buron. Her mentor, now in charge of 36, quai des Orfèvres, the headquarters of the *police judiciaire,* had finally broken his silence. Capestan had been summoned for August 9. Typical of the man: right in the middle of the summer break. A gentle reminder that this was no vacation, that she was unemployed. She would emerge from this meeting with or without her badge, stationed in Paris or the provinces, but at least the waiting game would be over. Anything had to be better than wallowing in limbo—this hazy, uncertain space where moving on was not an option. The *commissaire* rinsed her mug in the sink and told herself she would put it in the dishwasher later. It was time to go.

She crossed the living room, where the familiar pulsating double bass of a Stray Cats record was thrumming from the stereo. The apartment was spacious and comfortable. Capestan had not skimped on the rugs, throws, and ambient lighting. Her cat, snoozing away happily, seemed to approve of her choices. But the coziness was punctuated by traces of emptiness, like patches of frost on a lawn in springtime. The day after her suspension, Capestan had watched as her husband left her, taking half the apartment's contents with him. It was one of those moments in which life leaves you with a bloody nose. But Capestan was not one for self-pity; she refused to run away from what had happened.

Vacuum, TV, sofa, bed . . . within three days, she had replaced the essentials. That said, the round marks on the carpet were a constant reminder of the furniture from her former life. The wallpaper gave the clearest illustration: the shadow of a desk, the ghost of a bookshelf, the late lamented chest of drawers. Capestan would much rather have moved, but her precarious professional situation had kept her in this cage. Come the end of this meeting, she would finally know which path her life would pursue.

She removed the elastic band she kept on her wrist and tied her hair back. It had turned blonde, as it did every summer, but soon a deeper chestnut tone would start reasserting itself. Capestan smoothed her dress with a mechanical motion and pulled on her sandals, without so much as a flinch from the cat on the armrest. Only the pinna of the feline's ear twitched into action, tilting toward the door to monitor her departure. The *commissaire* hitched her big leather handbag onto her shoulder and slipped in the copy of *The Bonfire of the Vanities* that Buron had lent her. Nine hundred and twenty pages. "That'll keep you busy while you wait for my call," he had assured her. Waiting. She had had enough time to read all thirteen installments of *Fortunes of France* and the complete works of Marie-Ange Guillaume. Not to mention stacks of detective novels. Buron and his hollow words without dates or promises. Capestan closed the door behind her, turned the key twice, and set off for the stairs.

* * *

Rue de la Verrerie was deserted in the soft morning light. In August, at this early hour, Paris seemed restored to a natural state, cleared of its inhabitants, as though it had survived a neutron bomb. In the distance, the flashing light of a street sweeper gave off an orange glow. Capestan walked past the window displays of the BHV department store, then cut diagonally across the square outside the Hôtel de Ville. She crossed the Seine and continued to the far side of Île de la Cité, arriving at the entrance of 36, quai des Orfèvres.

She went through the enormous doorway and turned right into the paved courtyard, pausing to glance at the faded blue sign: STAIRWAY A, POLICE JUDICIAIRE SENIOR MANAGEMENT. Following his promotion, Buron had set up shop on the third floor, the cushy level for the force's decision makers. No gun toting on that corridor, even for the real cowboys.

Capestan pushed open the double doors. The thought of this meeting made her stomach lurch. She had always been a police officer, never considered any other options. Thirty-seven's hardly the age to go back to school. The restlessness of the past six months had already taken its toll. She had done a lot of walking. She had followed every single line on the Parisian *métro* at street level: 1 to 14, terminus to terminus. She was desperate to be welcomed back into the fold before having to tackle the suburban trains. Sometimes she wondered if she might be forced to run the length of the high-speed TGV train tracks, just to give herself something to do.

Face-to-face with the gleaming, brand-new engraved plaque bearing the name of the regional chief of the *police judiciare*, she gathered herself and knocked three times. Buron's deep, booming voice instructed her to come in.

2

Buron stood up to greet her. His basset-hound face was framed by military-cut gray hair and a beard. Everywhere he went, he wore a kind, almost downcast expression. He was a good head taller than Capestan, who was not exactly short herself, and a good stomach wider, too. But despite his hearty appearance, Buron radiated authority: no one joked around with him. Capestan smiled at him and handed over the Wolfe novel. There was a small scuff on the cover, which prompted a flicker of disapproval from the chief when he noticed it. Capestan apologized, even if she failed to see what the fuss was about. It was nothing, he said, but he clearly did not mean it.

Behind Buron, sitting in large armchairs, she recognized Fomenko, the former head of the drug squad and now deputy regional chief, and Valincourt, who had recently left a senior role at the *brigade criminelle* to become top brass at *brigades centrales*. Capestan wondered what these big guns were doing there. Given her current status, the prospect of her being snapped up by one of them seemed unlikely. She smiled at the lordly law enforcement triumvirate, sat down, and waited for the verdict.

"I have good news," Buron said, diving straight in. "The IGS investigation has wrapped up, your suspension is over, and you are formally reinstated. The incident will not go down on your file."

A huge sense of relief washed over Capestan. She could feel the joy coursing through her veins, and with it came a sudden urge to rush out and celebrate. But she managed to retain her focus as Buron continued:

"Your new post takes effect in September. You'll be heading up a new squad."

Capestan could not help raising an eyebrow at this. Her reinstatement had been enough of a surprise; entrusting her with a position of responsibility was starting to look suspect. Something about Buron's little speech had the effect of the crack of knuckles that usually precedes a punch.

"Me? A squad?"

"It's a special, force-wide initiative," Buron explained with a distant look. "As part of the police's restructuring that aims to optimize the performance of various frontline services, an ancillary squad has been formed. The squad will report directly to me, and will comprise some of the force's least . . . conventional members."

While Buron delivered his spiel, his associates looked bored beyond belief. Fomenko was studying the collection of old medals in Buron's glass cabinet without any real interest. From time to time he ran his hand through his white hair, tugged at the bottom of his vest, or gazed at the points of his cowboy boots. His rolled-up shirtsleeves revealed hairy, muscular forearms: a reminder that Fomenko could unhinge your jaw with one swing of his fist. As for Valincourt, he was fiddling with his watch in a manner that made it plain he wished it would speed up. He had clean, angular features and a dark complexion that brought to mind an old soul that had lived many lives. He never smiled and gave off a permanent air of irritation, like a monarch who takes offense at the slightest inconvenience. He was no doubt reserving his attention for more lofty concerns, an altogether higher purpose. Mere mortals would do better than to disturb him. Capestan decided to put them all out of their misery.

"And practically speaking?"

The casualness of her tone irritated Valincourt. Like a bird of prey, his head revolved abruptly to one side, revealing a powerful hooked nose. He shot Buron a questioning look, but it took more than that to ruffle the chief. Buron even allowed himself a smile as he edged forward in his armchair.

"Very well, Capestan, here's the bottom line: we're cleaning up the police to give the stats some gloss. The drunkards, the thugs, the depressives, the layabouts, and everyone in between—the people hamstringing the force but who can't be fired—are all to be absorbed into one squad and forgotten about in some corner. With you in command. Starting in September."

Capestan did not react at all. She looked toward the window, taking in the blue shades playing across the double glazing. Beyond the glass, she watched the gentle ripples of the Seine gleaming beneath the clear sky, giving her brain a moment to extract the meaning of this pitch from the men in suits.

A shelf. One big shelving unit, basically. Or rather a trashcan. A bunch of down-and-outs discarded into the same Dumpster; the department's shamefaced pigsty. And she was the cherry on top. The boss.

"Why me in command?" she said.

"You're the only one ranked *commissaire*," Buron replied. "Oddly enough, most people with a penchant for thuggery or drunkenness don't get much opportunity for promotion."

Capestan would have bet good money that this squad had been Buron's idea. Neither Valincourt nor Fomenko seemed to approve of the scheme: the former out of disdain, the latter out of indifference. Both of them had better things to do, and this whole business was a tiresome distraction.

"Who's on the team?" Capestan said.

Buron stuck out his chin and leaned forward to open the bottom drawer of his desk. He pulled out a thick, bottle-green leather folder and dropped it on his blotter. There was nothing written on the cover. The anonymous squad. The chief opened the dossier and picked out a pair of tortoiseshells from the lineup of glasses below his lamp. Buron had a variety of spectacles that he alternated depending on whether he wanted to appear reassuring, trendy, or strict. He began reading.

"Agent Santi, on sick leave for four years; Capitaine Merlot, alcoholic—"

"Alcoholic? So there'll be no shortage of personnel . . ."

Buron closed the folder and handed it to her.

"I'll leave you to study it at your leisure."

She tested the weight: it was almost as heavy as the Paris phonebook.

"How many are we? Are you 'cleaning up' half the police force?"

As the regional chief sank back into his chair, the brown leather issued a creak of surrender.

"Officially, around forty."

"That's not a squad, that's a battalion," Fomenko jeered.

Forty. People who had taken bullets, done days of stakeouts, piled on the pounds, and filed divorce papers for the sake of the force, only to be spat out into this dead end. They were being sent to a place where they would finally hand in their notice. Capestan felt sorry for them. Curiously, she did not count herself as one of them.

Buron sighed and removed his glasses.

"Capestan, most of them have been off the grid for years. There's no chance you'll even see them, let alone get them to do any work. As far as the police force is concerned, they no longer exist: they're just names, that's it. If any of them do turn up, it will be to swipe the stationery. Don't be under any illusions."

"Any actual officers?"

"Yes. Dax and Évrard are *lieutenants*, Merlot and Orsini are *capitaines*."

Buron paused for a moment and concentrated on the arms of his glasses as he twiddled them in his hand.

"José Torrez is a *lieutenant*, too."

Torrez. Better known as Malchance: the unlucky charm, the black cat you would never want to cross your path. Finally they had found a place for him. Isolation had not been enough—they had pushed him even farther away. Capestan knew Torrez by reputation. Every police officer in the country knew Torrez by reputation and would always cross themselves when he was nearby.

His story had started with a simple accident: a partner was stabbed during an arrest. Fairly routine. While the officer was convalescing, his replacement was injured, too. Occupational hazard. The next one took a bullet and spent three days in a coma. And the last guy had died, thrown off the top floor of a tower block. Any blame on Torrez's part had been brushed aside each time. He had not been responsible in any way, not even of negligence. But his aura became thicker than pitch: he brought Bad Luck. No one wanted to be on Torrez's team anymore. No one wanted to touch him; few would even look him in the eye. Except for Capestan, who didn't give credence to such things.

"I'm not superstitious," she said.

"Oh, you will be," Valincourt said, in a funereal tone.

Fomenko nodded in agreement, suppressing the shudder that rippled down the dragon tattoo on his neck, a souvenir of his days as a young man in the army. Nowadays, Fomenko wore a big white mustache that fanned out beneath his nose like a shaggy butterfly. Somehow the mustache didn't go too badly with the dragon.

Every time Torrez's name was uttered, a silence fell over the room for a few moments. Buron filled it.

"And finally there's Commandant Louis-Baptiste Lebreton."

This time, Capestan sat bolt upright in her chair.

"The guy from IGS?"

"The very same," Buron replied, spreading his arms resignedly. "I know, he didn't make things easy for you."

"No, he wasn't the most flexible. What's that fair-play fanatic doing here? IGS isn't even part of the *police judiciare*."

"A complaint was filed, something about a personality clash at IGS: basically an internal affair at the internal affairs division, and they decided they didn't need him anymore."

"But why the complaint?"

Lebreton might have been monstrously uncompromising, but no one could accuse him of being shady. The chief shrugged the question aside, feigning ignorance. The other two scanned the cornice of the ceiling, smiling mischievously, and Capestan realized that she would have to make do with the party line.

"Let us not forget," Valincourt said coldly, "you are hardly in a position to judge people for behaving aggressively."

Capestan took the hit without wincing. It was true: she was not without sin, and she knew it. A ray of sunshine spilled across the room and she could hear the distant reverberation of a pneumatic drill. New squad. New team. All she needed now was her mission.

"Will we have any cases?"

"Plenty."

Anne Capestan had the feeling that Buron was starting to enjoy himself. It was his little welcome-back joke, a knickknack to mark her brand-new position. After a decade and a half of service, she was back in first year, and this was her initiation ceremony.

"Following an agreement between police headquarters, the local branch of the *police judiciaire* and the *brigades centrales*, you will take on all the unsolved cases from every single squad and *commissariat* in the region. We have also relieved the archives of any closed cases that still have question marks. They have all been sent to your office."

Buron gave a satisfied nod to his colleagues, then continued:

"The headline is that the Île-de-France police force's record for solving cases stands at one hundred percent, and yours will be zero percent. One incompetent squad letting down the whole region. It's all about containment, you see."

"I see."

"Archives will send the boxes over when you start moving in," Fomenko said, scratching his dragon. "In September, when you've been assigned your premises. We're fuller than a Roman Catholic school at number 36, so we'll find you a little spot elsewhere."

"If you think you've gotten off lightly, then you're wrong," Valincourt said, still not moving an inch. "You should know that we're not expecting any results."

Buron made an expansive gesture toward the door: Capestan's cue to leave. Despite these less than encouraging final words, she had a smile on her face. At least now she had an objective, and she had a start date.

Sitting at the Café Les Deux Palais, Valincourt and Fomenko were drinking a beer. Fomenko helped himself to a handful of peanuts from the small dish on the table and munched them down purposefully, crunching them between his teeth.

"What did you make of her, Buron's *protégée*—Capestan?"

Valincourt nudged a single peanut all the way across his beer coaster.

"I don't know. Pretty, I suppose."

Fomenko burst out laughing, then straightened his mustache:

"Yeah, you can't miss that! No, I meant in professional terms. Be honest, what do you make of this squad?"

"It's a farce," Valincourt said, without a moment's hesitation.

3

Paris, September 3, 2012

Jeans, flat shoes, lightweight sweater, and trench coat: Anne Capestan was back in her police officer's outfit, and she was clutching the keys to her new *commissariat*. She was imagining that twenty of the forty might show up. If one in two could see the point in this squad, then it would be worth the effort.

Capestan, feeling eager and full of hope, strode past the gushing Fontaine des Innocents at a lively pace. The owner of a sports shop was winding up the graffiti-covered metal shutter, and the smell of fried fast-food was lingering in the cool morning air. Capestan turned to face number 3, rue des Innocents. It was not a *commissariat*—in fact there was nothing to suggest any link to the police at all. It was just an apartment building. And she did not have the door code. She sighed and went into the *café* on the corner to ask the owner. B8498. The *commissaire* converted it into a mnemonic to memorize it: Boat, Orwell (for *1984*), World Cup (for 1998, the only year France had won).

A barely legible "5" on a crumpled label on the bunch of keys indicated the floor number. Capestan summoned the elevator and went to the top. No chance of an official-looking ground-floor space with windows, neon lights, and passersby. They had been hidden away in the attic, with no sign or intercom on the street outside. The door on the landing opened up onto a vast, dilapidated, but well-lit apartment. The premises might have been short on prestige, but they had at least some charm.

The previous day, after the electricians and telephone people had finished, the movers had come to set the whole place up. Buron had told her not to worry: HQ would take care of everything.

As she entered, Capestan spotted an iron desk that was pock-marked with rust. Opposite it, a green Formica table was leaning crookedly despite the beer coasters shoved under the shortest leg, while the last two desks consisted of black melamine shelves perched on rickety trestles. They were not merely clearing out the police officers: they were clearing out the furniture, too. You could not accuse the scheme of inconsistency.

The parquet floor was dotted with holes of various sizes, and the walls were browner than a smoker's lungs, but the room was spacious and had large windows that looked over the square and offered an uninterrupted view beyond the old garden at Les Halles toward the towering Église Saint-Eustache, which jostled for space with the cranes that dominated the perpetual construction sites.

Navigating around a knackered old armchair, Capestan noticed a fireplace that had not been bricked over and seemed to be in working order. Could come in handy. The *commissaire* was about to continue her tour when she heard the elevator. She glanced at her watch: 8:00 a.m. on the dot.

A man wiped his hiking boots on the doormat and knocked at the half-open door. His thick black hair seemed to follow its own peculiar logic and, despite its still being early, his cheeks were already flecked with salt-and-pepper stubble. He stepped into the room and introduced himself, his hands in the pockets of his sheepskin coat.

"Morning. Lieutenant Torrez."

Torrez. So the bringer of bad luck was the first to roll up. He did not look as if he wanted to take his hand out of his pocket, and Capestan wondered whether he was afraid she might refuse to shake it, or if he was just a bit oafish. Unsure either way, she decided to dodge the issue by not offering her own, instead throwing him a toothy smile that flashed like a white flag, full of peaceful intent.

"Good morning, *lieutenant*. I'm Commissaire Anne Capestan, head of the squad."

"Yes. Hello. Where's my desk?" he said with a vague attempt at politeness.

"Wherever you like. First come, first served . . ."

"Can I take the tour, then?"

"Go ahead."

She watched as he headed straight to the room at the back.

Torrez was five feet seven of solid muscle. If the black cat thing was true, then he fell into the puma category. Compact and thickset. Before washing up here, he had worked at the third *brigade territoriale* of the second *arrondissement*. Perhaps he'll have some good local restaurant tips, Capestan thought. In the distance, she saw him open the last door at the end of the corridor, nod, and turn to her.

"I'll take this one," he called out.

He closed the door behind him, and that was the end of that.

Little matter: at least now they were two.

A telephone rang and Capestan looked around the room for it, scrambling around the various devices that were almost as eclectic as the furniture. Eventually she picked up a gray handset that was lying on the floor by the window. Buron's voice greeted her from the other end of the line:

"Capestan, morning. Just calling to let you know you have another recruit. You'll know her when she arrives—wouldn't want to spoil the surprise."

The chief seemed to be enjoying himself. At least one of them was having fun. After hanging up, Capestan switched the gray handset for an antique Bakelite job, dropping it on a zinc-top desk that she hoped would be serviceable after a wipe. She also scooped up a large lamp with a cream shade and a scuffed cherrywood base that had been lurking next to the photocopier, then took some wipes out of her bag along with a six-inch golden Eiffel Tower. It came from a souvenir vendor on the embankment: a present to herself on the day of her posting in the capital. She added her big red-leather planner and a black Bic ballpoint, and there it was—her office. Her desk was lined up at an angle between the window and the fireplace. Forty of them in the apartment was going to be a squeeze, but they would get by.

Capestan went to the kitchen to get a glass of water. It was a vast room equipped with a lopsided fridge, an old gas stove, and a low pine cabinet, the sort you would usually only expect to see in a chalet kitchenette. The cabinet was empty: not a glass in sight. Capestan wondered for a moment if there was even any water. She headed toward the French windows, which opened onto a terrace where some yellowing ivy was climbing a plastic trellis, cracking the building's brickwork.

In a corner, a sizable terra-cotta pot contained a heap of dried-out compost, but there was no sign of a plant. The sky was blue, and she paused for a moment to listen to the bustle of Paris below.

When she came back into the living room, Lebreton, the former IGS *commandant*, had arrived and was busy settling in behind the black melamine desk. His tall frame was bent double as he tried to open one of the boxes of files with an Opinel folding pocket knife. He was going about his task with customary calmness. Lebreton was as unswayable in his actions as he was in his opinions. Capestan could not help recalling the relentless, rigorous nature of his questioning. If the disciplinary panel had followed his recommendations, she would never have been reinstated. In Lebreton's eyes, she was an animal; as far as she was concerned, he was an obsessive nitpicker.

"Good morning, *commissaire*," he said, barely looking up before resuming his attentions to the cardboard box.

"Good morning, *commandant*," Capestan said.

A deafening silence fell over the room.

Now they were three.

Capestan went to fetch a box of her own.

Each with their own stack of cardboard boxes, Capestan and Lebreton spent the next two hours going through files with a fine-tooth comb. Every box was a veritable treasure chest of burglaries, ATM scams, smash-and-grab thefts, or the selling of counterfeit goods, and Capestan was seriously beginning to question the magnitude of their mission.

Their reading was suddenly interrupted by a ringing voice. They froze, pencils suspended in midair, as an almost spherical woman of around fifty appeared in the doorway. Her diamanté-encrusted cell phone was taking an absolute pounding.

"Well, you can go to hell, dickhead!" she screamed, her face bright red. "I write what I want! And do you want to know why? Because I'm not going to let some pint-size, pen-pushing stuffed suit tell me which way to piss!"

Capestan and Lebreton stared at her in amazement.

The fury smiled at them cordially, then turned away before erupting again:

"Lawyer or no lawyer, I don't give a damn. If you want to throw me under the bus, then fine. I've got nothing to lose. But if you want my advice, that wouldn't be your best move. Remember, if I want your prick of a lawyer to get piles in the next episode, he'll get piles in the next episode. That moron can make his own bed."

She hung up abruptly.

"Good morning," said the woman. "Capitaine Eva Rosière."

"Hello," Capestan replied, shaking the outstretched hand and introducing herself, still a little wide eyed at her entrance.

Eva Rosière. Buron's surprise, no doubt. She had spent years working at police headquarters at 36, quai des Orfèvres before discovering her true calling as a writer. Much to everyone's surprise, in under five years her detective novels had sold millions of copies and been translated into ten languages. Like any self-respecting police officer, she held lawyers in minimal esteem, lampooning them at every opportunity and drawing unashamed inspiration from the great and the good at the public prosecutor's office in Paris. She never took too much trouble to disguise the identities of anyone she did not like. At first, the legal eagles had taken it silently on the chin: self-recognition was as good as a confession; better to keep a low profile than cause a stir. But then a production company made contact with her, and she took an extended sabbatical from the police to embark on her next big adventure, namely creating a prime-time TV show. Ever since, *Laura Flames: Detective* has been essential viewing on Thursday evenings, broadcast on thirty-odd channels around the world.

At number 36, this sudden shoot to stardom ruffled a few feathers. If former policemen Olivier Marchal or Franck Mancuso want to go in search of fame in screenwriting, then fine. But for a woman—from the backwaters of Saint-Étienne, to make things even worse—to be blessed with a big brain and a vocal pen . . . it did not sit too well with the head honchos in Paris. Once she had made her fortune, Rosière had curiously applied to resume her duties as a police officer, without taking a step back from her screenwriting activities. And the police had been obliged to accept.

But what was permissible on the page soon became hard to swallow on the screen, what with its broader audience. She starting rubbing her *police judiciaire* colleagues the wrong way by flaunting her millions, and soon the top brass got fed up, too. The digs that started off as harmless banter started puncturing egos: you tend to be less forgiving of people when you envy them.

And so when the television series kicked off with stellar ratings, a veritable cabal formed as the administration set about trying to gag the artist. The fact that Rosière had washed up there today showed that round one had gone to the management. As for Capestan, she was glued to the series—she found it funny and, contrary to all the fuss, perfectly lighthearted.

Rosière smiled at Capestan, then looked hungrily over at Lebreton. Athletic frame, bright eyes, delicate yet manly features . . . there was no denying he was a fine specimen. The only thing marring his Hollywood good looks was a deep, vertical line running down his right cheek, like the seam of a pillow. Well accustomed to such close inspections, Lebreton leaned forward in a friendly manner and offered Rosière his hand.

"I've got two delivery men waiting downstairs with my Empire desk," the new arrival announced. "Where can I put it?"

"Okay, then . . ."

Rosière spun on her heel, surveying the layout of the apartment.

"How about I sub it in for this piece of crap, would that work?" the *capitaine* said, gesturing toward the other makeshift trestle table in the corner.

"That would work."

* * *

At 6:00 p.m., Capestan found herself standing in the entrance like a hostess who had been snubbed by her guests. She had busted a gut to memorize forty CVs, only to be left with three people, with no guarantee that they would show up the following day. She was not planning on forcing them, anyway. For each of them, landing in this squad was a punishment: the end of the road.

As if echoing the *commissaire*'s silent sense of defeat, Torrez crossed the room without so much as a glance at his colleagues. Rosière and Lebreton shuddered with a mixture of surprise and superstition as he went by. Capestan paused, then decided on a no-nonsense approach to gauge the other officers' commitment levels.

"Well, I'm planning on being here tomorrow," she said to the *lieutenant*. "But don't feel under any obligation yourselves."

With such a depleted team, the "yourselves" hardly meant a great deal anyway.

"I get paid to do 8:00 a.m. to midday, then 2:00 p.m. to 6:00 p.m.," Torrez said, unfazed and nodding his mule-like head. He tapped his watch, then added: "See you tomorrow."

Then he left, closing the door behind him. Capestan turned toward Rosière and Lebreton, waiting to see their reaction.

"We'll only be stuck here for a couple of months," Rosière said. "I'm not going to be stupid enough to let them fire me for abandoning my post."

She tugged at her charm necklace, fiddling with the various pendants dangling from it, mainly patron saint medallions.

"About Torrez . . . he's got his own office, right?"

Capestan nodded her confirmation and looked over at Lebreton.

"There has to be one case worth investigating," he said, allowing the briefest glimpse at his intentions before diving back into the cardboard box. "I'm looking for it."

And so there would be four of them. Not quite the twenty she had had in mind, but it was a start. All things considered, Capestan was pretty pleased.

4

The following day, they spent hours digging. Randomly picking at the wall of boxes lining the corridor, they skimmed through files in the hope of unearthing something worthy of further investigation. Rosière was the first to vent her frustration.

"Are we seriously going to riffle through all these cell phone thefts until we're blue in the face, *commissaire*?"

"There's every chance, *capitaine*. We haven't been sent here to hunt down a serial killer. Let's press on for the moment—you never know what might come up."

Positioned against the wall, Rosière looked unconvinced.

"Fine, let's keep playing grab bag," she said. "In fact, fuck it, I'm going shopping."

Capestan watched as she seized her coat with an expansive, theatrical gesture. Generally speaking, Rosière was not an inconspicuous woman: she had fiery red hair, red lipstick, and a shimmering blue coat. Capestan doubted there was a single shade of beige or gray in this eye-catching *capitaine*'s wardrobe.

"Hold on," Lebreton muttered.

He had just opened a file on his desk. Capestan and Rosière went over to join him.

"A murder. It was at the top of this one," he said, indicating a box stamped ORFÈVRES. "The case dates back to 1993 and concerns one

Yann Guénan. Shot dead. He was fished out of the Seine by the river police. His body got caught in a propeller."

The three officers considered this treasure haul, a faint smile playing over each of their lips. They let a few seconds go by in respectful silence.

"Do you want to take care of this?" Capestan asked Lebreton. Finders, keepers, after all.

"Gladly."

Time to see whether Sir Lebreton of Internal Affairs was as efficient at wading through the Seine and its floating bodies as he had been at the IGS Capestan had already worked out teams should an investigation come up: she did not want Lebreton, and no one wanted Torrez.

"*Capitaine*, you partner up with him," she said to Rosière.

"Perfect," she replied, rubbing her chubby hands with their multicolored rings. "So, what's this stiff trying to tell us?"

5

"Go on, marry me."

Despite his efforts to keep his voice down and stay discreet, Gabriel could not stop his words ringing around the Pontoise swimming pool. His proposal traveled across the water and bounced off the indigo tiles before echoing back, eagerly awaiting Manon's response.

It was the middle of the afternoon and the pool was all but empty, with the exception of a few determined regulars doing lengths. So long as Gabriel and Manon stayed out of their lanes, nobody minded their noisy chatter and splashing. Manon was swimming with an immaculate breaststroke, managing to maintain her rhythm despite Gabriel's spluttering attempts to keep up with her. She was smiling through the water running down her face.

"We're so young, Gab—"

Gabriel aimed for the start of each sentence to coincide with Manon coming up for air.

"It's not like we're minors," he said.

"Only just."

"Do you want me to prove I'm an adult?" he said, still delighting in his achievements of the day before.

He was lagging a bit and had to kick hard to catch up the two yards that Manon had gained on him.

"If you don't want a marriage, we could have a wedding instead? Or a civil partnership? A blood ritual! We could cut our hands with a rusty knife and shake on it?"

"You're not going to drop this, are you? This is already the thirtieth time we've spoken . . ."

They overtook an elderly woman in a floral rubber swim cap. She was too focused on her target to give them so much as a sideways glance. Gabriel had a target, too, and he had no intention of missing it.

"I could get down on one knee, you know. Even in the deep end. I'll get down on one knee even if it means drinking the whole damn pool. Look, have your big spectacle if that's what you want. Do you want a ring in a cake? Strawberries dipped in champagne?"

"Stop it, you'll make me drown, you lunatic."

Manon was gorgeous, and even soaked in gallons of chlorine she smelled wonderful. Gabriel was crazy about her. He was fooling around, splashing her with water as though they were bashful sweethearts from an American romcom. But in reality, every atom of his body was yearning for her answer: there was no joking about that. She had to marry him. She had to stay with him. She could never leave or run away or disappear from sight. He needed her by his side forever. If a piece of paper had the power to make that happen, even the tiniest amount, then he wanted to sign it.

"Please, Manon. I love you. And I plan to carry on loving you for the next fifty years," he said.

"But we've got so much time . . ."

He flicked his hair like a dog shaking itself down, his red-brown locks sticking to his forehead.

"Exactly, fifty years. Starting whenever you want."

She put her hand on the edge of the pool to catch her breath and look at him for a second. He stared into her eyes, so familiar with their every nuance, and he knew she was going to say yes. He prepared all his senses and engaged his memory, determined to save this moment. He had forgotten so many of the crucial points in his life—disappeared without any hope of retrieval—that he had etched this one into the innermost part of his brain.

"All right. Let's do it," she said, taking her time before adding, "Yes."

Gabriel went home with a real spring in his step. He was going to tell his father the news. But on boulevard Beaumarchais, a few yards from his house, he started to feel a lead weight in his stomach. And the closer he got, the heavier it became. It was a nuisance, a hiccup, a piece of gravel in his shoe: it would go away. He was not sure what it was doing there in the first place, but it would go away.

It grew from the size of a marble to a *pétanque* ball. Outside, he gave a short ring on the doorbell before letting himself in. He saw his father, sitting comfortably in his Voltaire armchair, turn his head and stand up to greet him. Tall, strong, solemn. He was like a cathedral, Gabriel's father. He took off his glasses and asked his son how his day had been, as he did every evening.

Gabriel launched in without any preliminaries:

"Dad, Manon has agreed to marry me!"

He seemed as though he was about to smile, but he did not really react. Gabriel thought he was a little shocked, caught off guard. Inevitably his father would think he was too young, that he wasn't ready yet.

"We were hoping to do it this spring, if possible. I'll be needing the family record book."

His father seemed suddenly to tense up, letting out the slightest of shudders. Gabriel saw a shadow fall over his eyes and stay there.

6

As she stepped inside what she was now calling, with justice, her commissariat, Capestan bumped into a bald man in a blue suit who must have measured a cubic yard. He had missed a patch shaving his chin, and his tie was stained with leftovers from different days, let alone different meals. On his jacket lapel was a Lions Club badge that he was trying to pass off as a *Légion d'Honneur*. Plastic cup in hand, he bowed his head courteously.

"Capitaine Merlot, at your service. To whom do I owe the pleasure?"

A powerful, toxic waft of red wine filled the air, forcing Capestan to hold her breath as she tried to answer.

"Commissaire Capestan. Good morning, *capitaine*."

"Delighted, dear friend," he went on lustily, not allowing the announcement of her rank to put him off balance at all. "Now, I have a meeting from which I am unable to extricate myself. I mustn't dally, but I do hope to have the honor of soon making your acquaintance more fully, since . . ."

Merlot spent a few more minutes pontificating on the importance of his meeting and the value of his associates before placing his empty cup on a pile of boxes by the doorway and promising to come back the moment his schedule permitted. Capestan nodded her consent, as though this *à la carte* approach to the job went without saying, then entered the apartment and quickly opened a window. She consulted her memory bank and brought up Merlot's CV: *Capitaine*. A "deskbound grandpa," as the nickname goes for those aging patrol policemen assigned to drafting reports. After thirty years doing vice with the *brigade mondaine*, he had been demoted to the bench. A notorious boozer and incorrigible chatterbox, he spent most of his time idling, though he was an undeniably gifted people person. Capestan hoped he would come back to swell the ranks once his fabled meeting was over and once he had popped a few aspirins. In the meantime, she already had enough of a job motivating her team of four—and her biggest job of all would be to persuade Torrez to work in tandem with her.

The day before, in a box sent over from the *brigade criminelle*, Capestan had found an interesting file lurking between a suicide and a road accident: an elderly woman strangled during a burglary. The perpetrator had never been found. The case dated back to 2005, and it warranted a fresh look.

Before going home, Capestan had dropped a copy of the file on Torrez's desk to start the ball rolling. If, as promised, he had arrived at 8:00 a.m. and barricaded himself in at his end of the corridor, then he ought to have made a start on it. Not that any of this was a given.

Capestan said a brief hello to Lebreton, who was wrestling with a tangle of electrical cables in an attempt to connect his computer to the internet. She dropped her handbag and coat on a chair next to her desk and automatically moved her hand to her belt to take her Smith & Wesson Bodyguard out of its holster. This lightweight, compact five-round semiautomatic pistol fired special .38-caliber shells: a present from Buron to celebrate her arrival in his team back when he was head of the antigang squad. But the revolver was not there. Capestan was no longer permitted to carry a weapon. She saved face by pretending to tighten her belt, then switched on her desk lamp.

The *commissaire* went to the kitchen to deposit the big red shopping bag she had arrived with. She took out an electric filter coffee machine, a box of six cups with various saucers, four mugs, some glasses, spoons, three packages of ground coffee, some sugar, dishwashing soap, a sponge, and a "Cheeses of France" dish towel. Reluctantly, she offered Lebreton a coffee, which he declined. She told herself not to bother next time.

Mug in hand, she sat down at her desk to study the murder of Marie Sauzelle, seventy-six, killed in June 2005 at her house on 30, rue Marceau in Issy-les-Moulineaux. Capestan opened the file. The first photograph was all it took to cut her off from the world.

The elderly lady was sitting on her sofa with an almost dignified air. She was blue. Red marks flecked her eyes and cheekbones, the tip of her tongue was sticking out from her lips, and an air of panic was still noticeable on her bloated face. But her hair was neatly done, held back by a tortoiseshell headband, and her hands were resting serenely one on top of the other.

All around the neatly arranged victim, the living room was a bomb site. Ornaments had been sent tumbling from the shelves, and the ground was littered with the debris of shattered porcelain animals. In the foreground of the photograph were the splintered remains of a pink poodle barometer promising fair weather. A bouquet of wooden tulips was strewn across the carpet. On the coffee table, another bouquet, of fresh flowers this time, mocked them from its vase, which had somehow been spared.

The next photograph revealed a different corner of the same room. CDs and all sorts of books were lying in a heap at the bottom of an oak bookcase. Opposite the sofa, the television—an ancient CRT model with a rounded screen—was showing the nature channel. One detail intrigued Capestan, who rummaged in her bag to find her fold-up magnifying glass. She pulled it out of its case and placed the polished-steel frame over the screen. In the bottom right-hand corner you could make out a symbol: a speaker with a line through it. The TV was on "mute."

Capestan pushed the magnifying glass to one side and spread the various photographs over her desk to get a complete picture.

Only the living room and the main bedroom had been turned over. The bathroom, the kitchen, and the guest room were unscathed. The *commissaire* quickly flicked through the reports: the lock on the front door had been forced. Capestan took a sip of coffee and thought for a moment.

A burglary. If the TV is on "mute," then Marie Sauzelle must have been watching it. You do not go to bed and leave your TV set on. She hears a noise and cuts the sound to make sure. The hallway was visible from the living room, so she must have given the burglar a shock. But instead of running away like a normal burglar, he decides to kill her. Then he sits her back down and, judging by her tidy appearance and the headband, he restyles her hair. After that, he trashes the living room, looking for money no doubt, followed by the bedroom, where the jewels had gone missing.

Capestan rotated the magnifying glass in her hands. This burglar struck her as somewhat unstable and irrational. Nervous, at the very least. Maybe a druggie, or a first-timer, something that always complicates investigations.

Next she tackled the coroner's report and the summary of evidence from the scene. Marie Sauzelle was strangled to death. Her body had been discovered much later, probably ten days after she was killed. The coroner had been unable to specify the time or day of her death. He noted the presence of a bruise on her right forearm, presumably the result of defensive action, but had not discovered any trace of skin residue beneath her fingernails.

As for the forensics team, they had not managed to find any DNA or fingerprints at the scene other than those belonging to the victim or her cleaning lady, who had been vacation in Le Lavandou (in the rain) at the time of the murder. "Some folk just have no luck," she had said, referring to the weather, not the murder.

Even though they had quickly come to the conclusion that this was a burglary gone wrong, the team from the *brigade criminelle* did explore other scenarios. The victim's telephone records did not turn up anything remarkable: fairly short calls from family members, administrative numbers, a few friends. Nothing suspicious in terms of bank transfers either, even though her current account had plenty in it.

The testimony of one of Marie Sauzelle's friends highlighted the extent of her community involvement, as well as her passion for tango: "She came along with me to a session a year ago and it completely changed her life. Marie took several hours of lessons a week, and every Thursday we'd go down to the tea dance at Balajo together. She'd always wear incredible outfits: split skirts and low-cut leotards. Despite her age, she still had it . . . Yup, she was talented, and she was so cheerful, too. Even when she was dancing, she couldn't stop herself humming along: *tam tam tadam, tadadadam, tam tam tam tadam* . . . It irritated her partners a bit, it must be said." Capestan grinned at the thought of the slick-haired grandpas grimacing as Marie threw them off their steps.

It was her neighbor, Serge Naulin, fifty-six years of age, who alerted the authorities. The victim's brother, André Sauzelle, sixty-eight, living in Marsac in Creuse, about four hours south of Paris, became worried that she was not answering his calls and asked Naulin to check if everything was all right. He had rung her bell without any success and, since "a nauseating smell seemed to be coming from inside," he called the fire department, who notified the police.

The transcript from the brother's interview ran to only two pages, but an appendix to the file established him as a bad-tempered, rough man with a history of domestic abuse. A perfect fit for a suspect, but he had been cleared: no incriminating evidence, no apparent motive, and a large geographic distance without any bank activity to indicate he had traveled. So the officers from the *brigade criminelle* turned their focus back to burglars operating at the time, and nothing had come up.

They needed to go back to square one: visit the crime scene and question the neighbors. It was seven years later, but maybe someone would remember something. A murder next door is not something you wipe from your memory.

* * *

As she stood up to go and find Torrez, Capestan noticed a head bobbing uncertainly in the doorway. It belonged to a lanky young man with thinning blond hair. He glanced up from the entrance, waved his hand, then disappeared abruptly. The *commissaire* recognized him as Lewitz, a transfer from the Nanterre branch of the *police judiciaire*, where the overzealous *brigadier* had written off three cars in three months. Along with Merlot's visit, he was the second person to vanish as quickly as he had appeared, and it was not even midday. It gave her confidence that her squad might swell in number after all, even if it was by one anticlimax at a time. Now they were seven.

Lebreton was making notes in Yann Guénan's file, waiting for Rosière to grace them with her fulsome presence. As he turned each page, he would tap his pen on his desk, like a drummer. At no point, however, did he betray a hint of nervousness. Never. Before joining the IGS, he had spent ten years as a negotiator with an armed response team at RAID. He was not easily flustered. The guy was the epitome of composure, with a dash of arrogance thrown in for good measure. He ignored Capestan as she passed him.

Through the door, the *commissaire* could make out the soft croon of Daniel Guichard's "*Mon Vieux*." Her knock was met with a good three seconds of silence, after which a "Yes" rang out, which Capestan interpreted as: "Who the hell is disturbing me and why?" She opened the door, determined to seem unfazed about disturbing him and show that she was in charge. Torrez was stretched out on a brown velvet sofa that had not been there the day before. Capestan wondered how on earth he had managed to get it up there. A mystery. Tacked to the wall was a child's drawing of a sun and a dog, or a cat, or possibly even a horse. A glance at the file on the lieutenant's knees suggested he was coming to the end of his read-through.

"I'm going to Issy," Capestan announced. "Are you coming with me?"

"I'm not going anywhere with anyone. No offense," he answered, his nose buried in the file.

On the shadowy policeman's desk, Capestan noticed a container of pencils surrounded by aluminum foil. In its center was a flower painted with red nail polish above the words HAPPY FATHER'S DAY. Capestan suppressed a smile, then softened her tone slightly:

"Listen, if you want to do any detective work from 8:00 a.m. to midday, then 2:00 p.m. to 6:00 p.m., then you need to come with me, your *commissaire*."

Capestan was also keen to avoid a showdown, but she needed a teammate who would work properly, and Torrez was the only one available. Whether he liked it or not, he would have to get used to it.

Torrez sized her up for a second; then a resigned expression swept across his features. Reluctantly he got moving, stooping down to pick up his sheepskin jacket.

"It's never me who ends up in the hospital," he warned her gloomily on his way past.

Staring at the *lieutenant*'s back, she replied in the same tone:

"Well, I'm happy to try my luck and see if I survive the week."

Key West Island, South Florida
January 18, 1991

Alexandre was swilling a glass packed with ice and rum on the wooden deck of his house, an elaborate white colonial-style construction. The condensation was making the glass slip between his fingers. Next to him, Rosa was sipping a fresh lemonade. She was eight months pregnant. The two of them were enjoying the gentle rhythm of their swing seat, the soft clack of their flyscreen door, and the scent coming off the bougainvillea. But Rosa, who was usually so active, was starting to get bored of her quilted cushion: she wanted to go for a little walk, just around the corner.

A new museum had recently opened and she thought it would be fun to take a look. The "Treasure Gallery" was exhibiting a modest selection of the booty that the famous Mel Fisher had recovered from the wreckages of two Spanish galleons. Alexandre was a diver himself, but the idea of paying to massage the ego of a guy flaunting his four-hundred-million-dollar fortune did not appeal to him in the slightest. But Rosa, the most sparkling treasure of all, insisted.

Alexandre never tired of looking at her. Rosa, the Cuban who had become a daughter of Florida like the thousands of others who had fled Castro. It was not so much her beauty that dazzled him, but rather the almost imperceptible quality of her movements, the flow of her gestures. Alexandre's stomach tightened at the sight of them, aware that they were the perfect foil to his own movements, his own gestures. There was an intensity to Rosa's eyes, a mixture of authority and melancholy that sent him into disarray. And she was expecting his child, something that would bind them together for centuries to come. So if she wanted to brave the sweaty, unwashed tourist hordes to get ripped off by Mel Fisher, then fine—he would go with her.

7

"Goddamn piece-of-shit handbag," Rosière grumbled as she looked for her mobile.

She put her monogrammed Vuitton down on the pavement and started bailing out items angrily, eventually finding her phone and flicking through her contacts until she reached Lebreton's number.

"Hi, it's Eva. Yes, I'm going to be in later than usual. My dog's decided to fuck with me this morning, I've been dragging him around the block for half an hour now and he's refusing to take a piss. No, we'll be fine without the vet, thanks. I know him, he's perfectly fine, he's just doing it to piss me off because he can tell I need to leave. Isn't that right, Pilou?" she said, addressing the dog. "Sometimes you think Maman's going to walk you to fucking Mont-Saint-Michel, don't you?"

Looking up at her with his delighted little face and eager paws, Pilote—Pilou to his friends—did indeed seem to think that Maman had nothing better to do than take him to Normandy and back.

"I've looked into our sailor," Lebreton said down the line.

"Aha."

Rosière was trying to gee Pilou into action with sharp, jerking motions of the leash, but to no avail: he would just sniff, sniff, then nothing.

"Tell me, Louis-Baptiste, would it be too much of a pain to come and meet me at home instead of at the *commissariat*? That way I can drag this tyrant around a little longer, and you can tell me all about our sailor boy over a coffee . . ."

"Whereabouts are you?"

"My place is on rue de Seine, number 27."

"No problem. I'll be there in fifteen minutes."

"It looks like an apartment building from the outside," she said, unable to help herself, "but it's a whole house actually. So just buzz when you're downstairs."

The previous evening, Eva Rosière had dropped in on the set of *Laura Flames*. She could not resist, even though she knew she had no reason to be there and her ego always took a bit of a hammering. Every time, she expected them to step back from their cameras and roll out the red carpet for her. She was ever hopeful that the actors, grateful for all those punch lines, might flash her a smile, or that the director, delighted to be working on such original action sequences, might greet her with a ceremonious handshake. But no, it never happened. After six triumphant seasons, and thanks to an ironclad contract negotiated by a fearsome agent, Rosière was rich. But on set, yesterday, as ever, the producer had met her with a tight-lipped smile, ushering her away as though he were returning a batty old woman to her bedroom. Deference—that was for the actresses. Scriptwriters just had to deliver the goods without making a fuss, sitting by themselves at their keyboard.

Rosière had to admit that she was crippled with loneliness, a problem that would never be solved by writing. She had not seen the abyss approaching. Back in the glory days when she was starting out as a novelist, she had managed to juggle being a mother and a policewoman, and her social life had still bubbled along. Success had taken hold of her, and with it the grip of money. Her parents were no longer around, and she had never married, but her son, Olivier, was still living with her while he tried to finish his degree in physiotherapy. He had been a typical student—scattering his stuff all over the apartment and leaving the kitchen a mess.

As nine-to-fives went, Rosière's time at police headquarters had been as cushy as anything: it was a constant source of juicy information, with officers from every department passing through. Colleagues, swivel chairs, gossip, and banter on the one hand; appreciation, coziness, and security on the other. She had lived a truly charmed life. But she had not been able to resist going for broke and pursuing television glory, so she had taken a sabbatical.

All of a sudden she was doing nothing but writing from dawn till dusk. Before long, the monumental demands of creating a series had drained her bank of ideas. There was not a drop of fiction left in her veins.

Without realizing it, in turning her back on the police, she had turned her back on her friends. Now her keyboard was her only colleague; just a screen to chat with. Olivier was the one thread that tied her to the world, her only link. A link that had become considerably more tenuous since his move to Papeete . . .

Papeete, Tahiti. Rosière had consulted the map: you could not get farther away from Paris.

In the last year of her leave of absence, her only human interactions were painfully brief, to negotiate a contract or attend a briefing. There was always a reason for any contact; a function of some sort. No more casual drop-ins or fly-by visits. In the morning, she saw nobody; in the afternoon, nobody; and in the evening, after she had been out to fetch some bread, she knew she would come home to nobody. Every week was made up of seven Sundays. What use was it being successful if you did not have anyone to show off to? Her life looked more and more like a poster warning against isolation.

So she went back to the police. At number 36, there was plenty to fill up her day and her pool of inspiration. Suddenly, everything came to life. She could make a racket without getting herself fired. At least that was what she had thought before they packed her off to this squad. She was optimistic, though. Apart from anything else, there were four of them, so she was well catered for when it came to company.

Rosière had gone digging for some info, and what she had found out through rumors, speculation, and snippets of overheard conversation had intrigued her. She was not at all upset to be working with

Capestan. The star pupil who goes off the rails, a loaded Kalash-
nikov with an innocent smile. Ideal ammunition for her next script.
Usually middle-class types didn't interest Rosière, but she could
not deny that Capestan was pretty sexy. And she was no pushover,
either. She had a natural authority to her, a strong force of will, but
she was not the sort to trample over others with her size-sevens.
Plus, she had taken on Torrez instead of throwing him to the dogs,
and that took guts. Rosière was also delighted to have snared the
Adonis from IGS, and on top of that, the murdered sailor's file
seemed promising.

She had not stopped thinking about the case and had barely
written a line all morning. There were a few upcoming episodes
on the back burner, but an author never wants to be faced with a
blank screen, so she had eventually managed to eke out a few words.
Hence the delay to the mandatory second dog-walk and the subse-
quent strike action: Pilote was a stickler for timekeeping.

How was one to go about investigating a case that dated back twenty
years? The file was flimsy, with no trace of interrogations or potential
leads. The officers at the time had screwed up, the lazy bastards.

Rosière, planted in the middle of the pavement, took a cigarette
from her pack and lit it with her gold Dupont lighter, which had
LAURA FLAMES engraved on it. She blew the smoke out through her
nose. The murder of an out-of-work sailor had not caused much of
a stir. His widow had kicked up a fuss at the start, but before long
she had hit the bottle. Rosière wondered if she was still drinking
today, as the world continued to turn a blind eye. She imagined a
scene with the woman and her red wino's nose, then switched it to
TV format and tried to come up with a dialogue that was long on
emotion without being too tear-jerky. Pilou took this pause as his
cue to relieve himself.

Eva Rosière was still gazing at the tip of her cigarette when Lebreton and his broad shoulders appeared in her line of sight. Such a
hunk, she thought to herself. What was he doing in this dead-end
squad? He did not fit the no-hoper profile. She stubbed her cigarette
out on the toe of her Louboutin.

"Anything to report?" Lebreton asked, nodding at the dog.

"Yes, this plane tree finally gave him some inspiration. Right outside my door. We do a full lap of the neighborhood and he ends up pissing on my steps. Come on then, Pilou, are we going to do our trick?"

At these words, the dog immediately hopped through the open door and did a series of pirouettes—around to the left, then the right, and repeat—diligently cleaning his paws on the brush doormat.

"Good boy," Rosière congratulated him, then turned to Lebreton. "Coffee?"

The two of them were perched on her large, white-leather L-shaped sofa, with Guénan's file carefully laid out on the smoked-glass table. Lebreton stirred his coffee, placed the teaspoon on the saucer, and opened proceedings with a calm voice:

"So we have Yann Guénan, a quartermaster in the deck department of the merchant navy, who, after a brief spell of unemployment, had taken a job on one of the *bateaux-mouches*. When he was thirty, he married Maëlle, a maternity nurse four years his junior, and they had a son together: Cédric. He was five at the time of his father's death. The three of them had recently moved to rue Mazagran in the tenth *arrondissement*, not far from Maëlle's sister."

"Yup," Rosière said, grabbing one of the black-and-white photographs. "When they fished him out, he'd been glugging down river water for some time and the fish had started taking chunks out of him. His skin's so see-through he looks like a jellyfish. Shit . . . those guys from the river police did well not to puke when they had to handle this custard tart! They could only narrow down his time of death to the closest week."

"We should count from when his wife declared him missing," Lebreton said.

"That gives us July 3, 1993, then. The last time he was seen alive, he was leaving a bistro near quai Branly."

"Long way from home . . ."

"But it is by the river," Rosière said, instinctively toying with her necklace.

"Fair point."

"But hold on, the murder dates back to 1993. Hasn't it expired?"

"No, because the widow lodged a protest in 2003," Lebreton said. "She brought fresh information that turned out not to be so fresh. But a *juge d'instruction* looked into it anyway, so the case was given a new lease on life."

Lebreton paused for a moment and shifted his weight on the sofa, before saying:

"Three months to go. Then it's all over."

He took out a pack of Dunhills and raised his eyebrows to ask for permission. Rosière nodded, taking it as her cue to rip the cellophane off a new pack of Vogues. She lit one and took a long drag, trying her best to look like Marlene Dietrich as she exhaled, then ostentatiously lay her gold lighter on the table. The smoke rose up to the ceiling in ribbons. Pilou was kipping happily at their feet, stretched out on an authentic black and fuchsia Persian rug that had set her back six big ones.

That was what it took to furnish a place on the chic Left Bank. Hers was some way off a full-blown mansion, but it was still a pretty house. Two thousand square feet spread across three levels: more than enough for one adult and her dog. And how about rue de Seine for an address! Rosière had bought it two years earlier, all courtesy of her international royalties. She had sold tons of books in Europe, Japan, and Latin America. After this vanguard from the books, the TV series rolled in without any resistance. Ever since, as a token of respect, she had been learning Spanish. And she had added Our Lady of Luján, the patron saint of Argentina, to the medallions on her charm necklace.

As Rosière refilled her coffee cup, she wondered whether it had been a good idea to serve it in a china teapot. Maybe that was not the done thing. She made a mental note to look it up. The Aubusson tapestry hanging on the wall framed Lebreton's aristocratic features very nicely.

"The first bullet pierced the right ventricle," he resumed, "and the second shattered his spine. Both bullets found their target, so we're definitely dealing with an experienced shooter firing from point-blank range. The coroner figured they were nine-millimeter bullets."

"The most common caliber. Next the coroner will be telling us that our guy was wearing jeans and sneakers, and we can narrow it down from there . . ."

Lebreton smiled, scratching his cheekbone.

"In any case, we can't confirm a thing: they didn't find any cartridges, and the killer removed the bullets with a knife. There's a nice, clean, cross-shaped incision in line with his heart . . ."

"A real pro," Rosière said.

"Exactly. A cautious pro, too. He weighed Guénan down with a diver's weight belt. It's a standard model, and naturally there weren't any fingerprints."

Lebreton ran his hand through his thick hair and stubbed his cigarette out thoroughly. He was thinking.

"The murderer's a man," Rosière said. "Yann Guénan was a big guy: you'd need some brawn to tip him overboard, especially with the weight belt on. No witnesses, no noise, professional approach . . . I'd put good money on it being the work of a hit man. A contract. An execution. Not definite, but that would fit."

"I thought about that. I started looking into it this morning, but our access to the archives is limited. The thing is, it doesn't appear Guénan belonged to a gang of any sort. If this was a settling of scores, it wasn't anything to do with organized crime."

Lebreton slowly removed some papers from his jacket pocket and unfolded them.

"Two months before his death," he said, "he was on board the *Key Line Express*."

"Aha," Rosière said, having no idea what he was referring to.

"It was a ferry that operated between Miami and Key West Island. It sank in the Gulf of Mexico. Forty-three dead, including sixteen from France. The ship owner was American, but the ferry was built in Brittany, in the shipyard at Saint-Nazaire. And Yann Guénan showed up there at the start of June."

Rosière leaned forward and tickled her dog's fluffy ear. His tail twitched lazily and he let out a contented sigh.

"The officers questioned the shipbuilder, but nothing came of it," Lebreton said.

"And the widow, what does she think?" Rosière said, sitting up straight.

"She's still living on rue Mazagran—she's agreed to see us tomorrow."

"Great! Shall we drop by the *commissariat*? I was hoping to take a couple of measurements."

The two of them stepped into the sun-drenched street. Rosière turned the key in the lock, setting off the alarm that no code could ever neutralize: the yapping of a dog in distress. She turned to Lebreton to seek his approval, but her appeal was met with silence. Inside, Pilou was letting out a mournful whine, sniffing at the gap beneath the door. Rosière caved in.

"Okay, I'm taking him," she announced.

Lebreton nodded his assent, but he said nothing. He was not one for throwaway comments, not about anything; he was more the sort to maintain a friendly yet uncompromising attitude, happy to leave others to face up to their responsibilities. No chance of getting let off the hook with him. Rosière opened the door and the dog leapt into her arms as if he had been locked up for a decade. Lebreton started heading for the Seine.

"Where are you off to?" Rosière asked.

"To the *commissariat*."

"On foot?"

"It's ten minutes away . . ."

Rosière let out a puff.

"You're so cute," she said, at which point she twirled a set of car keys and zapped a powerful-looking Lexus—a gleaming black full-hybrid luxury—parked on the corner of the street.

8

Twenty minutes later, the Lexus was still purring at the lights on rue Dauphine. A yellow pine-tree air-freshener was fluttering beneath the rearview mirror. Lebreton looked out at the tourists from the passenger seat as they snapped away at Pont-Neuf and the statue of Henri IV. With their sleeves rolled up and windbreakers tied around their necks, they were enjoying the mild weather and the lovely view down the river. Even walking backward, they were going faster than the cars.

"You married?" Rosière said, gesturing toward the silver rings on Lebreton's left hand.

"Widowed."

"Oh, I'm sorry. For how long?"

"Eight months and nine days."

Rosière cleared her throat awkwardly, even though her instincts were screaming at her to probe further.

"What was her name?"

"Vincent."

"Ah."

Every time, without fail. The same "ah" that carried a mixture of surprise and relief. So this was not a real broken family; we were not dealing with a proper tragedy. Lebreton had lived with Vincent for twelve years, yet everyone seemed to think that he was not experiencing any real pain. Or at least not the same pain. Louis-Baptiste Lebreton had grown accustomed to it, but every "ah" was like being stabbed with a spike. By the end of the year he would resemble a porcupine. This squad was no different from all the others.

The few remaining minutes of the journey were dominated by Rosière's embarrassed silence. Lebreton carried on gazing at the crowd casually. Soon, however, they pulled up alongside the Habitat on rue Pont-Neuf, and Rosière spotted some striped canvas deck chairs that she absolutely had to look at. She parked at an angle across a loading bay and bundled her partner into the shop.

She picked four to be delivered to rue des Innocents, along with a round iron table and some chairs to brighten up the terrace at the office. Rosière was already on to the next thing, and her most urgent plans concerning Lebreton now revolved around making him lug a potted rhododendron plant from quai de la Mégisserie to the terrace at the *commissariat*. The *commandant* was quite happy to offer his services, not that she gave him much choice in the matter. Rosière dropped him at the foot of the building and went to find somewhere to park.

Up on the landing, shrub in hand, Lebreton managed to knock on the door with his elbow. He heard some shuffling footsteps followed by a furtive slide of the steel flap covering the peephole. After two turns of the key, the door swung open to reveal a familiar face: Capitaine Orsini. A sudden coldness fell over the *commissariat*. Maybe a window had been left open somewhere—or maybe it was simply Orsini's being there.

Lebreton set down the rhododendron and shook the icy hand of the former investigator from the *brigade financière*. He was only fifty-two, but he looked a good ten years older. He always wore the same gray chinos, with a white shirt and black silk scarf (navy blue every once in a while). Maybe a V-neck sweater in the same tones to keep him warm in the winter. His shoes were the only thing with any sparkle—the *capitaine* could not bear sloppiness of any kind.

Orsini had taught violin at the Lyon Conservatory until he was thirty-four before passing his exams for the *police judiciaire*. A curious change of career, especially since he loathed the police and always seemed intent on bringing down the force: on more than one occasion, Lebreton's internal investigations had been substantiated by evidence gathered by Capitaine Orsini. In the informant's defense, he had raised only well-founded corruption cases, backing up his accusations with persuasive proof. He provided plenty of ammunition not just for the IGS, but also for the press. If this irreproachable individual had landed in this squad, it was because of his address book and his penchant for keeping journalists in the loop with every secret at the HQ. He had never been reprimanded for his failure to respect confidentiality, but some *divisionnaire* must have considered him to be the source of one inside story too many and decided it was time for him to go elsewhere—to hell, for example. Exit the bean spiller; enter one more soul into the lost brigade.

Orsini was going to have a field day with his new colleagues. Lebreton could not help thinking that his arrival did not bode well for Capestan.

Eva Rosière checked that she had not left anything in the driver's door. She ran a grateful hand over the Saint Christopher sticker on the dashboard, then gripped the handle of her leather bag on the passenger seat. Before getting out, she turned to her dog, sitting at attention on the back seat.

"Listen up, Pilou. As with most places, I'm fairly certain dogs aren't allowed here, but we're going to give it a shot. So behave yourself—understood?"

"Yep!" Pilote replied, concise as ever.

"Good. Now be polite to everyone. Especially the boss."

9

The traffic along the river was fine, and the scooters weaved in and out of the cars like a flock of starlings. A few minutes earlier, Torrez had needed to take a moment when the beat-up carcass of the 306 rolled into view. Capestan had tried to explain with a reassuring smile that this Peugeot—along with a rusty Renault Clio and a Renault Twingo missing its bumper—represented the extent of the squad's fleet of cars. Clearly the state allocated its vehicles according to merit.

Torrez had initially refused to take the wheel, but Capestan had insisted: she hated driving, always preferring the pleasant opportunity for contemplation in the passenger seat.

The 306's interior was a perfect match for its bodywork. A screwdriver was wedged in the door to stop the window from falling down; the knob of the gearshift had been ripped off, reducing it to a long greasy bolt that you had to grip with some force to get it into first; electrical wires spilling out of the radio compartment jiggled up and down to the rhythm of the journey; and the fuel gauge was flickering around the zero mark. The two police officers had not exchanged a word in this hazardous cockpit since leaving the parking garage. At the lights on Pont de Grenelle, Torrez finally said:

"Finding a burglar seven years down the line . . . this should be a laugh."

"We'll need to get creative, that's for sure."

The *lieutenant* raised two thick eyebrows and set off again. His optimism was a joy to behold.

Fifteen minutes later, they were parking at the top of rue Hoche, a stone's throw from the Issy-les-Moulineaux town hall. In the square, a stone monument boasted the grandiose inscription IN MEMORY OF THE FALLEN AND ALL VICTIMS OF WAR. No qualms about casting the net wide in this neighborhood: honor be to those at both ends of the rifle, throughout the ages and across the lands.

Capestan and Torrez waited for a bus to maneuver itself into the terminal, then set off toward rue Marceau.

The ramshackle house at number 30 was narrow and tall. It comprised one upper story with a loft above, as indicated by a dormer window in the tiled roof. Outside, the yellow paint on the shutters was flaking off, the render was crumbling, and a greenish sludge was oozing from the gutter. On the tinplate letterbox a worn, discolored sticker saying NO JUNK MAIL PLEASE was peeling off at the corners. The rusty gate creaked as Capestan pushed it open to give them access to the overgrown minuscule garden. The *commissaire* climbed up the three front steps and rang the bell. No answer.

"It looks uninhabited," Torrez said, stamping down the tall grass with his thick rubber soles.

"Agreed. Even if it's not, it has been neglected for some time."

Torrez stooped down to slip his hand between the base of the wall and a scrawny boxwood. He pulled out an old piece of fluorescent orange tape, the sort used to cordon off crime scenes.

"From the time of the murder, you think?"

He handed it to Capestan, holding it between thumb and forefinger for her to inspect.

It seemed unlikely. Seven years is a long time. The *commissaire* thought for a few moments before making up her mind.

"Let me ask the neighbors. Stay here."

* * *

She came back ten minutes later. The couple at number 28 had only moved in a few years ago. A lady had answered the door, a little girl clinging to her leg with pigtails that stuck up like palm trees. The commissaire had held up her ID with a smile, prompting the mother to send the girl inside to play.

The newcomers had never heard about the murder, and Capestan could not help thinking that the details might spoil their evening, not to mention the next few months. But the young woman had been able to confirm one thing: they had never seen anyone in the house next door.

Capestan went back to Marie Sauzelle's place, where Torrez was waiting, absentmindedly scraping the sole of his boot.

"Are we going in?" he said.

They were eager to avoid wasting time requesting permission from a *juge d'instruction*, so Capestan nodded. After a quick scan of the area, the *lieutenant* took out his lock-picking kit and manipulated the mechanism like a true pro.

"The dead bolt hasn't been locked," he said with surprise in his voice.

The wood had swollen and the door scraped against the frame as it opened. Capestan and Torrez were barely across the doorstep when they stopped suddenly in complete disbelief.

Only the body was missing. In seven years, nothing else had moved. The floor was still covered with upturned drawers, scattered books, and broken glass. Curled-up rubber gloves from the forensics teams were lying on the coffee table, while the powder used to dust for fingerprints was smudged across the door handles and furniture. The teams had left it as it was, and no inheritor or real estate agent had spruced the place up, even to sell it at a knockdown price.

"Ever seen anything like it? A crime that hasn't been cleaned up for seven whole years?" Torrez said.

"No. Especially not in a house that would be so easy to sell."

They made a start on their inspection. Compared with the photographs from the police report, the décor had turned gray from the dust. The spiders had made the most of the owner's absence to weave their webs with great enthusiasm. Anne Capestan tried to picture the corpse on the sofa. Taking care not to trample on the shards of porcelain, she picked up a clear acrylic photo cube. There was a picture of Marie wearing a black-and-white djellaba as she perched on the back of a camel. On one of the other sides, she was grinning as she leaned at an angle next to the Tower of Pisa. Capestan turned the object over in her hands. The following photograph was all yellowed and featured a young man with a strong family resemblance—the brother, no doubt—standing next to a racing bike, holding it by the handlebar and wearing a polka-dot cycling jersey. Next up was a young couple—Marie and a slender, blond-haired man—posing beneath an apple tree. Finally, a photograph of Marie in jeans and sandals, drinking from a bottle of mineral water outside Buckingham Palace.

Somewhere, perhaps even in this city, was the man who had killed this lady, snuffing out her wonderful lust for life. And to this day he had never had to face the smallest consequence.

Capestan carefully laid the photo cube on a bookshelf, beside a box full to the brim with multicolored discount coupons. Torrez, his hair all over the place, was darting around the room, scowling as always like someone who had just crashed his car. He was relaying the start of the report aloud from memory:

"Marie Sauzelle, seventy-six years old, sister of André Sauzelle, sixty-eight. Both originally from Creuse. Marsac, to be precise. I'm from Creuse too—Dun-le-Palestel," he added, his face brightening for a brief moment. "Brother still lives there. Marie was married, but not for long: her husband died in Hanoi during the Indochina War. No children. She was formerly a primary school teacher."

He fell silent and seemed to be thinking hard as he glanced around the room. One detail was bothering him.

"A burglar who strangles someone . . . that's rare."

"He was trying to shut her up, no weapon available . . . The thing I find more out of the ordinary is that he took the time to sit her down again," Capestan replied, gathering up a trinket that had miraculously survived and replacing it on a shelf.

Sitting the victim down again was an unnecessary precaution that gave the burglar away as an amateur. He was frightened and strangled her in panic, then immediately registered what he had done. Overwhelmed with remorse, he sought to make amends, like a child clumsily gluing a vase back together after smashing it with a football.

Torrez was now inspecting the entrance, hands on hips.

"The lock's been replaced, but the dead bolt is the same as before. And it's intact. That means it can't have been closed when the burglar forced the lock."

"Yes, otherwise he would have had to kick it down, more or less."

Just as she was about to pick up a CD of tango music from the rack, Capestan froze: she was thinking back to the police report.

"The dead bolt wasn't closed, but the shutters were. That's strange. Normally you'd close the shutters and double-lock at the same time, wouldn't you?"

"Yes, definitely."

Torrez was fretting about something. He let out a sigh before continuing:

"On the other hand, old people can forget stuff. Last Sunday, my mother came over and she was still holding a little garbage bag. She'd caught the *métro*, bought some chocolate *éclairs*, punched in our door code, and taken the elevator without once thinking to throw it away. It was like she was hoarding. Although I'm not complaining about the *éclairs* she brought—nice ones, and plenty of them, too. When it comes to remembering where the *pâtisserie* is, everything's still working fine."

Capestan could not help smiling at the *lieutenant* as he voiced his concerns about his mother: what a good son. But he was undoubtedly right. A memory lapse was possible. Maybe the same was true of the muted television she had found so intriguing. Burglars do not come bursting in at prime time—far too risky. No, they come during the small hours, around three in the morning, when the old ladies have switched off their TVs. Capestan's initial thought about that "mute" symbol had been that something was awry, but maybe the explanation was much simpler: Marie Sauzelle had just gone up to bed and forgotten to turn off the TV.

The body had been found on the sofa, a chunky, rustic three-seater with a varnished wood frame. Capestan moved toward it. A piece of fabric from the back had been removed for analysis. The armrests and cushions were still intact, and on them the *commissaire* noticed an embellishment that she would have recognized anywhere: cat hair. The beige floral velvet was covered with the gray and white strands that indicate feline domination.

She instinctively gathered a few specimens and rolled them up in her palm.

She did not remember reading a thing about any animals in the police report. What had become of this cat?

Capestan went into the kitchen. Not a single bowl on the tiled floor. If the cat had indeed fled through the burglar's legs, its bowls would still be in place. It did not make sense.

She headed back to the living room to explain the issue to Torrez, who offered his conclusion very matter-of-factly:

"It died before the burglary. Maybe even a long time before: cat hair takes ages to deteriorate. Same with rabbits. It never ever goes away."

Torrez paused for a moment as he in turn observed the sofa.

"You know what," he said enthusiastically. "My son has a rabbit. He named it Casillas, like the Spanish goalkeeper. Only our Casillas is constantly leaving his area. Basically, the rabbit goes around eating all our electric cables. One day he's going to get one hell of a shock."

Capestan looked at Torrez as he shook his head. For a man with a reputation as a lone ranger—silence, curses, and all that jazz—he was turning out to be astonishingly talkative now that he was up and running. Torrez blushed suddenly. He had gone too far, become too familiar, been too remiss about who he was. Capestan could see his self-awareness gradually creeping back: harsh frown, lowered chin, tight lips. He returned to being the thickset, hirsute, brooding man with his hackles up. This black-haired cinder block was beset by dark clouds. To avoid embarrassing him any further, Capestan headed up the stairs at the end of the hallway.

On the upper floor, a dark, narrow corridor led to the bedroom, where a ray of sunlight shone through a cloud of dust. The musty smell caught in Capestan's throat.

The large room was covered in mauve wallpaper and was furnished with a sleigh bed and matching bedside table, all of which was dominated by a crucifix. A shelf on the wall displayed an ancient collection of Asterix books—first editions, Capestan noticed, pulling one down. The parquet floor was slippery with dust, but little by little the *commissaire* got used to the odor and slowly released her breath. On top of the chest of drawers, a little figurine of an Ancient Egyptian goddess stood next to a jewelry tree laden with bracelets. Capestan opened the lace curtains. The window looked out onto the back garden, which was also completely overgrown. In one corner, a watering can with a dented spout had practically disappeared into the rampant grass. The gravel path was being swallowed up by moss and daisies. There was no way out of the yard, so the burglar must have entered and exited via the front door. Yet there had not been a single witness.

Capestan let go of the curtain and headed toward the adjacent bathroom. None of the toiletries had been moved. For seven years, Marie's ghost had been allowed to continue her existence without any disruption to her routine. A tube of Émail Diamant toothpaste, a small glass bottle of rose water, an old-fashioned bristle hairbrush, some violet soap, and cotton balls of various color in a large glass dish. There was also a tube of red lipstick in a small terra-cotta bowl. Marie Sauzelle had been quite the coquette.

A sudden inkling forced Capestan to return to the bedroom. The bed was still made. So Marie Sauzelle had indeed been downstairs watching television when the murderer entered the house. He had dropped by unannounced in the early evening, like an old friend.

* * *

Torrez was still in the living room when Capestan came back down-stairs. A long, curling thread suggested that one of the belt loops on the *lieutenant*'s sheepskin jacket was starting to come away at the seam. Torrez checked his watch.

"Midday. I'm going for lunch. Let's meet outside number 32, Serge Naulin's place, at 2:00 p.m.?"

Without waiting for a response, he walked out.

Commissaire Anne Capestan was left on her own, her arms held out in a gesture of helplessness.

10

Two hours later to the minute, Torrez came rolling down the street like a rhinoceros.

"I was doing some thinking on my break," he declared.

The two officers were standing on the pavement, keeping their distance from the house owned by Serge Naulin, the man who had alerted the authorities. A badly pruned laurel hedge was shielding them from the windows on the ground floor.

"Since the murder, the house has never been put up for sale. It seemed odd to me that no squatters had come flooding in, so I wondered . . . Do you suppose the brother's paying someone to keep an eye on the old place? No idea who."

So maybe the brother was prioritizing security over sanitary measures. Interesting.

A plaque above the letterbox read MONSIEUR NAULIN.

The man who opened the door was still in his pajamas and a burgundy dressing gown. He possessed a sort of greasy softness that somehow allowed him to be both thin and fleshy. He raised his droopy eyelids and studied Capestan with a crooked smile, in no apparent hurry.

"Lieutenant Torrez and Commissaire Capestan," she said drily, showing him her badge. "We won't disturb you for long, we just have a few questions about your former neighbor, Marie Sauzelle. She was murdered seven years ago. Do you remember?"

"Of course," he said, letting them in.

The man deliberately did not move far enough aside, obliging Capestan to brush past him. She held back a shudder of disgust before forcing her way through roughly.

"The street was blocked off for ages after that horrible event. Would you like something to drink?" he offered in a smooth voice. "I have some schnapps, or perhaps a *crème de cassis*?"

"We'll be fine, thanks," Capestan replied curtly.

A few patches of stubble intruded on Naulin's otherwise bare cheeks, while his long, thinning hair was slicked back in a scraggly ponytail. He was clearly cultivating a bohemian look, desperately trying to come across as sensual and seductive. Seeing that Torrez was at the ready with his ballpoint and notebook, Capestan made a start:

"Did you know her?"

"A little. We conversed from time to time . . . The usual good-neighbor things, nothing more."

He lit a cigarette, which he held between the tips of his slender fingers. Half the filter vanished when he brought it to his crimson lips.

"Were there any other burglaries in the area around that time?" Capestan asked, looking away from this distinctly unappetizing spectacle.

"No, just her house. Even though she was by no means the most well-heeled person on the street . . ."

"Did you hear anything that night? Any details that came back to you later on? Someone you saw scoping out the house beforehand, or anyone hanging around?"

"Nothing," he said, puffing out smoke. "Nothing remarkable."

"Did she seem at all anxious in the days before?"

Naulin stroked the corner of his lips with a yellow-stained finger, not bothering to think before giving his answer.

"Perhaps," he said. "Though she wasn't a worrier by nature. Would you like some cookies? I have some stashed away in a tin."

Capestan didn't want booze and she didn't want cookies. Capestan wanted new information, something specific, anything to relaunch this investigation and give them a fresh line of inquiry. She wanted to honor the memory of Marie Sauzelle, and she also wanted her squad to succeed where others had failed.

This Naulin guy was prevaricating. He was displaying the smugness of someone who was sitting on what he knew, taking pleasure in keeping it warm. Capestan dropped the questions about the burglary and chose a different tack:

"Anyone have a grudge against Marie Sauzelle? Any locals, for example?"

Naulin did not seem pleased with this abrupt change of tone.

"Of course," he said reluctantly, taking a deep inhalation. "She was a bit of a battle-ax and could be very stubborn, often without taking much heed of other people. The Issy–Val de Seine property group, for starters . . . now they were hardly enamored of her!" he said with a sardonic chuckle.

"Why do you say that?"

"A new media center was supposedly going to be built right here. Bernard Argan, the developer, offered her a fortune for her place . . ."

"How are we spelling 'Argan'?" Torrez interrupted.

Capestan let him note it down before continuing:

"She didn't sell?"

"No . . . Bless her soul, she never wanted to, the silly bitch."

Torrez jerked his head up, the tip of his ballpoint still touching his notebook.

"Your house is just next door," Capestan said, trying hard not to blink. "Did she consult you before sending them away?"

"No."

"You must have had to turn down a lot of money."

"Two million euros. It was a tidy offer, at the time."

Naulin seemed to have no qualms about providing such a wonderful motive. Maybe he organized the burglary to frighten Marie Sauzelle and pressure her into moving, and it turned sour? Capestan rejected this thought before it had even fully taken shape. Naulin was still looking at her through the slits of his lizard-like eyes: he had cast his rod and was waiting for her to take the bait. No doubt he'd have an alibi for the time of the crime. She did not want to give him the pleasure of announcing it, so she chose to let him stew in silence instead.

"I was in Bayeux," he said, as if reading the *commissaire*'s mind, "at my parents' place. I only came home two days before discovering the body. I didn't kill her. Just as well I didn't bother, because as you can see, her death hasn't changed a thing. They ended up building the center over by the boulevard."

"So the brother refused to sell, too?"

"There's no hiding anything from you two."

"He even pays someone to keep an eye on the house. That's the real bummer," Capestan said, playing him at his own game.

"Me. He pays me," Naulin replied, stubbing out his half-smoked cigarette in the overflowing ashtray.

"You're not working terribly hard," Torrez chimed in. "We walked straight into the house in broad daylight."

"I didn't say he paid me well."

So Naulin was the one in charge of security. Maybe this was the piece of information he had been brooding over so mysteriously since the start of the interview. The man did not know much, but he packaged it in such a way as to swell his own sense of importance. Or perhaps he was throwing them a dummy with this admission. Capestan decided not to push any further until she had dug around in his past a little. It was time to call it a day.

After a few more questions about the discovery of the body, the officers gratefully hauled themselves off the foam sofa that had swallowed them up. They left a contact number, just on the off-chance that Serge Naulin hit upon some memories or some compassion, and left after the customary farewells.

* * *

Torrez ripped a flyer off the windshield that promised him unbeat-able prices on full leg waxing.

"Nice guy, wasn't he?" he asked, scrunching up the ad before tossing it into a nearby trashcan.

Capestan opened the passenger door of the 306 and practically dived in, despite its lingering smell of stale tobacco. Once Torrez was inside, too, she delivered her verdict:

"There's something not quite right about the guy. And there's something not quite right about his connection with the brother, either."

"You think it wasn't a burglary after all?"

"No, I do, because *crim* said so. They did work on the case for a while, to be fair to them. I just don't know," she admitted, rolling down the window to let in the warm afternoon air.

A sticker on a road sign was saying NO TO AUSTERITY! On a bench on the square, in the shade of a plane tree, two young women chatted as each of them rocked a buggy.

"We'll need to take a look at Naulin. He might be hiding something."

"I'll take care of it when we get back," Torrez said before start-ing the engine.

He pulled out of their space in silence, cautiously avoiding the cars that were hurtling recklessly down the street.

"And the brother," he said once they were on the move. "Seven years later and he hasn't sold? Having the place watched? Strange behavior."

"The brother. I don't think we should make up our mind before we've seen him. We need to go down there."

"In this car?" Torrez exclaimed, the tinge of concern in his voice not quite disguising his excitement about going back to Creuse.

"Let's take the train and hire a car down there. Our budget is only supposed to cover local journeys, but it's set for forty people. There are still only about four and a half of us, so we should get away with it."

Capestan thought for a second longer. It would also be good to meet the police officers from the time and find out what led them to conclude that it was an isolated robber.

"No," she said, turning to Torrez. "I'm not buying the burglary theory at all."

"Neither am I."

11

They drove back on the other side of the Seine and had to slow down when they were level with place de la Concorde. Capestan gazed across the square, with its obelisk and street lamps surrounded by little clusters of tourists on Segways. They advanced in short bursts, stiff with apprehension and smiling nervously as they clung to the handlebars of their mobile platforms. They had all of Paris before their eyes, but most of their excitement was focused on their thick rubber tires on the pavement. Thanks to the traffic jam, Capestan had time to appreciate this whirligig. When the lights finally went green, the 306 stalled. Torrez glared at the windshield menacingly, took a deep breath, and turned the key. The engine revved back into action just as the lights went red again, setting off a deafening blast of horns that almost ruffled the seagulls occupying the bridge. Twenty yards later, they were met by yet another holdup.

Torrez sighed and drummed the steering wheel impatiently.

"Let's stick the light on . . ."

He took his eyes off the traffic for a second as he searched the dashboard, then under the passenger seat. Nothing.

"There isn't one," Capestan confirmed wearily.

"What about a siren?"

"Afraid not: no siren, no lights. We're an auxiliary squad and we do get a budget, but it doesn't cover everything."

Bearing in mind the state of the office, the computers, and the cars, Capestan had resigned herself to such setbacks.

"So it doesn't cover sirens?"

"Not for equipment. We get the hand-me-downs and the surplus. Or the stuff that's gone out of fashion. And sirens are still in."

"How are we supposed to work without them?"

"We're not in any great hurry. Our case is seven years old. A few minutes here or there . . ."

The car was still at a halt and Torrez was staring at the *commissaire* in silence. She felt as if she had just told him he was transferring to Minsk.

"I'm sorry," she said.

"You know what," Torrez said after a few seconds' hesitation, "I've been a cast off for years. Before it was just me, but now there's a whole team of us. As far as I'm concerned, that's progress."

The brake lights on the Volvo ahead went out, and they were on the move again. Torrez joined the right-hand lane, taking care to avoid a bike that was studiously ignoring the cycle path six feet to its side. The *lieutenant*'s face suggested he was chewing over a question but was hesitant about spitting it out. Capestan knew precisely what it was, and decided to give him until Châtelet to come out with it. He finally cracked at Saint-Germain l'Auxerrois.

"Did you really shoot that guy, then? That's quite something to pin on you bearing in mind . . . what you'd done before."

Bull's-eye. She had plenty more to say on the matter, but she trotted out the familiar phrase instead:

"Self-defense."

Torrez screwed up his face with skepticism and kept his hands tight on the wheel. The second question would come soon. The same inevitable follow-up. But Torrez abstained: he was saving it up for later.

They arrived at boulevard de Sébastopol and pulled into the Vinci parking garage, where a few spaces were reserved for the squad. One of them was filled with a sumptuous jet-black Lexus.

"What the hell is that?" Torrez said.

"My guess is it's Rosière's car."

"I bet she's got a siren."

12

When Capestan and Torrez reached the landing, they noticed that the door was locked from the inside with the key still in it. She had to stoop to ringing the bell to get into her own *commissariat*. The sound of barking came from inside, and she couldn't for the life of her think what was going on. Lebreton opened the door, a furious dog at his feet. He nodded at them and returned to his conversation, the little hound walking alongside him.

All four of them went to join Rosière, who had furnished her Empire desk with remarkable opulence: a chic leather blotter, an intricately gilded pen holder, and a bronze lamp with false candles and a shade with the Napoleonic bee-print pattern. She had also unashamedly expanded her territory, adding two large armchairs—upholstered in stripy green-and-cream satin—opposite her own mahogany throne. Sitting in one of these chairs was a woman with blonde curly hair. She was holding a file and turning the pages in a perfectly measured manner. A new recruit, the *commissaire* thought to herself.

"I found it in that cardboard box," the young woman explained, pointing to one at her feet marked DRUG SQUAD. "Supposedly a closed case, something about a dealer operating in parc Monceau."

She stood up when she saw Capestan.

"Good morning, *commissaire*, I'm Lieutenant Évrard. I used to be in the gambling task force, but they transferred me here. When I found out you were in charge of the squad, I thought . . ."

She held out her hands in a manner that roughly translated as "got to be worth a try." Capestan put on a welcoming expression at the same time as returning to her internal list of CVs. Évrard . . . *lieutenant*, yes, but also a compulsive gambler who had been banned from all casinos and sidelined for suspected foul play involving underground gambling dens. She looked perfectly clean-cut and open, with big innocent blue eyes. Not your everyday bluffer—that must have been a bonus for her.

"Hello, *lieutenant*. Delighted to have you on the team. Is that your dog?"

"I'm going to get a coffee," Torrez said, heading into the kitchen.

Évrard suddenly turned pale. She had just recognized the notorious Malchance and was automatically reaching for a salt shaker or a lucky charm of some sort. She thrust her hands into her pockets and managed to regain a semblance of calm. After pouring his coffee, Torrez looked at her irritably and then disappeared down the corridor to his office.

"Whose dog is this?" Capestan said again.

"Mine," Rosière answered. "You don't mind, do you? We can say he's a police dog . . ."

"He's not even eight inches high, your police dog."

"Don't listen to that lady, my little Pilou. She's talking nonsense," Rosière said in a falsely consoling tone, then added: "He's got flair, you know."

Capestan felt the need to assert a basic level of authority. But the dog plonked his rear on the floor as if it weighed three tons and stared back at her with his ears and nose in the air. His enormous paws and disproportionately large head gave him the appearance of a perpetual puppy. In any case, Capestan had never been overly fond of authority.

"What breed is it?"

Rosière answered by numbering on her left hand:

"There's some corgi, like the Queen of England has, then some dachshund, some mutt, a bit of pooch, and some mongrel. He's even more hybrid than my Lexus," she chuckled, delighted either by her joke or by the dog itself. "His name is Pilote, but you can call him Pilou."

"Oh, I can? He won't get upset?"

Rosière smiled, leaned down, and tickled the neck of her dog, who stretched his muzzle as far forward as possible to take full advantage of his mistress's attentions. Capestan was about to go and join Torrez when Merlot appeared in the doorway. He greeted the mere commoners in the room with a gesture that was almost as expansive as his waistline:

"Ladies and gentlemen! And canines," he added, acknowledging the world's least effective guard dog.

After much bowing and scraping, Merlot made the most of the introductions to plant an enthusiastic kiss on the hands of the unfortunate Évrard and Rosière, whom he had never met before. Reeking of cheap wine that was potent enough to strip wallpaper, he embarked on yet another round of urbane conversation. He held forth one way and the women recoiled; he held forth another way and the women fainted. Lebreton, whose height gave him access to purer air, listened for a few moments without losing his balance, then retired to his desk.

During a brief respite, Capestan turned to Évrard:

"That case about the parc Monceau dealer that you were talking about just now . . . is it a murder?"

"No, it's all to do with badly cut coke. It just seems strange that they never wrapped it up despite having all the info they needed. Parc Monceau is full of kids—a dealer's going to do some damage."

"Absolutely. Can I leave you to take a look with Merlot?"

It meant a blow for Évrard's sense of smell, but it came down to simple arithmetic. The young *lieutenant* shrugged resignedly. She knew all about the tyranny of numbers.

Reaching through the gaps in the bulletproof glass, Alexandre picked up the gold ingot. It was both heavier and softer than he had previously imagined it would be. This was the museum's big attraction, its main marketing hook. As you came in you had to hand over your ticket in exchange for a little oval sticker that was patted authoritatively onto your chest, with black lettering on a gold background that read I LIFTED A GOLD BAR. Never let anyone say that a trip here is futile.

Alexandre felt the delicate touch of Rosa's palm on the bare skin of his forearm.

"I don't feel so well . . . ," she whispered, the same way she did when she wanted breakfast in bed.

"If it's because you want me to steal that emerald for you, then my answer is no," Alexandre joked. "There are cameras all over the place."

"No. No. It's my water, I think . . . ," she said, gripping his arm more tightly.

Gasping for breath, she took hold of Alexandre's hand and slid to the floor, where she lay down. Water. What water?

"Are you going to give birth here? Now?"

"Yes, I think so, yes."

"We're in a museum, you can't give birth here . . ."

Sweat was forming on his wife's dark forehead and she smiled. She wasn't going to give in: she was absolutely serious that this was to be the place, right in the middle of the display cases of the Mel Fisher Museum, where she would bring her son into the world.

13

Outside, a thin mist was obscuring the stars in the gray night. Only the blue neon sign on the hotel opposite illuminated the room. Sitting on his sofa, his bare feet on the drab parquet floor, Louis-Baptiste Lebreton was smoking with all the lights off. He could have stayed like that for hours, with the red standby signal on his television as his only witness, a static contrast to the flickering ember of his Dunhill. His bass guitar, a Rickenbacker 4001, was hanging on the wall so as not to wake the neighbors. The glass-fronted poster for Bowie's Hammersmith Odeon show cast the occasional reflection, which Lebreton would follow for an hour, sometimes two, before going to sleep. He woke up, then he smoked. Most of the time, he waited until 6:00 a.m.—that was when normal people got up. Add in a shower and a coffee, and soon it would be 7:00 a.m. That was an acceptable time to set about the day. Lebreton never left a single task unattended: life had dealt him more time than tasks. He stubbed out his cigarette and sat back on the sofa to wait.

In three hours, he would pay Maëlle Guénan a visit. He was not that interested in the inquiry, and certainly not in the godforsaken squad, but this was the way of the world, so on he would go, if only to stay in the frame. At least Rosière was funny. As for Capestan, he was not expecting anything there.

* * *

Seven o'clock. In the chest of drawers, Vincent's T-shirts were still stacked in an immaculate pile. Lebreton had ironed the ones that were drying on the rack before the accident, then folded them up in the drawer. Maëlle Guénan's husband had been dead for twenty years. After all that time, surely the pain was enveloped beneath several thick layers of film. One layer per year, maybe. Or maybe not. Lebreton did not know; he only hoped.

As for him, eight months later and he still had the impression that he was sleeping under a shroud, that he was showering in a mausoleum. Each room, each item of furniture, each creak of the floor evoked the exact same feeling as a year before, when he looked forward to opening the door and everything in the apartment seemed useful. Nowadays, its contents were just souvenirs; Lebreton could neither bear to stay nor leave. In this place, every action carried a subtitle. He wandered into the kitchen to have breakfast, which he ate standing up to avoid sitting at the table alone.

They had lived together for twelve years. Throughout those twelve years, Vincent had sliced his bread over the sink to avoid making a mess, and each morning Louis-Baptiste had come through and run the tap to chase away the soaked crumbs. Even now, whenever Lebreton approached the sink, he did so hunched up and overcome with nausea. In the fridge door was the last in a long series of empty jars of *cornichons*, which Vincent insisted on keeping until Providence intervened to throw them out. Lebreton had never touched anything, and the jar had stayed put, full of vinegar, its green plastic contraption still hanging in the middle. Louis-Baptiste, who never ate cookies, kept three packages of Saint-Michel *galettes* in his cupboard, one of which was half-empty. On the bookcase in the living room, the first volume of The Farseer Trilogy had been shelved the wrong way up. Volume two was sitting on Vincent's bedside table, dog eared. The table actually belonged to Louis-Baptiste, who had been given it by his family, but he liked to call it "Vincent's bedside table." It was on Vincent's side of the bed. Lebreton hadn't changed the sheets for eight months. And Friday night drinks were now every night drinks. At thirty-nine years of age, he was already "the ghostly, the widowed, the disconsolate"—all he was good for was quoting this single line from Nerval.

Lebreton put on his black jacket and zipped up his boots, giving the former a brush and the latter a buff. His body, crippled by loss, had become a straitjacket. He wanted to rip it off and run, the way people flee the capital for the countryside. He wanted to leave this all behind, just for a weekend. As he closed the door behind him, he wondered how long it had taken for Guénan to remake her bed.

It was bucketing down. At the café on the corner, Lebreton found Rosière and her dog sheltering beneath the awning of the terrace. The rain was making a racket on the canvas. Rosière seemed to be coming off second best as she tried to open her paper packet of sugar. Pilou leapt up on seeing Lebreton, causing the table to lurch to one side, spilling half the coffee and making Rosière drop both sugar and paper into her cup.

"Shitty fucking table . . . ," she said before looking up at the *commandant*.

Maëlle Guénan lived on rue Mazagran not far from here, and they had agreed to meet here before heading on together. Lebreton sat down next to Rosière, stroked the dog's head, and signaled to the waiter for a coffee.

"Morning, Eva. Are you planning on bringing Pilote, too?"

"No, I'll leave him in the Lexus. He should be fine for half an hour with the window open a crack. Might even help us avoid the car getting swiped."

The rain hammered into the awning as the pedestrians hurried along the pavement, while some of them huddled in the doorway opposite the bar, staring at the sky to make sure they didn't miss a clear spell. A gale was picking up, flipping umbrellas and blowing flyers down the street. The water in the puddles was rippling and a rumble of thunder announced the next downpour.

"Savage day," Rosière said, trying to reassure the dog cowering between her ankles.

"That's a funny expression—where does it come from?" Lebreton asked.

"It's a Loire thing, I'm from Saint-Étienne. What about you, you're not a Parisian, I hope?"

"No, I'm from outside Dijon."

Lebreton's parents lived in the sticks, in that lowland expanse that rushes past on the train, and that you run away from as a teenager in favor of the hustle and bustle of Le Marais. The *commandant* drank his espresso in one shot, then placed enough change in the saucer to cover both of them. The rain had calmed, as if gathering its strength for the next bombardment; a window of opportunity in the storm that they could not afford to miss.

"Shall we?"

The dog seemed to think the invitation was directed at him, and he jumped to his feet and started wagging his tail frantically.

"Do you remember the *Key Line Express* shipwreck?" Maëlle Guénan asked as an opener.

Rosière was struggling to concentrate, knowing that Pilou was all by himself in the car. Poor little thing. What with the storm, too, he must be overcome with distress and worry on those honey-colored leather seats. On top of that, she always found these preliminary interviews tiresome—nothing useful ever came out of them. Rosière usually saw them as an opportunity to establish a picture of the witness, nothing more. She was always on the lookout for the moment when the emotions started to come through. Only at that point would you get any leads worthy of the name. Shit, the nice lady had just asked her a question—what was it again? Oh yes . . .

"No, before our investigation I had never heard of it."

Maëlle Guénan nodded sadly. At almost forty-four years of age, she was wearing jeans with various colors of butterfly sewn onto them, and her baggy mauve cotton sweater was starting to fray at the elbows. She smiled, pushed back her hair with her chewed fingers, and moved her feet together. A silver, star-shaped badge twinkled on the laces of her sneakers.

"Same with me, I have to admit," Lebreton added from his magisterial height.

Lebreton: Such a waste, Rosière thought to herself. There had even been a twinkle in Guénan's distant eye when she saw the stud.

"It's crazy," Maëlle said. "Twenty years and no one remembers it anymore. People remember the *Concordia*, the *Estonia*. . . , but the *Key Line*? Nothing. Too far away. Or maybe not enough deaths. Although there were forty-three. Forty-three deaths, you realize. Maybe it's because there weren't enough French people among the victims."

A laminated floral-pattern tablecloth covered the kitchen table, where Maëlle had invited them to sit down. They could feel the non-slip padded protector underneath. The corners had worn through with use, revealing the dark wood below. The straw chairs were threatening to collapse—Rosière and Lebreton kept still and watchful as a precaution. Along the wall were three fake brass portholes, under which was a series of gold-framed photographs showing a boy growing into a fine-looking young man: Cédric, their son, no doubt. On a side table, a bizarre instrument with a grille, also brass, drew Rosière's attention. A compass, she figured.

"Can I offer you a cider?" Maëlle said, her voice so soft they had to lean forward to hear her.

Cider! So that was her poison, Rosière thought. Cider? Goodness gracious, old girl . . . Well, reputations don't come out of thin air. Rosière was about to pick up the compass-thingy to have a look, but Lebreton's glare stopped her just in time.

"Two ciders would be lovely, thank you," he said, with his half-silky, half-shattered tone.

Maëlle appeared to live an austere life. She looked like the sort of person who dreads opening the mailbox. Next to a white playpen in the corner of the room, a see-through plastic box was overflowing with teddy bears, colorful bricks, and scuffed toys. Her childcare toolkit. Once Maëlle had come back with an already open bottle of cider and three glasses, Lebreton picked up the thread:

"Your husband was on board when the ship sank, is that right?"

"He was never the same after that," she said, sitting forward in her chair. Her eyes stayed glued to the glass in her hands. "It was all he thought about. He'd wake up sweating in the middle of the night. He spoke about it all the time: the panic on board, the people screaming and stampeding over each other. Some people take their traumas to the grave in silence, but with him it was the opposite. I think he told me the story of every person on that ferry. For weeks he spoke of nothing else. He wouldn't even listen to our little boy when he came home from school. In the evening, he'd sometimes go off on a tangent halfway through a film, telling us about the girl he'd seen punching a granddad in the face. He'd wake me up in the night to share some episode that had come back to him. Like the man who jumped overboard shouting 'My glasses, my glasses!,' his hands pressing against his face to make sure he didn't lose them, while his wife tried to cling on to a rubber life ring. Women trampling over teenagers, people yelling in different languages, and so many other horrors. It was terrifying to hear. Of course Yann saw some heroic behavior, or just some good, altruistic acts. But those didn't stay with him; he spoke less about them. He did love the story of a Frenchwoman whose husband had yelled at her, 'Save what you can.' And in her panic, she'd grabbed the first thing that came to hand: a plastic salt shaker! Yann went to see them again after the shipwreck. The woman had kept the salt shaker in a glass cabinet. 'I'd take this over my jewelry box any day: it's precious to me,' she had said. Yann liked that couple."

"Did anyone have any cause for complaint regarding your husband's conduct during the accident?" Lebreton said, leaning forward.

"No, no one. And after hearing the survivors' condolences at his funeral, I can be absolutely sure of that: Yann behaved like a true sailor."

Rosière was admiring the living room's ochre wallpaper. Really gives a room some oomph, wallpaper: more crisp, more refined.

"Could anyone have wanted to harm him?" Lebreton asked softly.

"Are you joking?"

The abruptness of her tone yanked Rosière from her decorative reverie. They were getting to the heart of the matter, when the accusations would start flying thick and fast. Maëlle Guénan simply could not believe she was being asked this again:

"Jallateau! It's all his fault—Jallateau, the shipbuilder. There's no doubt he was behind the murder. When it came to foreign clients, he skimped on safety checks and materials. The bow doors were too weak: they gave way and the ramp flooded. After taking on water, the ferry keeled over in less than an hour. On top of that, the public address system on board was defective, so the passengers didn't know which deck to go to. Yann wanted to sue the crook. He built a case and contacted as many passengers as possible—Americans, Cubans—to get them to testify. He visited the French passengers one by one—it took him weeks. He prepared a document this thick," she said, holding her thumb and forefinger two inches apart. "Then he went to Saint-Nazaire to see Jallateau. And three days later, he was dead. No illness, no accident. A bullet."

She stared at them in turn, her eyes gleaming. She was exhausted by all this injustice, drained by the delays and inaction.

"And to this day, there hasn't been a single arrest."

When Lebreton and Rosière came out onto the street, the rain was still running down the windows, though the sunshine was doing its best to break through the charcoal-gray clouds.

"Jallateau the powerful versus Guénan the insubordinate. The lone ranger heading into battle with nothing but his pants and a pocketknife—always makes for a juicy story," Rosière said amidst blowing her nose. "On the other hand, the shipbuilder must have known that he'd end up as suspect number one."

The *capitaine* rolled her hankie into a ball and slipped it up her sleeve, then let out a squeal of delight as she saw that both Lexus and dog were intact. Pilote bounced up and smeared the windows with saliva.

"The original detectives didn't find a shred of evidence against him," Lebreton replied. "But he may well have called in a gun for hire. Or maybe someone just used their own gun: a trial would have put lots of jobs at risk. When the guys at the shipyard saw Guénan showing up with his case notes, it must have made them sweat."

"True. And sailors aren't renowned for being the brightest."

"Unlike police officers—remarkable how quickly they managed to solve this case," Lebreton said mockingly.

Rosière took his point with a nod.

"Jallateau's company is based at Sables-d'Olonne nowadays," he continued. "He must have gotten fed up with ferries—now he's taking commissions for luxury catamarans. I think this calls for a day at the seaside."

"Couldn't agree more," she said. "Hey, it was pretty nice, the wallpaper in her living room, don't you think? We could do with a bit of that at the *commissariat*."

Évrard closed the door to her teenage bedroom, with its starlit ceiling, poster of Scorsese's *Casino*, and single bed. For the past six months, she had been back with her parents. She headed through to the hallway and picked her windbreaker off the polished-wood coat stand. Before leaving, she poked her head into the kitchen to say good-bye to her mother, who responded with a "knock 'em dead."

Out on the pavement, Évrard absentmindedly checked the contents of her pocket through the waterproof material. Her lucky euro was there, safe and sound. Her last euro: the one she didn't gamble away; the one she could use to rebuild her life. At times she had been tempted to throw it into the Seine, just to see what would happen. It was all a load of claptrap, anyway. Even the worst gamblers know that you can't get your life back on track with one euro. So what did you need? That was the real question.

14

"Right, he's refusing," Capestan announced as she came into Torrez's office.

"Did he tell it to you in so many words?"

The *lieutenant* rested his elbows on the reams of printed sheets spread across his desk. He seemed surprised that Valincourt had even agreed to take her call.

"No, I got one of his assistants, who relayed a message from the *divisionnaire*: he can't see us right now, but we shouldn't hesitate to contact him at a later stage or to bring a *précis* of the investigation to his attention, et cetera, et cetera."

Capestan sighed. Out of all the officers connected with the Sauzelle case, the only one still in the region was Valincourt. He was already a big cheese at the time, so he had done more overseeing than actual investigating and was therefore unlikely to remember a great deal. On top of that, the *divisionnaire* was hardly the most available or accommodating resident of number 36.

Torrez was frowning with the resignation of a man who had always endured refusals from his colleagues. He gave Capestan a faint smile before reverting to his standard prickly expression as he continued running through Naulin's criminal record.

The *commissaire* stood there looking vacantly at Torrez, waiting for a decision to materialize. According to his assistant, Valincourt was at the shooting range in La Chapelle. In ordinary circumstances, she could have gone along and played the chance-encounter card, but bearing in mind she had been relieved of her weapon, she was not really supposed to go there anymore. Valincourt would know that she was there to force his hand. Not that that was a big drama.

"I'm going to see him," she declared suddenly. "It'll be harder for him to send me packing face-to-face."

"If you say so," Torrez said, in a pessimistic mumble.

Arriving at porte de la Chapelle, a part of Paris shorn of even a glimmer of charm, Capestan passed beneath the overpass to the Périphérique and pulled into the upper level of a run-down parking garage. She rang the old, unmarked button of the intercom and, after stating her name and rank, pushed open the steel door. The shooting range was on the top floor and the graffiti-covered elevator was out of order, so Capestan took the stairs, the *rat-a-tat* of the revolvers marking the way. On every floor, the doors were bricked up with cinder blocks, behind which she imagined the endless ranks of empty parking spaces in the darkness. This place really made you wish you had your weapon.

At the top, she showed her ID card to the old man smiling at her through the grille. Above his counter, some surveillance cameras were relaying a grainy black-and-white picture. The elderly guard struggled to hide his surprise at seeing her again and murmured a few words that she couldn't properly hear. In her uncertainty, she nodded and made her way toward the large, neon-lit room that served as a clubhouse.

The place was pretty much deserted. No one was playing pool or foosball. The walls were covered in James Bond film posters, and a few plastic plants supplied the room's only dashes of color. Two men were practicing in a gallery with a glass back, similar to your average squash court.

The *commissaire* was ill at ease, physically feeling the absence of the Smith & Wesson at her waist. Like a champion freestyler at the edge of the pool without her swimsuit, she stood in the doorway and tried hard to keep her dignity as her eyes searched for Valincourt.

He was sitting by himself at a table for four, with the case for his weapons resting on the chair next to him. He was drinking coffee from a plastic cup and reading a newspaper. Behind him, the large glass cabinet full of club medals and trophies seemed to honor his senior-ranking status. As he looked up and saw her, a brief grimace of disapproval contorted his distinguished features. With a reluctant motion of the hand, he invited her to come and join him, already anticipating the reason for her visit.

As she walked up to him, Capestan was all smiles. This was an opportunity to glean some information, so best to approach it as delicately as possible. She quickly slid into the chair opposite Valincourt, turning her back to the room.

"Good morning, Monsieur le Divisionnaire, and thank you for—"

"Make it quick."

Determined not to be ruffled, Capestan nodded and cut to the chase:

"As I explained to your assistant, we are reopening the Marie Sauzelle case. She was killed in 2005 in Issy-les-Moulineaux. It's a while back, I know, but you worked on the case and I was wondering if you had any lingering impressions about it."

Valincourt searched about in his memory for a few moments.

"Yes, Marie Sauzelle . . . There had been a spate of burglaries around the area at that time. First-time novices under the control of some big racketeer. The poor woman heard something, the guy panicked, and he killed her," Valincourt said, shaking his head slowly. "At her age, she didn't stand a chance."

He seemed genuinely sickened by it, wearing the characteristic expression of the police officer lost in his memories, painfully running through the long list of people he had never managed to arrest. In spite of his stiff appearance, the *divisionnaire* was displaying a certain sadness, and Capestan was surprised to detect a glimpse of the man behind the mask. She did not, however, lose her train of thought.

"It's strange, but for a first-timer, the guy didn't leave a single trace . . ."

"What do you expect me to say? It was a first-timer with gloves. Any idiot with a television and eyes knows that trick."

"True. And what about Marie Sauzelle—what sort of a woman was she?"

"Well, when I met her, she was fairly dead," Valincourt said curtly.

Of course she was, Capestan thought. That was not what she had meant, and he knew it. The brief interview that the *divisionnaire* had agreed to was not about to turn into a conversation. Facts: nothing but the facts. Capestan got the message.

"Yes, so I imagine. I was referring to the testimonies you must have collected at the time."

"The testimonies . . . Why would you want to investigate the character of the victim of a burglary?"

That was the end of that. One way or another, the next few minutes would put the original *brigade criminelle* inquiry in the spotlight. Either the *divisionnaire* was aware of some inconsistencies and would rush to defend his squad; or he was convinced that their conclusions were well founded and would fight tooth and nail to protect his team. Double or quits.

Subtle variations and phrasings of the same sentences whirled around Capestan's head. She felt as if she were trying to dislodge a sea urchin without touching the needles. Eventually she took a discreet breath and went for it:

"The thing is, in my mind, there are a few details that don't fit with the burglary theory. The dead bolt, for example . . ."

Valincourt's eyes flashed with scorn, the sort reserved for the lowest of the low.

"Hold on, hold on, Commissaire Capestan. Let me just make sure I'm hearing this right: are you insinuating that our inquiry was deficient?"

Valincourt was digging in his heels. She needed to adjust her aim to avoid having their talk brought to a premature close.

"No, not at all. I'm simply questioning—"

"You're simply questioning?" Valincourt cut her off, then proceeded to give her both barrels with a deadpan expression and chilling voice: "Listen, I understand that you need to keep busy down in your little rat-hole. And I appreciate that mediocre officers love nothing more than questioning the integrity of their predecessors. But your squad is a dead end, not a development scheme. So don't waste my time with your 'questioning.' If you want to feed on our scraps, young lady, then be my guest. But at least have the decency not to come begging for our help."

"Young lady" . . . Why not "pretty little thing" while we're at it, Capestan thought to herself. The master was really starting to pull rank, and she managed to resist the urge to kick back with an "old man." She nodded in silence. Deep down, he was right. And she had run the risk of a snub by turning up uninvited.

She had not hit upon any new information, and she had already been given her marching orders.

The room was starting to fill up. An officer with an affectedly casual manner came over to greet Valincourt with great ceremony. He had a shaved head and a leather jacket and was carrying a gun case big enough to house an acoustic guitar—not that he looked the type to bash out a Dylan cover. He made a surprised face on spotting the *commissaire*, smiling out of the corner of his mouth, as did the next two colleagues. Capestan was fuming, but she still offered her hand out of politeness as she stood up.

"I'll leave you in peace, Monsieur le Divisionnaire," she said. "Thank you for your time."

He shook her outstretched hand and smiled an artificial smile at her. He hesitated a moment, then said:

"If you must look elsewhere, try the brother. But mind how you go with him: he was a nasty piece of work."

Capestan nodded, then made for the exit under the sneer of her colleagues, smarting from the blow to her pride. As she opened the door, she made out the unmistakable sound of a Beretta automatic pistol. A shiver of envy ran down her spine.

15

It was early afternoon, and Évrard and Merlot were sitting on a bench in parc Monceau, carrying out surveillance on a junkie. In reality, Merlot was brazenly attempting to school Évrard in the subtleties of chess. She listened to him patiently, all the while thinking that the good *capitaine* was too drunk to count to five. But the weather was mild and the park was pretty, so Évrard passed the time placing accumulator bets based on the alternating numbers of wheelchairs and tracksuits, skirts, and trousers. There was nothing sociological about her people watching: just numbers and the voice of Merlot, her *croupier*, in the background.

Opposite them, the junkie was scratching the inside of his arm distractedly and tapping his foot. He was getting impatient, wondering what the hell he was doing in a park in the snazzy eighth arrondissement. He glanced at them nervously, and for some reason their presence seemed to calm him. Évrard looked at the man next to her in his mustardy trousers through the corner of her eye, then at her own worn-out black Converse sneakers and wondered, once again, what she was doing with her life. Two wheelchairs, one pair of trousers, three tracksuits, one skirt.

A man was striding down the central pathway. Évrard was on her guard. Nothing really marked him out from the crowd other than the fact he was a little more scruffy and pale than the others.

And the fact that he was screaming "Asshole! Asshole! Asshole!" at the trees, the sky, and the passersby. Yet another person that Paris had forsaken. Évrard felt a sudden envy for his unbridled freedom, for the free fall that comes when you cut the final cord, the last restraint. She let the heady idea register, then breathed out to bring herself back to reality. The stakeout. Her job. Her chance to get back on track. Merlot was saying something.

"And so I advance my rook, hazarding a guess at my impudent opponent's response . . . Ah, ah: no diagonal. Do you not realize? In public, no less!"

Évrard nodded in agreement, but her attention was back on the druggie under their surveillance. He was sitting bolt upright: must be someone coming. Bingo! A young man with a raver's complexion and dressed in a blazer, skinny jeans, and a thin tie was sitting next to the junkie on the bench. They were pretending not to know each other despite having a conversation: it was a ridiculous sight. Right there, perched on a bench in the middle of the park with their vacant expressions, they suddenly shook hands. Notes passed between fingers and the crackle of tin foil around the bag of coke could be heard from where the officers were. They were dealing with first-rate cretins, and Évrard wondered how this moron had managed to avoid getting busted sooner. He left the bench and Évrard discreetly nudged Merlot's elbow, startling him.

"What on earth is wrong with you?"

Well, this was what the morons were up against. Évrard jerked her chin in the dealer's direction, and Merlot hauled himself up with great difficulty to start tailing him. When their target stopped to take off his aviators and check his smartphone, Merlot stopped in his tracks.

"No need to follow him a step farther," he said. "I know where he lives: Villa Scheffer in the sixteenth. He's the Riverni boy."

"Riverni . . . Isn't he a minister or something?"

"Secretary of state."

"Not hard to see why the case was closed, then. This dealer didn't strike me as a fast runner, let alone someone who might crawl through the net. So there we have it. Let's call Capestan," Évrard said.

"Absolutely. There's a *café* on the corner: they ought to have a telephone."

Évrard chose not to point out that she, along with the rest of the world, had a cell phone. Always best to indulge your colleagues. She went into Café Carnot and ordered a raspberry kir. Merlot was beaming: a highly satisfactory outcome, and all thanks to him.

16

Capestan managed to extract herself from the elevator dragging a dark-pink shopping cart filled to the brim with logs. She backed into the *commissariat*, pulling her cargo toward the fireplace. The room was thick with the strong smell of wax, and the parquet was gleaming like a horse chestnut fresh out of its shell. A broom wrapped in a wax-soaked cloth was leaning against the wall behind Lebreton's chair. Capestan greeted the *commandant* first, then Rosière, who was squashing a teabag against the side of her mug as Pilou lay curled next to her blue stilettos. The three of them greeted her in return. Torrez and Orsini were no doubt both holed up in their respective offices. The *commissaire* unfolded the brass fire screen that she had slid down the side of the trolley and started stacking the logs to the right of the fireplace.

"So?" Rosière said, plopping the teabag in the green leather wastebasket beside her desk. "How are things looking with the old lady?"

"A bit blurry, for now. Tomorrow we're off to Creuse to question the brother. How about your sailor?"

"The wife's convinced the shipbuilder from the Vendée did it, so we're off to the seaside. But we have to wait till the day after tomorrow—we needed to make an appointment."

"Vacations all around," Capestan said. "Are you taking the train? We've got the budget, if you want—"

"No, we'll take the car. I prefer it that way, and Louis-Baptiste doesn't mind," Rosière said, glancing at her partner, who nodded. The dog, intrigued, trotted up to the pile of logs and sniffed them, clearly intending to contribute a squirt of something inflammable.

"No, Pilou! Buzz off!" Capestan shouted, pointing at Rosière's desk.

The dog's face turned in the direction of her finger, but his paws didn't move an inch.

"The whole dog, please Pilou, not just the head," Capestan insisted.

The dog obliged, but only because he had been distracted by an unfamiliar face: Évrard was hanging her navy-blue windbreaker on the hook by the door.

"Good morning, *commissaire*, we tracked down the dealer's address," she said. "Villa Scheffer in the sixteenth."

"Wonderful!" Capestan said to the *lieutenant*, bursting into a smile, a log in each hand. "Quick work, very efficient. The nation is forever indebted to you."

Évrard was visibly disappointed: the one time she received any praise for her work, she would have to dash their hopes.

"Well, there's no point getting too excited. He's the son of the secretary of state for family and the elderly, Riverni. Which no doubt explains why the file was squirreled away at the bottom of a box. I guess we're not allowed to apprehend him."

"Yes, yes, of course you can," Capestan insisted with great optimism. "If he leaves his house carrying drugs, then bring him in."

Rays of sparkling autumn sunshine were spilling into the room, hitting the back wall and making it shimmer in their heat. This was no day for negative thinking.

"Commissaire, I don't mean to take issue with you, but if the file ended up here, then it means that two years ago an even bigger squad was told to back down. And they were fully operational. I don't think they left it behind for our sake."

"Hey, we're fully operational, too. I'm not saying we'll succeed, I'm saying we'll try. If no one stands in our way, we'll push on."

That was how she wanted things to be. They already faced enough obstacles without having to invent their own. The least they could do was wait and see.

Évrard's big, innocent blue eyes were wide open, but she was still uncertain. She did not much care for a trip to the sixteenth to spend hours negotiating with the family lawyer, only to go home empty handed after a good dressing-down. Capestan could see where she was coming from—her own encounter with Valincourt had been far from pleasant—but her squad must not be resigned to its fate; they could not wallow in indifference. That was what the top brass wanted. If they started surrendering without even trying, then they may as well not bother getting out of bed in the morning.

"We don't even have a holding cell," Évrard said, motioning around the apartment.

Capestan laid down the logs she'd been holding, rubbed her hands together, and pulled a Swiss Army knife from her enormous bag. She walked straight over to the bathroom, unscrewed the latch, and fastened it to the door of one of the offices at the end.

"There you go," she said, closing the knife, "there's your cell. That should work just fine for starters. Catch young Riverni red handed like the good police officers you are, and if there are any complications, play dumb and call me."

A smirk played across Lebreton's lips, who had been listening all along. Évrard, still skeptical, nevertheless slipped off to telephone Merlot, who had stayed behind at Café Carnot "just in case."

Capestan had not expected an arrest to be in the cards so soon. She would have preferred to spend a bit more time getting her bearings before rushing headlong into the game, especially as it involved contravening the powers that be. But she wasn't about to let her officers be sidelined. Admitting to them that their investigations were futile would hardly make for a motivational team talk. This squad had to be good for something. Good for what remained to be seen: she should find out in a couple of hours. The least she could do was keep a close eye on them when it came to crunch time. Her eyes met Lebreton's again. The *commandant* tapped his pen on the edge of his desk and tilted his head to one side to show that, like her, he was looking forward to hearing the verdict. She gave him a quick smile and returned to her shopping cart.

From the bottom of it, she lifted out a pair of antique-style andirons embellished with goddess figurines. She lined them up on either side of the fireplace, perfectly parallel, then rubbed her hands together again to get rid of the thin layer of rust they had left behind. Rosière came over to admire the installation.

"Classy. I'm thinking a big mirror to go on top. Gold frame?"

Rosière needed little encouragement in this department, but Capestan nodded her approval anyway. As a matter of principle, she always tried to reward good intentions.

"Have you got one?" she said.

"Of course. Let me make a quick call," Rosière said loudly, grabbing the telephone on her desk.

"We'll need a crystal chandelier, too," she added, the receiver clamped against her shoulder.

"A chandelier?"

Capestan felt the stirrings of a whirlwind.

"As you wish . . . ," Capestan said, knowing full well she was about to unleash a war machine.

17

One hour later, a gilt-bronze mirror and a crystal chandelier had appeared in the main room. Capestan and Rosière were celebrating the arrival in the deck chairs on the terrace, each sipping a cup of steaming tea. It was a mild autumn, perfect for the twin pleasures of the log fire and the terrace. The hurly-burly of the Parisians teeming around the fountain rose up toward the rooftops: laughter, piercing voices, ringing cell phones, the bells of bicycles, and the beating wings of the pigeons. A pair of djembe drums could be heard pounding in the distance, their soft rhythm setting the perfect tempo for the midmorning dawdlers. Lebreton came out and propped his elbow on the stone edge of the terrace as he lit a cigarette. The lull seemed to go on forever in the warmth, staving off the threat of the ringing telephone. Eventually it came, shattering the silence, and Capestan, ever the good soldier, stood up to answer it. Time for Buron's verdict.

She took a breath and picked up. It was indeed the chief, and his tone was far from friendly:

"Your officers are over at Riverni's, is that correct?"

"That's correct. Unlike your own highly qualified, utterly perfect son, Monsieur le Directeur, young Riverni is peddling some pretty low-grade coke—"

"Capestan, what exactly are you trying to do? I forbid you to arrest or even question him."

"Excuse me?"

"Not one single *juge d'instruction* will take on the case. Just like last time, and that was with proper police officers," Buron said. "We've tried it all before. Don't bother wearing yourself out."

"I don't feel worn out. In fact I feel in great shape."

"Capestan, please, this is not a laughing matter. Do you want to know how limited your options are? Let me spell it out for you: none of the investigating judges even know your squad exists. You simply don't have the weight for this sort of case."

That final sentence really riled Capestan. She listened first to the silence, then to the tone at the other end of the line before resignedly hanging up. There was no point fighting if the public prosecutor's doors were closed.

However much she had seen this coming, a flush of annoyance rose to her face. She was really angry. Fine, Buron had laid out the rules from the start, but to be gagged so quickly was hard to take. Her squad deserved better than that; they would do better than that.

The adrenaline was coursing through her veins. Capestan took a deep breath to try and dismiss the dark clouds overwhelming her, to think of a way around the barriers the chief had erected. Standing in the middle of the room, she screamed at no one in particular, hoping she'd be heard from the terrace through to the back offices:

"Does anyone here know Divisionnaire Fomenko?"

Her question was met with silence, and she was about to rephrase it when Rosière, mug in hand, rippled into the living room.

"I know the dragon well," she said in a husky voice, her grin heavy with innuendo.

Capestan was not at all sure she wanted to hear the details, but it was good news nonetheless.

"Listen, Buron's refusing to let us nab Riverni. Our team is being forced to back down, officially at least. But surely the drug squad will have more to say on the matter. Fomenko is still tight with his old team: he might persuade them to check out the boy or, failing that, at least lend us a hand. But first we need to get him on our side. Might that be doable?"

"Sure, why not," Rosière said casually. "But should we really be so bothered about this dealer?"

"Absolutely. If we give in this easily, it will discredit all our future actions. We'll look like a bunch of clowns."

"And we are not a bunch of clowns . . ."

"Precisely."

With her left thumb, Capestan traced the path of the scar running down her other index finger, a delicate reminder of a tumble she took while roller-skating, the first of many lessons in prudence she had failed to learn from.

"Let's be smart about this, though," she said, lowering her voice but keeping all her determination. "Our future depends on our ability to indict the Riverni boy. If this kid goes before a judge, we're back in the game."

"Very good, then. Very good," Rosière said, her fingers lingering on the medallions around her neck. She was glad to discover that there was still another chance at a lucky break.

18

Évrard and Merlot had stayed put in Riverni's neighborhood, waiting for the telephone calls to go up and down the hierarchical hill
before making a decision. After her talk with Buron, Capestan
had called them on-site and instructed them to wait for eventual
reinforcements. Évrard told her that there was a small enclosure
in the center of the Villa and that they had seen the boy hide his
stash beneath a flagstone in a metal box. So they knew where to
search if and when they got permission. The officers had rung the
bell anyway to ask a few routine questions, taking care not to give
their game away. This had not gone down well with the little brag-
gart, and it looked as if things were about to take a turn. Merlot
had intervened with great authority, confronting the young man
without a grain of hesitation, despite being a foot shorter and thirty
years older. Within seconds, the young lion had run off to kick up
a fuss with Papa.

Évrard had been greatly impressed by this sudden show of
strength from Merlot, whom she had written off as a fully certi-
fied buffoon. She felt a fresh wave of confidence in her partner, and
along with wanting to nab their irritating dealer, that made two
solid reasons to wait for Fomenko's cavalry.

* * *

Unfortunately, Rosière came back empty handed in the late after-noon. Fomenko had seemed to give it some thought before saying that he "couldn't be bothered with that kind of bullshit": the boy was so small-fry that that there simply wasn't any point bringing him into custody. The *divisionnaire* was damned if he was going to fill out endless piles of paperwork for a little brat who (flicker of a smile) would walk free in fifteen minutes. Not to mention the boy's father, who would block any attempt to advance the case for the next ten years. "If we were talking Escobar at the height of his powers, then maybe, but this dumb prick? We're better off drop-ping it," Fomenko had said. Rosière had been happy to see an old friend—and even happier to swipe a bag of Moroccan weed on her way out—but she was also deeply sorry that her diplomatic mission had failed. She hated to be the bearer of bad news.

"Okay," Capestan said. "Thanks for trying anyway, *capitaine*."

Ultimately, today had been quite a lesson. Fomenko had turned down her appeal outright, a little more courteously than Valincourt had, but just as firmly. In summary, Buron was blocking any official action and the gods of number 36 were refusing active collabora-tion. The squad was on its own. Completely alone. She could either hang around on the sidelines or she could force the issue. After all, she still had one secret weapon.

Capestan set off down the corridor and knocked on the first door on the right. The walls of the office were already adorned with post-ers from the most prestigious productions at the Opéra de Paris. A gentle aroma of mandarin was emanating from an essential oil dif-fuser, and the soft trill of France Musique played over the radio. On a tall smoked-glass table sat a large stack of law books, including an ancient *Dalloz*. Capitaine Orsini was scribbling away in a notebook. Orsini: the velvet-gloved snitch; the *police judiciaire*'s very own lie detector. Capestan's trump card. He looked up at her, all ears.

"Capitaine Orsini? May I ask you to lend a hand with an investi-gation? We have a team in position at Villa Scheffer in the sixteenth. They'll bring you up to speed."

Sitting on a chair beside his daughters' bunk bed, his feet tucked in to his polka-dot slippers, Torrez was reading *Clementine Does Hip-Hop* in his fine baritone. His daughters, deep in concentration, were each twisting a strand of black hair, one of them staring at the ceiling, the other at the bottom of her sister's mattress.

After a knowing pause designed to build the tension, Torrez turned the page. The simple drawing depicted a dance studio with a television and a DVD player.

The DVD player. It was still in Marie Sauzelle's living room. Burglars wouldn't bother with that sort of thing anymore, but back in 2005 . . . The murderer had trashed the place in a hurry. Was this an oversight, or were they on the hunt for a burglar without a swag bag?

19

Gabriel was in his bedroom gazing at the photograph of his mother. This picture in its old black-plastic frame was the only one left of her in the whole apartment. One by one, the others had deserted the walls and then the shelves. Not that there had ever been an awful lot: they simply didn't have that many.

Gabriel had drawn dozens of portraits of her from this photograph. Most of his attempts—charcoals, watercolors, even cartoons—had stemmed from this picture. He had made prints of sixteen of them, all the same size, which were now pinned above his chest of drawers in four rows of four. Each one had a very slight variation in her features, making it look as if his mother was aging.

He heard a knock, and suddenly his father's silhouette filled the door frame. In the days since Gabriel had announced his engagement, his father's face had occasionally twitched into a smile, but it was clear his heart hadn't been in it. Gabriel had wanted to reassure him, to tell him that he might be young, but that he wasn't going far, that he would come over on Sundays, Saturdays, midweek—all three if necessary. But his father was not the sort of man you could speak to like that. He was not the sort who needs his hand held.

He was still standing in the doorway, wearing his same old blue woolen cardigan that was bagging at the elbows, and clutching a hammer and a screw. He seemed to be there purely by accident, and Gabriel decided to tease him:

"I'm not sure what odd jobs you're planning on doing, but I can't help thinking you'd be better off with a nail. Or a screwdriver."

His father smiled and pretended to only just notice it was a hammer.

"I was starting to wonder myself. This wall's not being very cooperative . . ."

As always, Gabriel felt a tinge of embarrassment at being caught with the photograph frame. He tried to find an excuse at the same time as fishing for some paternal approval.

"I'm sure she would have loved Manon," he said, pointing his thumb casually at the portrait. "She fits the perfect daughter-in-law profile, don't you think? She would be proud, wouldn't she?"

"Without a doubt."

Gabriel tried hard not to hope for a follow-up. He turned to rummage for a nail in his pot of stationery, pushing aside the Marvel figurines littering his desk.

"How old was she when you met?" he said, then held out a nail he had salvaged from a pile of paperclips, screws, and elastic bands.

"Thank you," his father said, slipping both nail and screw into his pocket. "She was twenty-six, I've told you before."

"She looks older in this picture."

His father flinched, as if about to turn the frame over, but he checked himself in time, thrusting his hand back in the pocket of his gray trousers, embarrassed by his sudden gesture. Gabriel shifted his gaze to the window and looked out at the cars lining up on boulevard Beaumarchais. They were in all colors next to the gray of the exhaust fumes, revving their engines at the red lights as they waited for them to change. Even before the lights turned green, the drivers were in first gear, nudging forward four measly inches.

"And Manon's parents are pleased?" his father asked, his voice a little louder. "We must have them over for dinner. I'll let you fix a date."

Gabriel could hardly believe his ears. Dinner? People at their apartment? This was progress . . . To hide his happiness—no, his total elation—he carried on facing the window, closing the blind on the traffic, not that it did much to block out the sound of the cars. Once he had managed to tone down his smile, he dug his cell phone out of the side pocket of his Bermuda shorts: his lucky beige ones, which he thought made his calves look good. Before Manon, it would never have occurred to him that calves could even look good. But now he wore them constantly, no matter how cold it was.

"I'll call Manon straightaway and ask her."

The moment of awkwardness surrounding the photograph had passed.

"And the family record book . . . Have you managed to have a think?" Gabriel asked, unlocking his cell phone.

"Yes, yes, I'm taking care of it. But there's a chance it may take a while. You understand, don't you, Gabriel?"

"Yes, of course, Papa."

But actually, no, Gabriel was not sure he did understand. Come the spring, he would officially be taking the step into adulthood. Manon might see this as just an adolescent thought, but she also knew that he'd already taken this step a long time ago.

She was his passion, his refuge, and he was going to marry her. The reality still had not fully dawned on him, and each time he thought about it a little puff of warmth would take him by surprise. His chest was tight with a joy so palpable that it overwhelmed his grief, turning it instantaneously into something else, something like nostalgia.

Gabriel sat down at the edge of his bed, facing the photograph of his mother. She had bequeathed him her olive complexion and the perfect oval of her face. For Gabriel, the notion of perfection stopped at his ears: the left lobe had been torn off when he was barely two years old. A dog, so his father said, but Gabriel didn't remember. Same with the missing half of the little finger on his right hand: he didn't remember a thing.

His mother. He still had no idea what happened. When Gabriel was small, his father used to talk about her often. Then the source dried up. Each of Gabriel's questions was gradually silenced by the tears his father desperately tried to hold back. It made for a horrific spectacle, the giant with the red eyes. Gabriel was not a torturer by nature, so in time he simply gave up, deliberately protecting himself in the thick cotton batting of the unsaid. Soon he would be a father, too, and then it would be his turn to answer. And he would have nothing to say. This was unthinkable. The time had come to search for the truth: an investigation—a serious one—was required.

20

"It is—it's a very real danger," Torrez repeated to an impassive Capestan.

With each response, she raised her eyes to the heavens. She was standing in front of the Clio rented car, her fingers touching the handle of the passenger door. The final travelers were drifting out of the parking lot at gare de la Souterraine, relieved that it was all over. The train had arrived an hour late from a journey that ought to have taken less than three. A piece of vandalized cable had fallen onto the tracks. After traveling through miles of beautiful country-side, they had found themselves at a standstill in some lovely bit of urban sprawl, on a railway speckled with patches of yellow grass and lined with a jumble of fences, undergrowth, and cable drums. The window through which Capestan contemplated this grim industrial scene was spattered with droplets of detergent. Their train had no dining car, and the refreshments cart had been ransacked long before it reached them in standard class. After going halves with Torrez on the few remaining Ricqlès pastilles that she kept at the bottom of her bag, Capestan promised herself that next time she would be more lavish with her state budget and travel in first class.

Worst of all, however, had been listening to Torrez apologizing for the delay for the entire journey. However much Capestan tried to persuade the lieutenant of his probable innocence in the cable affair, he had continued to grumble: "It's because of me, it's because of me." He feared that this unfortunate hitch had set an ominous precedent.

Torrez could not let go of his jinx, and Capestan began to wonder whether this feeling crept into his private life, or whether it was exclusive to his role as a police officer. Whether it was the mark of Cain or the sword of Damocles, Torrez had no shortage of baggage.

Behind the wheel of a freshly vacuumed car, gazing out on the countryside of his beloved Creuse, the lieutenant calmed down a bit. A smile was obviously a step too far, but his eyebrows had returned to something resembling a normal position. As the road wound through hills, fields, and forests, Capestan felt carefree, delighted to see the word "autumn" shift from an abstract term to a reality. The monochromatic town and the evergreen mountains were in the past, and nature was now putting on a glorious Technicolor show for them: red and orange oaks, the brown of the horse chestnuts, and yellow for the beeches. Each species paying its own tribute to October. The verdant prairies put the finishing touches on the eco-idyll they saw before them. No noise, no gray, and everywhere the primeval smell of the wild. The air was pure and fresh, cleansing every cell and flushing out the foggy heads of the city dwellers. It was enough to make Capestan giddy. Torrez picked up on it, puffing his chest as though it were a personal compliment.

At the far end of a village, an imposing eighteenth-century house came into view. A scarlet Virginia creeper covered the facade of the two-story house, reaching up to the roof's slate tiles. Traces of rust on the iron shutters indicated that they could do with a lick of paint. From the street, Capestan made out a note on the shabby door.

She pushed at the garden gate, which let out a quiet squeak, and walked up the path, gravel crunching underfoot. Good, honest sounds, she thought, returning to her whimsical reverie. André Sauzelle had left them a message: *I'm at the pond. The fishing hut on the little island.*

Before returning to Torrez, who was waiting with his back to the car, Capestan noticed some large balls of fat hanging in several of the trees for the birds. Strange, she thought: it wasn't even winter yet.

"André Sauzelle is waiting for us in his fishing hut. I feel like swinging by the churchyard before going to find him."

"You want to say a quick prayer?" Torrez said in surprise.

"No. That's where Marie is buried. I just want to check something."

Back in the car, Torrez, hampered by his sheepskin coat, took two attempts to buckle his seat belt.

"Aren't you hot with that on?" Capestan asked.

"I am a bit now, but it'll be perfect in a month. Plus it has pockets," Torrez said, turning the key in the ignition before finally admitting: "I don't like the cold."

The churchyard was perched on the hillside above the village. They saw the dark outline of the bell tower and the cock of the weathervane slicing through the deep azure sky. The fields stretched for as far as the eye could see, dotted with reddish-brown cows. At least the dead could rest in peace with a lovely view. They had to climb a bit higher to reach the Sauzelle family vault, which was sheltered from the wind by a stone wall.

The marble and the inscriptions were in an impeccable state. The headstone was resplendent, with no trace of moss, rain, or earth, all perfectly maintained and surrounded by fresh flowers. Three rows of azaleas filled a lush flowerbed, its perfect edges suggesting the use of a gardener's line. The chaos of the house in Issy was still vivid in Capestan's memory: André Sauzelle might have closed the door on that, but when it came to his sister's tomb, surely he was not keeping it spick and span for show?

The *commissaire* had seen what she had wanted to see. Torrez was still by the entrance to the churchyard, looking uneasy as he read the notices on the community board. Capestan came down some steps to join him again. Just off the walkway, a plaque with the pledge WE WILL NEVER FORGET YOU had fallen over and was lying half-buried in the ground, with one of its corners chipped. Capestan looked at all the photographs of the dead smiling for posterity. They only existed in this little patch, wedged inside their overelaborate frames.

"Shall we go?"

"It's a trap," Torrez said with a gloomy voice.

"Not this again . . ."

Torrez tapped his knuckle against a yellow leaflet, the way you knock on a door:

"Sauzelle's got no business in that hut. The fishing season has finished."

Capestan brushed the risk aside with a shrug, while Torrez shoved his hands in his pockets and stared at his boots.

"We shouldn't go there. I've got a bad feeling," he said.

The *lieutenant* was insistent, and his contagious anxiety was starting to irritate Capestan. In trying to play the role of Cassandra, he was simply inviting disaster. The *commissaire* was not one for superstition, but she did have an aversion to die-hard pessimism.

It took them a couple of minutes to get to the pond. Two children were screeching with delight on the seesaw in the playground. Further on, the wooden hut could be seen nestling among the oaks and horse chestnuts of a little island, which they reached via a low embankment that served as a dam. The shade from the huge trees meant that every inch of the ground was covered in moss, and the air was thick with the smell of damp earth. They walked toward the hut. The door was open. The carpet of twigs and dead leaves crackled underfoot. Torrez made a slight motion toward Capestan's arm, trying to make her hold back, but she refused to hold back. If the *lieutenant* was going to get over these nervous niggles, she would have to prove that she could work alongside him without the whole world crashing down. She gave a firm knock on the wooden door and stepped inside the hut.

The small room was pitch black. Capestan's eyes had no chance to get used to the darkness, because a violent blow struck her on the temple, sending a piercing pain through her skull. As the adrenaline flooded through her body, a single thought jolted through her mind just before she collapsed: "Whoever you are, when I wake up, I will kill you."

21

"You won't take me like this!" Sauzelle yelled feverishly.

Torrez, hands in the air, was standing six feet from the shotgun aimed at his chest. The weapon, an old Browning that must have dated back to the seventies, was shaking in the man's hands, but his face was determined. Sauzelle kept glancing worriedly at Capestan, who was still laid out by the doorway. It was hard to tell whether he was afraid she might wake up or not wake up.

Torrez, who was unfortunately all too familiar with such situations, tried to rein in his frantic emotions. He was not going to lose his partner—not again. A steady stream of blood was running from her left temple. She appeared to be breathing, but her face had gone terribly white and she was not moving.

He had warned her . . . Why hadn't she listened? Despite his gnawing anxiety, Torrez managed to pull himself together. If there was to be any hope of rescuing the situation, he would have to stay focused.

Sauzelle was nervous. His blue eyes, small and alert, were darting in every direction and strands of gray hair stuck to his sweat-covered forehead. Torrez needed to restore some calm to the confined space of the hut. It was up to him to prevent the situation from escalating. He found his voice, taking care to keep a measured tone:

"No one wants to take you away, Monsieur Sauzelle. We're just here to ask you some questions."

"That's not true, I had a warning! You're here to take me to prison, but I won't go! Not at my age!"

Sauzelle's voice was strained and he was clinging tight to his weapon. Through a mix of desperation and sheer panic, he was refusing to go down without a fight. This state of mind meant there was a good chance of his letting off a shot. He was struggling to articulate his words, but they continued tumbling out:

"Same as last time, you tried to pin the murder on me before you came up with the burglary story . . ."

"You don't believe it was a burglary?" Torrez said.

"No, of course not! But it wasn't me!"

Interesting. The brother had his doubts, too. Surely he had his reasons: they just needed to figure out what those were in order to move the investigation forward. The investigation? First things first, they needed the *commissaire* to survive safe and sound. Torrez should never have agreed to be her partner. Not her, not anybody. He shouldn't have given in.

Capestan's motionless body was still stretched out on the dark, dank floorboards. Above her, a khaki oilskin was hanging from a big, rusty nail. A pair of rubber Wellington boots, also khaki, had toppled over, and the heel of one was touching Capestan's head.

"Why don't you believe it?" Torrez said, still trying to calm the aggressor.

"I don't know. Because of the flowers. Marie hated cut flowers— she never bought them."

This line of argument was even more speculative than their thoughts about the DVD player, the closed shutters, and the missing cat.

"Someone might have given them to her."

Sauzelle nodded his head vigorously—that's just what he was coming to:

"Yes, exactly—the murderer."

"Or someone else—a boyfriend . . ."

Torrez saw Capestan twitch. She was coming to. Torrez knew he must not let Sauzelle notice: he had to distract him somehow. A cluster of fishing rods and tangled nets occupied a corner of the hut, just within Torrez's reach. He was reluctant to knock them over—too risky. The old man was on edge, and it would only take a slight surprise for him to pull the trigger. A verbal intervention would be a more sensible approach. Torrez took a deep breath and went for it:

"You didn't mean to kill her, it was only an accident."

Sauzelle reared at the accusation.

"No! It wasn't an accident, but it wasn't me. Why would I have killed her, anyway?"

"The house. A couple of million."

"But I haven't sold it."

Capestan opened her eyes. After a moment, she discreetly brought a hand to the side of her head. She could feel the blood on her fingers and a fierce expression came over her that Torrez had never seen before. She sized up Sauzelle and prepared to act.

"Plus, you have a history of violence," Torrez said.

"Me?"

The old man seemed genuinely amazed. Torrez nodded at the shotgun and Sauzelle's face contorted with embarrassment. The lieutenant turned the screw:

"A man who beats his wife can just as easily kill his sister."

Sauzelle lowered his weapon in astonishment.

"Me? I never touched Minouche! What are you saying?"

In a fraction of a second, Capestan gathered herself and pounced on Sauzelle. She bundled him to the floor and grabbed the barrel of the shotgun in one hand, wrenching it away from him roughly, shoving it to the other end of the hut. Sauzelle stood up with his back to the wall, but Capestan didn't let him regain his balance. She seized him by the throat and pinned him upright against the wooden boards, which quaked under the strain. She held him like that, arms straight and hands tight on his windpipe. Sauzelle's blue eyes bulged with terror. In that brief instant, Torrez thought she was going to kill him, and he started forward to intervene, but Capestan abruptly released her grip. Sauzelle sank to his knees and spluttered to regain his breath.

22

The pharmacist pushed down on the pedal of the metal trashcan and threw in the alcohol-soaked sterile pad.

"All cleaned up," she said to Capestan, who stood up from the gray footstool where she had been sitting to have her wound examined.

Standing before the shelves of medicinal infusions, Torrez and Sauzelle both looked as guilty as the other as they observed the end to the procedure. Traces of bruising were starting to break out on Sauzelle's neck. He wasn't hurt, but Capestan felt uneasy all the same. He was nearly seventy, and she had displayed a level of aggression applicable for a man half his age.

They left the pharmacy under a clear blue sky. An airplane had left a vapor trail in its wake, a stratospheric oddity that you only seemed to see in the countryside. After installing Sauzelle in the back seat of their car, Capestan and Torrez leaned against the vehicle to discuss their plan of action.

The man had taken two police officers hostage and threatened them with a gun. He had even knocked one of them out. At the same time, even though she could justify it as self-defense, Capestan's response had been disproportionate. And the *commissaire* was anxious to spare herself another hearing with IGS—she did not have enough points left on her license. As for Torrez, he was reluctant to sustain another blow to his reputation. They agreed not to press charges against Marie's brother. All that remained was to ask him a few questions.

Sauzelle, still a bit shaken up, watched them through the car window, waiting for the verdict. Capestan motioned to him to lower it, which he did promptly. He welcomed the news of his exemption with relief and gratitude, then asked straightaway—aware that this might be pushing it—whether he could answer their questions at the same time as doing his round of deliveries: this whole incident meant he was running late.

As soon as they arrived back by the pond, Sauzelle opened the back of his white van, which had the words VERGERS SAUZELLE stamped on its side, and took out a crate of apples, offering the officers two of the shiniest specimens. Torrez accepted with the fulsome thanks of a well-mannered schoolchild; Capestan declined with a shake of the head. Her scalp was throbbing and she still felt unsteady on her feet. She gave Torrez a meaningful glance, prompting him to take the lead—she would observe from the background, giving her temper time to calm down. The *lieutenant* bit into the apple before beginning, opting for a less mild approach in order to maintain their upper hand.

"Did Naulin tell you we were coming?"

"Yes. He told me that you'd questioned him, that you were on your way, and that you'd almost certainly be arresting me . . ."

Sauzelle was standing in front of the back of his van, wiping his hands on his trousers, a washed-out pair of jeans with a neat crease running down each leg. The man didn't really know what to think anymore.

Torrez held out his apple to Capestan, then took out his notebook and pen to scribble a few words down.

"Did you get along well with your sister?" the lieutenant asked.

"Yes, we were very close."

"Despite living two hundred miles apart?"

"It's not that far, just a little drive. And we spoke on the telephone all the time."

"You're right, it's not that far, just a little drive . . . You could easily have made it there and back in one night to kill her."

"No, absolutely not, I never left the area. Plenty of people will tell you—"

"Plenty of people can't be monitoring you every day, and certainly not every night."

"That's what your colleagues said last time."

"And what was your answer back then?" Torrez said, his pen hovering over his notebook.

"I hadn't bought enough gas for a journey that long . . . Anyway, that hardly matters. Nothing. I said nothing, but I never would have killed Marie."

Sauzelle swiped a stray curl of hair away from his forehead with a thick hand. His beige workman's jacket was fraying at the elbows.

"You know," he resumed in a dull voice, "we had lost both our parents. She was a widow, I was divorced. Neither of us had children. She had lots of friends, but I—I only had her."

Capestan took a few steps back, taking the apple with her. Nearby, four trees with thin trunks and bright-yellow leaves had been pruned into a spherical shape. They looked like giant matches that had been planted there to light up the green grass.

The smooth, syrupy surface of the pond shone like mercury. In the middle, a solitary duck was tracing a silvery furrow, following a decisive, unswerving trajectory. This duck knew where it was going. Unlike the murderer, Capestan thought to herself. He had been floundering, zigzagging. First he had brutally killed her with his bare hands; then he had sat the body back down and straightened her up with some dignity. He had strangled her, yet he had fixed her hair. There had been too many emotions bound up in such a staunch body. He had been unable to control them. Sauzelle fitted the profile, but did he have a proper reason to kill his sister?

Torrez, who had forgotten all about his apple, pressed on with the interrogation. By his reckoning, they had dispelled any suspicions about the brother and were now investigating other potential leads. So the *lieutenant* adjusted his line of attack and slipped into collaboration mode: a one-man display of good cop, bad cop.

"Was she on bad terms with anyone?"

"Maybe that property developer, the one in Paris . . ."

"Oh yes?" Torrez said, his voice at once gruff and encouraging.

Capestan wondered how he managed that. The lieutenant was able to string together questions and registers. It wasn't hard to see that he was an officer well accustomed to working alone.

"She was refusing to sell, but he was insistent," Sauzelle said. "But to go from that to . . . I didn't pay much attention, in any case."

"She was a retired teacher, correct? Can you tell us about her? Her life, her personality . . ."

"Yes, of course. But in all seriousness, do you mind if I start my rounds? You can fit in the van; it'll be a bit tight up front, but we're not going far."

Torrez looked over at the *commissaire*, and she nodded her consent.

They jammed themselves into the front seats and Sauzelle tore off at full speed.

"Where are we going?" Capestan said, returning to the fold.

"Bénévent-l'Abbaye. They have a three-day antiques fair there every autumn. I keep the bar stocked up with apple juice," the brother said, nodding at the cases of bottles in the back of his Berlingo.

The way into the village was blocked off for the fair, and Sauzelle had to move the barriers aside to reach the place de l'Église. On the way, they had learned a little more about Marie. A chance posting had sent her to Paris, where a woman of her vitality had gotten into the swing of things right away. She loved traveling, and on the death of her husband, she had taken a trip around the whole of Europe—by herself. She had also been hiking in the Holy Land, crossed the Atlantic to visit the Americas, and roamed across India and the Middle East. Sadly none of these voyages had yielded a second husband. Aside from that, Marie was passionate about tango, tarot, movies, and Asterix comics. Her cat was even called Tunafix. André Sauzelle could not remember if it had died by the time of her murder, but it wasn't something he had ever given much thought to.

Still misty eyed, the brother hauled out a few cases of bottles from his van and shut the door with his elbow.

"Give us a hand, big man," he said, offloading one to Torrez.

He thought better of trying it with Capestan, but she had the feeling that he had been tempted. The three of them headed to the beverage tent, and while Sauzelle chatted to his customers, Capestan and Torrez decided to sample his wares and a cheerful lady in a floral apron served them some juice that was murkier than the waters of the Seine. They went and sat on one of the benches and observed the gathering as they sipped at the nectar.

"I've been thinking back to the unforced dead bolt, the muted television . . . Marie muted her TV to go and open the door—I'm sure of it. She knew her attacker."

Torrez nodded in agreement. He had evidently arrived at the same conclusion.

"The brother fits the bill pretty well," he said.

"Yes . . . Even if I do find him less violent than the description in the file . . . ," Capestan began.

Torrez nearly choked on his juice. After regaining his breath, he pointed at his partner's mangled temple.

"Okay, but not really violent . . . ," the *commissaire* maintained. "Unstable, more like. Good profile, but he doesn't have a motive, he cared about his sister, he hasn't received a huge inheritance, he hasn't sold . . ."

"Maybe he's patient. Or he doesn't have the means to pay her inheritance taxes. We'd have to check the title deeds, do a bit of digging. And the motive could well relate to something else: family resentment, some sort of betrayal . . . Perhaps he couldn't bear sharing her affection."

Not so farfetched, Capestan thought to herself: this happens frequently where blood relations are concerned. Torrez traced a finger around the rim of his cup before saying:

"And Naulin? Naulin's not a bad fit."

Torrez had done his homework and found out that Naulin had a record for drug offenses. He peddled morphine and opium in the sixties but had been toppled by the next generation of dealers and seemed to have gone into early retirement. His current source of income was no less opaque.

Capestan chewed it over for a moment.

"He certainly looks like a tricky customer," she said. "I just don't know if the sale falling through is a solid enough motive. But then neighborhood spats are always tough to call . . ."

"You start by pumping up the volume on the TV and end up poisoning the dog . . ."

". . . or warning a suspect that the police are on their way. Just in case he had to get rid of any incriminating evidence."

The square was buzzing with various traders and stands of charcuterie and other local produce. A lady was sitting in a deck chair embroidering the doilies she was selling. Leaning against her stall was a bicycle with a NOT FOR SALE sign flapping in the breeze.

Capestan went to fetch two slices of *pâté aux pommes de terre* on cardboard plates, which they ate in silence with their fingers, enjoying the spectacle of the fair. In a vehicle that opened on the side like a pizza van, a man of about fifty gazed adoringly over his wares: a six-foot line of Kinder Surprises in tight formation, arranged by series in transparent boxes. The man was glowing, proud to be displaying his life's work. At a tiny stand next to him, his wife was nonchalantly threading wooden beads onto charm bracelets.

Sauzelle came over to break up their lunch party. Capestan put down her slice on the greasy cardboard and asked the question that been bothering her:

"Why did you never clean up the house? There are companies who can do that for you."

"Out of the question. Someone killed my sister. And the police let him get away with it. They closed the case. If I cleaned the house and sold it, that would be the end of that—just move on to the next thing. And then what? The house will stay as it is until this mess gets sorted out."

So the house is to stay and blight the city, Capestan thought as she studied the old man. A mass of bricks and memories that provided a blot on the landscape. So long as his sister was prevented from resting in peace, that street would not sleep easy. The *commissaire* recognized genuine, righteous anger when she saw it. This man was waiting for a conviction. He scratched his cheek and stared at the ground for a moment before starting again:

"This is where Marie is, not there. Here is where it counts, where it has to be tidy, well maintained. In the churchyard."

"One last thing, Monsieur Sauzelle. Was she wary by nature, or might she have opened her door to a stranger?"

"She was confident, but within reason. Strangers were better off outside than in."

"Is there anything other than the flowers that's stopping you from accepting the burglary theory?"

Capestan did not believe in intuition. Intuition was just a detail that occurred at the back of your brain. It needed to be brought forward for analysis, to be scrutinized in the nerve center. She needed something else: an uncharted feeling about his sister's death; a telephone conversation, perhaps.

"What did she say the last time you were on the telephone?" Capestan said.

Sauzelle scrunched up his face as he tried to remember, then suddenly he lit up:

"That's it! She had an evening, with one of her associations or clubs . . ."

"Tarot? Tango? Residents' association?"

"I can't remember. Hold on, she said it was something 'not very cheerful, but close to her heart.' That's it. That's the last thing she said to me," Sauzelle said in a distant voice, rubbing his nose with the back of his hand. "So, shall I take you back to your car?"

"Yes, thank you," Capestan said, getting to her feet.

She looked for somewhere to throw away her cup and saw a trash can that already had a good foot and a half of plastic cups spilling out of it. She managed to balance hers on top, and Torrez gave her his so she could perform the feat again. On their way to the van, the *lieutenant* stopped at a stand and bought two pots of honey. He handed one to Capestan.

"Here. To support local business," he said with a serious expression.

"Thanks," Capestan said, slightly taken aback. "I'll bring it to the *commissariat* so that everyone can enjoy it."

"As you wish."

Pushed up against the rear wall of the room, giddy from the deafening screams and crying, Alexandre squeezed her hand in his and stared through the windows at the back.

"One more try! I can see his head!" the midwife said, urging her on.

The girl from reception was standing next to them, gawking unashamedly at the event. Even the director of the museum had joined the party, wearing a striped polo shirt and a toothy smile fit for a lottery TV presenter. Alexandre would have chased them off right away, but he hadn't seen them come in. The midwife's encouragements became more intense and Alexandre started sweating buckets.

Outside he could hear the hustle and bustle of Mallory Square. Tourists were gathering in droves around the plaza and along the docks. At that time of day, they turned their backs on the jugglers to admire Key West's finest spectacle: sunset over the Gulf of Mexico. The expectation surrounding this moment of pure beauty spread across the entire island, forcing it to pause for a few minutes to catch its breath. His son was to be born here; he was to be born now.

His first cry shattered the silence.

One breath later, the child took hold of his father.

One step later, Alexandre was by Rosa's side, and they squeezed each other's hands. Both of them were stunned into silent admiration of the cherry-red infant, all sticky and wrinkled.

"Gabriel . . . ," the new mother murmured.

He was there.

For almost nine months, they had thought about this presence that would become the mainstay of their lives, yet they had never seen his face. Now they were meeting him for the first time. They welcomed him with tears streaming down their cheeks, proud mammals dazzled by their cub.

The midwife swaddled the newborn in a large terry towel, onto which the emotional director planted an I LIFTED A GOLD BAR sticker.

Before Alexandre could protest, Rosa burst out laughing. She was right, he thought to himself. A wild commotion broke out in Mallory Square: the crowd outside had burst into rapturous applause as the last rays of sunlight disappeared. Gabriel had been born, surrounded by treasure, before the whooping adulation of a crowd celebrating his star.

His arrival could not have been more auspicious.

23

Évrard had organized an impromptu darts tournament by pinning a target to the door at the end of the corridor. Two rooms down, Torrez must have been hoping against hope that no one would hurt themselves, but in the main arena it was all fun and games. Although not entirely: Capestan had just won her fourth round in a row. Out of four.

"I think we should play without her," Rosière announced, plucking her dart from the outermost ring.

Évrard, Merlot, Orsini, and even Lebreton nodded enthusiastically before returning to their mark, which had been painted directly onto the wooden floor.

"That's mean," Capestan protested, although secretly she was delighted.

Each time a player threw a dart, Pilou set off like a mad dog, then trotted back confusedly, one ear pricked and the other down.

"It's a fair point: having a shooting champion does slightly kill the fun," Évrard said.

"It's nothing like firing a pistol!"

Capestan had won silver in the twenty-five-meter pistol event at the Sydney Olympics in 2000. Twelve years later, she was not even allowed to look at a gun.

"Whatever," Évrard said, lining up the tips of her sneakers with the red ochre.

The telephone rang in the living room.

"There you go, you're all off the hook," Capestan called out with a wry smile, knowing it would be for her.

She went to her metal-top desk and cleared away the samples of English wallpaper that Rosière had submitted for group discussion. She picked up the telephone and sat down in her swivel chair. It was bound to be Buron, all set to deliver the roasting of the century.

Earlier that morning, Riverni's outraged face had been plastered across the front of every newspaper in the city, free and paid-for alike. The pages that followed contained ruthlessly precise and formidably well-informed articles about Riverni the Younger's misdemeanors. Orsini, like the seasoned pro that he was, knew how to unleash a good story. He lit the fire online, kindled it by providing *Le Canard enchaîné* with the necessary documents, and by the eight o'clock news, which had no choice but to run it, the whole thing was up in flames, only for the sparks to land on the following morning's dailies. Orsini always delivered the goods; the journalists knew how reliable a source he was. Buron must have been glued to his telephone all morning.

Capestan held her breath as she picked up.

"Typical," Buron said. "I suppose I should have seen this coming!"

"Good morning, Monsieur le Directeur. It was too tempting, yes. Only seems just."

"Just? Just! Do you know what Riverni wants to do with your 'justice'? He wants to fire the whole group of you!"

Buron was almost choking. Capestan pictured his scarlet face, bow tie ready to detonate. His receiver must be gleaming after that almighty shower.

"Permission to shed a tear?"

"It's not tears you'll be shedding, Capestan! You are intolerable: you'll never change. Senior management, police headquarters, the ministry . . . the whole goddamn barnyard has been on my case since seven o'clock asking where this leak came from. It's not a leak, it's goddamn Aqualand! You didn't pull any punches. You didn't stop at telling the press about the boy and his cocaine; you had to tell them about his father attempting to hush it up."

The game of darts had resumed without Capestan, and the players were having a lot more fun. She always found it fascinating how much people hate losing—herself included.

"You left me with no choice. And you know it," she said.

"You always have a choice. And you routinely opt for the one that appeals to your pride."

"The squad's pride," Capestan corrected him. She distractedly leafed through the wallpaper samples, eventually settling on the red ochre.

"There we have it. Fine. I didn't tell HQ that it came from your squad. That wouldn't have done you any favors, Capestan. Let me remind you how close you were to going to the slammer. I decided to protect you. I'm not asking you to thank me—"

"But I do thank you, wholeheartedly. Thank you, Monsieur le Directeur: thank you very much. I'm grateful for your understanding and for your exemplary discretion," she said, surprising herself with her tone.

It wasn't insolence. She often tried that with Buron, but usually in less tricky situations as a way of lightening the mood. Not that he ever took offense: he was more than aware of the endless, unswerving admiration she had for him. Her respect for the chief was never genuinely in question. But her response had clearly been out of tune with the reprimand she had just received. It was like a sudden flash of inspiration. Capestan wouldn't have been able to explain such a sudden, uninhibited display of nonchalance; this sense of play acting. Buron, however, far from reprimanding her, copied her benign tone:

"And apart from this, how's the squad? All going well?"

After a few minutes of lighthearted conversation, Capestan hung up, only for the telephone to ring again immediately, like a rebound.

"Did you forget something, Monsieur le Directeur?" she said.

There was a moment of hesitation at the other end, shortly followed by an oily voice that Capestan recognized with a shudder of revulsion.

"Good morning, *commissaire.*"

"Monsieur Naulin, hello," she said. "What can I do for you?"

"I just wanted to let you know that a young man just rang my bell looking for Marie Sauzelle."

"Did he now? For any reason in particular?"

"He just wanted to talk her, or so he said. He was very surprised and extremely upset to hear that she had died seven years ago."

"What did he look like?" Capestan said, pulling a pad toward her and picking up a ballpoint that turned out to be a dud. She tested three others by scribbling on the back of the wallpaper samples, ultimately finding a red rollerball that did the job. Why was it never the blue or black ones that worked?

"Like a sort of young, squirrelly boy with reddish-brown hair. A ruddy complexion, almost as red as his hair. Around five foot eleven. A handsome boy, but gangly—not grown into his body, if you know what I mean. Timid, eyes darting all over the place. The lobe of his left ear was missing. And perhaps a finger, but I'm not entirely sure. He was wearing an orange zip-up hoodie, and one of those new cartoon-style T-shirts . . ."

"Manga?"

"Absolutely. He was also wearing beige Bermuda shorts and enormous sneakers, you know those ones that make them look like Mickey Mouse."

Capestan could hear Naulin smiling: he couldn't resist a bit of humor.

"And a bright-green bike helmet . . ."

His precision was remarkable, suspicious even. Capestan had been around there the day before. She had wanted to share her thoughts surrounding the welcome she had received in Creuse thanks to his efforts. She had come for an explanation, but Naulin had stalled in classic fashion, denying any responsibility, then played the impenetrable, enigmatic card as soon as she started asking questions. Exasperated and still reeling from the blow to her temple, Capestan had rattled him a bit, but Naulin had nothing new to report. The *commissaire* should have gone easier on him. She left convinced that the guy was guilty, but she still didn't have anything firm to go on. Naulin obviously woke up this morning and decided to make himself seem more innocent. Now here he was—description at the ready—providing the perfect smokescreen.

"Did he leave a name?"

"Unfortunately not."

Well, there you have it.

"Shame, but thanks all the same, Monsieur Naulin. Your sketch was extremely precise," Capestan said, with a hint of irony.

"Always eager to help," he said in his unctuous tone.

Capestan said good-bye and hung up. She stood there for a few moments studying the notes on her desk. In the end, she tore off her jottings from the piece of wallpaper and went to knock on Torrez's door, waiting for his response before entering.

The *lieutenant* was sitting on his sofa reading through André Sauzelle's tax records—paying particular attention to the inheritance—by the light of an adjustable architect's lamp that he had bolted to a stool. On the floor, his old cassette player was issuing a melancholy Yves Duteil number. The heat in the room was suffocating. A new poster had been pinned to the wall: a junior football team—Paris Alésia FC—made up of three rows of youngsters in oversized shorts bookended by two coaches in undersized tracksuits.

Capestan relayed Naulin's telephone call word for word and Torrez noted down the description for himself.

"What do you make of it?" the *commissaire* said, rubbing the scar on her index finger.

"A nice present, all wrapped up with a ribbon."

"Exactly. Without a name, either. I'm struggling to see how the details hang together. A young guy with red hair and a hoodie . . . wearing Bermuda shorts at this time of year? Clearly he doesn't feel the cold," Capestan said.

"When it comes to clothes and teenagers, the weather's the last thing on their mind."

"You've got a teenager, too?"

"You name it, I've got it," Torrez replied earnestly. "We might be able to run a search on the bright-green bike helmet. Not a typical color—must come from a specialist cycling shop. If we find one in Decathlon, though, we're screwed."

"Let's just pretend for a second that this kid exists outside Naulin's imagination: could it have any importance? A boy visits an old lady who's been dead for seven years. Why?"

Torrez scrunched up his dark eyes, hunting for a clue, a key, an opening.

"Former pupil? Remember she used to be a teacher," he said.

"Yes, maybe. Listen, I'll look into the helmet and we'll bear the description in mind, but let's not fret too much about this. It's a tip-off from Naulin, after all."

Capestan was by the door, about to leave, when the evening event mentioned by André Sauzelle came back to her.

"Did you find anything about a function or a meeting of some sort in Marie's calendar?" she said.

"No, no I didn't: in fact I wanted to talk to you about that."

Torrez held up a finger to try and detain the *commissaire*, and with his other hand he searched through the documents scattered across his desk.

"There wasn't anything written in her schedule, so I thought about checking her mail to see if she'd received an invitation. But . . . have a look," he said, digging out a piece of paper from the *crim* file. "Turns out there wasn't a single letter in the list of evidence recovered from Sauzelle's house."

"Maybe they didn't see anything worth picking up," Capestan said.

"That was my initial thought, but I went to check the premises," Torrez replied, exuding professionalism. "I searched the writing desk in the living room, the drawers under the bookshelves, the hall table: nothing. Apart from an electric bill and a letter about some competition from a mail order company, there wasn't a single envelope."

"You're right, that is strange. Especially for someone so involved in clubs and community life."

"The murderer took her mail—I don't see any other way around it. If you want my opinion, he didn't just know the victim, but the two of them took part in some sort of activity together."

Before Capestan could say even a word, the *lieutenant* held up one of his big mitts in surrender:

"I know, I know, only one thing to do: check to see if there's a record of anything with the local clubs."

The game of darts was finished. Capestan went through to join the team in the kitchen. The doors onto the terrace were wide open, and Lebreton and Rosière were out there smoking. Évrard had her hands clasped around a cup of coffee. Orsini, rigid as a watchtower, was surveying them all. Capestan went over to him and drew him to one side.

"*Capitaine*," she said, "my approach may seem naïve to you, but—"

"Don't worry, *commissaire*," he cut in. "When it comes to this squad, I am not banking on reporting anything I see to the IGS or the press. I denounce only the corrupt. They may be in prison, they may be in office, but they are never discarded. No offense intended, but the actions of cretinous officers in the naughty corner do not concern me in the slightest."

"Well, you've been posted here, too," Capestan said, eager to take a stand against Orsini's disdain for his colleagues.

He cordially acknowledged her point, rearranged his navy-blue silk handkerchief, and smiled:

"I consider my role to be more of a supporting one, *commissaire*."

Capestan nodded her agreement and walked away from the *capitaine*. That final remark had given her pause, and she moved it to the back of her head to let it simmer away.

She opened the fridge and poured herself some fruit juice before going out for some air herself. Merlot completed the gathering on the terrace, holding a spoon in one hand and the pot of honey from Torrez in the other. Without any consideration whatsoever for future consumers, he plunged the spoon into the pot and put it directly in his mouth. As he was about to plunge it back, Capestan leapt forward to rescue the honey.

"That's a present from Torrez," she said, fully aware that this might discourage anyone else from touching it.

Merlot thought about protesting for a second, then brought all his attention to bear on the spoon, which he licked with delight:

"Honey, my children. Honey! Is it not truly marvelous what nature gives us?"

Pilou sniffed in agreement, desperate for some to fall.

"It doesn't 'give' us anything," Rosière objected, wagging a chubby finger at Merlot. "It takes hundreds of little bees working their asses off for months to build up their supply, only for a human to pop in at the end and steal the whole lot like some goddamn gangster. It's one wing forward and two wings back for those poor bees. Back they go to square one! Nature 'giving' . . . Honestly! We steal it and that's that! 'Marvelous,' *pfff* . . ."

Rosière often concluded her diatribes with a melodramatic "pfff." Merlot carried on smiling, nodding as he admired the spoon, apparently pleased for Rosière to have her say. Merlot loved his life. His ego functioned with eye-watering simplicity: all glory and gain was for him, and everything else was of no consequence whatsoever.

At the far end of the terrace, Orsini was now removing the dead leaves from the rose-bay. He had supplied the press with a wealth of remarkably detailed information relating to the Riverni case. Capestan had seen it coming, but even so the end result had surpassed her expectations. The perennially chic old-school *capitaine* filled both hands with leaves before disposing of them in the kitchen trash. Capestan realized that, deep down, she had never been afraid of Orsini. From the start, she had regarded him as a solution, not a threat.

The *commissaire*'s thoughts returned to Buron, whose reprimand had gone above and beyond, despite the fact that—as he acknowledged at the start—he hadn't been at all surprised by her conduct. The *directeur* knew Orsini, and he knew Capestan even better. As much as she hated to admit it, she became extremely predictable the moment she was backed into a corner. She responded badly to arbitrary bans and did everything she could to bypass them. Buron had known that for a long time. All of a sudden, Capestan became certain that she was being played. Like a fiddle. And she hadn't kicked up the smallest fuss. Now she needed to find out why.

An impulse made her turn to Merlot, who had left his spoon lying on one of the deck chairs.

"*Capitaine*, may I ask you a favor?" she asked.

"But of course, my dear girl. At your service."

"If any of your contacts has heard anything about a spat between Buron and Riverni, I'd like to hear about it."

24

They had left in the middle of the night. The deserted streets of Paris filed past them. The windows of the apartment buildings were pitch black, and the occasional sound of traffic seemed muffled, as if coming from far away. At a red light, Lebreton had spotted a small group of tipsy thirty-somethings smoking outside a club, spotlit by the neon sign above the entrance. Soon they would be joining the Périphérique, where the Lexus could finally open herself up, like a dog off its leash in a field.

Lebreton was driving smoothly, savoring the engine's barely audible purr. The leather seats were as cozy as anything, and the orangey glow from the dashboard cast a soft light on their faces. Pilote was lying peacefully in the back on his fleece-lined blanket, letting out the occasional snore. For once, Rosière hadn't doused herself in boatloads of Guerlain, and the Lexus's new-car smell prevailed. Lebreton had prepared a playlist for the journey: a few country classics, some California surf tunes, and a handful of Otis Redding numbers. A soundtrack for a road trip to the coast.

Rosière had been asleep since they got off at the A11 after Saint-Arnoult, only waking up when they had to slow down for the Roche-sur-Yon toll booth. She stretched and leaned down to grab her handbag, insisting on paying, but Lebreton had been too quick with his card. As he pulled away, she asked a question that she must have been sitting on for a while.

"Is it true you used to be a RAID negotiator?" she said casually.

"Yes. For ten years."

Ten years that went by in a heartbeat. Lebreton had adored that job. It had been all about action, composure, discipline, and listening. Identifying peaceful solutions in the heat of crazed situations; focusing on the last line of defense—negotiation—before the guys with guns and balaclavas came storming in. Ten years of training, honing his skills, and he had never been bored for a second. The *commandant* had an instant flashback to the day before, back in their *commissariat*, where he had noticed that his computer keyboard was missing its A and ENTER buttons.

Lebreton chose not to expand, so Rosière took the reins:

"RAID, that's pretty classy. What took you to IGS?"

"Nothing took me—it wasn't my decision."

During the recruitment phase, Lebreton had never mentioned his sexual orientation. The rapid-response unit was like testosterone HQ, rife with prejudice, and he had wanted the job. And he had gotten it. After that, his performance had placed him beyond suspicion.

"Why?" Rosière said, twisting in her seat so she could see him more easily.

"Do you know what it's like to be gay in the police force?"

"For starters, I'm guessing the word 'gay' doesn't come up much . . ."

Lebreton smiled.

"Yes, for starters."

And then Vincent had arrived on the scene. The years went by and he grew tired of keeping secrets. One morning, on the banks of the Canal Saint-Martin, Lebreton and his boyfriend had bumped into Massard, a RAID *commandant*. Lebreton had introduced Vincent, making no bones about who he was. At the time, Massard had played the worldly, liberal card, not that they were seeking any reaction at all.

"When the word got out, I was transferred in two weeks flat. They promoted me to *commandant* to sweeten the pill."

The IGS: the elephant graveyard, the end of the earth, the hole. Lebreton did not think it was possible to descend any lower. At least, not until Capestan's squad came along. In the end, however, the work hadn't been entirely without interest. There was a constant stream of officers mistaking their ID badge for a blank check.

"Is it true you grilled Capestan while you were there?"

Prime example, Lebreton thought to himself. Batman syndrome. He kept this to himself, however, and simply turned away. The leaves on the trees at the top of the embankment running alongside the divided highway had turned yellow, while the countryside that appeared in the rearview mirror from time to time was still green.

"The last time she slipped up, yes," he confirmed, then turned to Rosière and said: "But I'm not supposed to discuss it, sorry."

He thought back to the case. Two children kidnapped by a teacher. It had taken Capestan six months to locate them. When she arrived at the premises, she killed him: simple as that.

"It was self-defense, wasn't it?" Rosière insisted.

"Indeed."

If you can call it self-defense when the guy is standing fifteen feet away armed with a pen, and Capestan shoots him three times, right in the heart. Not exactly where you aim if you're planning to immobilize a suspect. Capestan maintained that she had been unable to adjust her line of fire. Coming from an Olympic silver medal markswoman, that was verging on the unreasonable. Lebreton still couldn't believe the top brass had let it slide.

"Then what happened after the IGS? How did you end up with us?"

Pilou started gnawing at the armrest, causing her mistress to raise an authoritative finger. The dog calmed down, stopped, let out a powerful yawn that finished with a satisfied squeak, then made a half turn and went back to sleep. Dawn was gradually lighting up the inside of the car, and with it came an urge for coffee. The orange sun blazed through the back window, streaming down the road in a straight line. Lebreton felt like he was riding down the freeway, and he was longing for a bit of silence for company.

"Well?" Rosière said with the persistence of a hammer drill.

The *capitaine*, with her honest warmth and uncomplicated energy, was in the mood for exchanging secrets, and Lebreton could not shake her off without hurting her. He veered into the fast lane to overtake two trucks.

"Vincent's death was a shock," he said blankly. "But two weeks after the funeral, I was back at work."

Lebreton remembered how he felt wandering aimlessly along the corridors, unable to find his office in the confusion. Colleagues patted him on the back sympathetically, commiserating as far as they deemed necessary.

"I couldn't concentrate, so I went to the *divisionnaire* to request some unpaid leave."

"And he said no?"

"He said that it would be a big inconvenience for him."

Lebreton had mentioned bereavement leave. Damien, who had lost his wife the year before, had taken a much-needed break, four months, to straighten himself out. The *divisionnaire* was aghast and said: "You can't honestly make that comparison!"

A billion explanations would not have been enough to open that brute's heart. Lebreton had had his fill: enough self-justification, enough toeing the party line. If even the officers in charge of cleaning up the police were guilty of discrimination, then something needed to be done.

"So?" Rosière said, keen as ever for the next installment.

"I filed a complaint on grounds of discrimination. I took it right to the top, both at police headquarters and the Ministry of the Interior."

"And what did they do?"

"Nothing, of course. Internal affairs was hardly going to investigate internal affairs."

"Your *divisionnaire* got away with it just like that?"

Taking his eyes off the road just for a moment, Lebreton aimed a wry smile at his copilot:

"Which of us is sitting next to you in the car?"

The sign indicating the road into Les Sables-d'Olonne put an end to the conversation. Lebreton and Rosière wound down their windows in perfect synchronization, and a gust of humid, salty air came rushing into the car. The dog sat up in the back and moaned impatiently. Rosière held her hand outside and splayed her fingers to feel the breeze, while Pilote dug his claws into the armrest and tried to clamber up front to reach the window and catch that promising smell of seaweed. It was 8:00 a.m., too early to turn up at the shipbuilder's, but perfect for a coffee break by the sea.

Lebreton passed through the barrier to the outdoor parking lot at the fishing port and slid the Lexus into a diagonal space, applying the hand brake and cutting the engine. Before getting out, Rosière returned to Capestan: something kept bothering her about the stray bullet.

"Her partner wasn't there to cover her . . . Maybe she got the jitters?"

"In our squad, she chose to team up with Torrez. Torrez," he said, to ram home his point. "Capestan's not afraid of anything."

25

Capestan was afraid of everything. After showering and dressing, she went back to the bedroom to close the windows that she had flung open to air the place out, then drew back the duvet, taking care to remove the revolver from under the pillow. She had placed it there the night before; she placed it there every night. It was her old spare gun, now simply her gun, thanks to the administration confiscating her Smith & Wesson. She could no longer sleep without it. She felt Paris lying in wait for her behind the door, and she needed her piece like others need sleeping pills. Her job had broken her. It was a career she had chosen out of preference rather than sheer bravado, a way of disrupting the neatly mapped-out trajectory for young girls: further education, then an appropriate husband. Enthusiasm and a sense of duty had taken her far, but compassion and emotiveness had pushed her into a corner. And Capestan had been afraid ever since. Not that she had become deflated: losing her self-respect would have meant the end. She was better at containing her fear than her fury, fully aware that they were two sides of the same coin.

Earlier that morning she had decided to examine the Sauzelle case out of doors, to see whether the ins and outs would seem any different in the fresh air. The sun was faint but it was shining nonetheless, and she settled for a chair in the Jardin du Luxembourg.

Facing the pond, she had split her time between rereading the various facts and observing the procession of passersby.

She had called the land registry office on her cell phone, followed by the Issy-les-Moulineaux town hall, and finally the Issy-Val-de-Seine property group to follow up on the Bernard Argan lead—the developer that Naulin had mentioned. She had found out that the contracts for the alternative media site had been signed a month before Marie Sauzelle's murder. So at the time of the crime, Argan had no reason to apply any pressure: one more suspect they could cross off the list.

With her mind at peace from the calm of the park, Capestan headed down boulevard Saint-Michel, reflecting on the fine scent of autumn as she passed under the horse chestnuts. She reached the quai above the Seine and admired Notre-Dame to her right, so magnificently authoritative, passing judgment on all the souls of Paris.

On the other side of the quai, she saw a dog sitting at the foot of a pedestal. It was a Rottweiler. Capestan didn't have anything in particular against Rottweilers, but she was glad that Rosière had gone for the Pilote format. As always, the *commissaire* looked up at the owner to see if he resembled his dog. He was sitting with his legs hanging over the wall, and no question he looked even less friendly than his dog. The man patted the stone patch next to him to encourage the animal to join him, but it was afraid and refused to jump: it didn't know what emptiness lay behind the wall. The Rottweiler folded back its ears, tail between its legs, but the owner insisted, yanking the leash and shouting at it to jump. A wave of fury pinned Capestan to the spot. The dog was scared to death—the guy needed to back off with his vicious commands. Capestan couldn't cross because the lights were green and the cars were flying past. The animal was lying flat on the ground now, and the stumpy owner had come down from his perch to stand over it in a menacing fashion. The *commissaire* could see him screaming at the poor thing, and he looked like he was about to hit it. Capestan was ready to explode with anger. It felt as if she had a hundred hornets buzzing around her head, and a red mist started blurring her vision. She paced around the pavement as the cars rushed past, glaring up at the light. She was going to cross the road, grab the bastard's head, and smash it against the wall until he stopped yelling at his dog. She could already hear the bone crunching against the stone, so in her mind she moderated the force of the impact, but only by a touch. A primal, apelike aggression was pumping through her veins, and she responded to its beat. Suddenly the cars all stopped and the pedestrian crossing opened up before her. On the other side, the Rottweiler had managed to jump up and was sitting there with its tongue hanging out, appreciating the respite. Next to it, the scumbag owner was lighting a cigarette. Capestan was breathing heavily as she crossed the road. An irrepressible anger was still pricking at her temples, goading her on to kill the bastard. His dog had not died today, but maybe it would tomorrow. The *commissaire*'s sense of reason was hammering away at her skull, begging her to unclench her fists: the emergency was over; you don't kill for that. She was not allowed to kill. The message forced its way through and prudence seeped back into her pores. Capestan swerved abruptly, redoubling her pace toward the bridge and the office beyond.

It was getting worse and worse. Now even dogs were sending her to the edge. Before long she'd be unable to face up to the ordeals that came with police work. Like skin that becomes allergic following exposure, instead of toughening over time, she was softening; her defenses were crumbling, and she was becoming entirely susceptible. Soon she would be totally unfit, as savage as the scumbag back there. As she walked along, she rolled her entire being into a corner of her subconscious in an effort to calm down.

Fury. Killing a man but saving a dog.

Capestan stopped on the bridge.

What if Marie's cat had been alive at the time of the burglary? The food and water bowls weren't there anymore, but the killer could always have taken them. What if he had decided to spare the cat? To adopt it?

What sort of murderer would do a thing like that?

Sitting down to enjoy a helping of smoked herring and potatoes in oil, Merlot poured himself a large glass of Côtes-du-Rhône, then thumped the cork back in with a veteran hand. As he lifted it to his lips, a flash of inspiration brought the glass to a standstill.

"Is that Rosière not unattached?"

A lusty smile crept across his face, and a hand came up to his bald pate to slick back a curl of hair that had long since disappeared. Old habits die hard. The *capitaine*'s head bobbed up and down.

"Ho ho. And Capestan, too," he said to himself, full of confidence.

26

Rosière and Lebreton walked around the fishing port to reach the pier, where two lighthouses, one green and one red, faced each other on opposite sides of the channel. The green one was slightly tilted, like a palm tree assailed by one storm too many. The view encompassed the vast bay of Sables-d'Olonne. Little waves were rolling in from the ocean, which was still calm at this early hour. Up on the long promenade hugging the beach, a waiter in an apron and sneakers was laying the tables on the terrace of Brasserie Le Pierrot.

They sat down and ordered a coffee, along with a bowl of water for the dog. Once their order had arrived and the waiter had gone back indoors, Rosière took a deep breath and summarized the facts before they went into battle.

"Objectively speaking, it's simple enough: if Jallateau doesn't talk, we've got nada, diddly-squat. He's our number one suspect; in fact he's our only suspect. If he doesn't give us the hint of a confession or a fresh lead, then we're back to square one. And we'll have to tell the widow that in three months the case will lapse and that it's time to move on."

"The last time the police questioned this guy they came back empty handed," Lebreton said.

"The last time the police questioned this guy they did a shitty job of it. Up to us to prove we're better."

Rosière unwrapped the *biscuit* that came with her coffee and gave it to her dog, who took it delicately between his teeth, gobbled it up in one gulp, then looked at her eagerly, all set for round two. Rosière looked at Lebreton, who surrendered his speculoos.

"You look like you've got a plan," he said.

"No. But we're not going in stark naked—I've got something up my sleeve. We'll win him over with a fake commission."

"I'm not convinced that's admissible, Eva—"

"Oh my little Loulou, you are sweet. Listen—we have to make do with what we've got. He's loaded and lawyered up, and we don't have any cargo whatsoever. We need to come in at an angle. This Guénan business goes way back—he won't suspect a thing. Let's go in softly-softly, talc up his balls, then grab them."

Lebreton stirred his coffee in silence for a few moments. If they went in like their predecessors, they would come away with the same results. Rosière was right about that. Better to mix things up.

"Fine," he said, setting his spoon down on the saucer. "I will be amazed if it works, but I'm listening."

At 9:15 a.m., they left the Lexus at the Marée parking lot next to a thirty-eight-ton ship unloading huge polystyrene boxes full of sardines and walked to Jallateau's company headquarters. Between the seaweed and the bird shit, they were getting a good dose of the local fragrance, Rosière thought. There were few people around, and the *capitaine* was the only woman. The men gazed at them: they were hardly your average tourists looking to get off the beaten track. Gigantic concrete towers loomed overhead, dominating the rusty corrugated-iron roofs of the warehouses. The grinding of the cranes competed with the squawking of the seagulls, and farther along the masts of a thousand yachts swayed clumsily in the wind. The sea smelled of oil here. They arrived at the glass doors of a long, single-story building, above which were the words JALLATEAU SHIPBUILD-ERS in blue lettering.

"Let's smoke him out," Rosière said. "Best celebrity smile, now."

* * *

At the reception, a young man with ash-blond hair asked them if they had an appointment.

"Yes, at 9:30," the *capitaine* said. She had been careful to make an appointment. "Madame Rosière and Monsieur Lebreton."

"Absolutely. For a forty-two-foot catamaran."

"Indeed."

They did not have long to wait before Jallateau arrived. He greeted them and introduced himself in a friendly manner. He was wearing a gray suit and pointy shoes. The guy looked like a desert buggy ready to tackle a dune: thick, bumper-like eyebrows protecting his steely glare. Rosière realized it might not be so easy to hoodwink him after all.

They went into his office, their shoes sinking into the thick carpet, which was pristine and beige. There were shelves running the length of the wall exhibiting model boats and a few framed newspaper articles. At Jallateau's back, a wide sliding window looked out over the mouth of the channel. On the far bank you could make out the waterfront with its endless row of low multicolored houses. For Rosière, the charming view made focusing on Jallateau's ugly face all the more painful.

She kicked off her con artistry while Lebreton kept an eye on the shipbuilder's reactions. Jallateau was tight lipped as Rosière relayed her spiel, and when she finished he looked at them both in silence. He brushed a few pencil shavings off his desk, then clasped his hands together.

"You don't want a boat."

"How dare—"

"Buying a boat is the stuff of dreams, and you're not dreaming," he said with a contemptuous smile. "So. What do you want from me?"

Rosière needed a plan B. Supplier? Mafia? Insurer? She racked her brains as quickly as she could, but Lebreton beat her to it:

"Commandant Lebreton and Capitaine Rosière. We're investigating the murder of Yann Guénan."

Jallateau shut down immediately. An icy chill swept through the room. The silence lasted an age, pulsing with an electric tension.

"Police," he said.

The businessman's body language had lost all semblance of customer-facing courtesy, and his shoulders squared up as he sat forward in his chair.

"I wasted enough time with you back then," he spat with the tone of a dockworker. "Get lost!"

Lebreton braced himself as he opened up his file.

"First we'd like to ask you a few questions."

"I've heard them all before: I didn't like them then, and I won't like them now," Jallateau said.

"Guénan came here with a dossier about the *Key Line* shortly before his death. Did you have anything to hide?"

"Nothing, absolutely nothing!" Jallateau exploded. "It's a fantasy dreamed up by the filth! Nothing but mass paranoia. Don't start running after me with your conspiracy theories again. Do you really believe that this shipwreck hasn't been examined with a fine-tooth comb? Have you read the results of the public inquiry into the ship? There are six fucking volumes, a foot thick! Experts, engineers, insurers, judges, inspectors . . . my offices were full of them for months! Americans, French, even Cubans! Ten years of official investigation and they've got nothing on me! And do you know why? Because I've got nothing to do with that fucking accident! They should never have set sail in that weather, end of story. Now get out!"

The two police officers stayed where they were. Jallateau's face had turned purple and his hand was shaking as he pointed at the door.

"I said fuck off!"

"What do you think?" Lebreton said, turning to Rosière. "Should we fuck off? Does that sound good to you?"

"No, not so much. I like it here—we've got a nice view across the harbor."

Outside, a Zodiac was coming up the channel, its sausage-like sides bouncing off the choppy water. Lebreton looked back at Jallateau:

"We've had a good think about it, and we have decided to stay."

For a moment, Rosière wondered if the sailor was planning on throwing a punch. His torso swelled, but he thought the better of it. Lebreton's powerful physique had that effect—it had been one of the secrets to his success as a negotiator. Wearing a foul expression, Jallateau chose to glare at Rosière instead.

"The experts weren't on board the ship," she said, relishing the situation. "Guénan was. Did he blackmail you?"

"I've got nothing else to say. If you want to stay, fine, but I have some reading to do."

Jallateau gathered a pile of documents, picked up a pen, and started crossing out a few lines from the first page. After a short while, Rosière opened the outer pocket of her handbag and took out her cell phone, then made a show of browsing through her contact list.

"Loïc Cleac'h—does that name mean anything to you? I know I have his number here somewhere . . ."

Jallateau knew the Breton businessman extremely well. As Rosière could have read in any number of publications, the millionaire had just ordered the biggest luxury catamaran ever built in his shipyard. She brought the cell phone to her ear.

"He'll be relieved to hear that—according to the experts—your boats don't sink. It's ringing," she said, pointing at the earpiece.

The shipbuilder dropped his pen on his paperwork and rubbed his eyes before interrupting:

"Okay, okay."

He was tired of this business. Lowering his tone slightly, he continued:

"Listen, no disrespect to the memory of Guénan, but he wasn't the sharpest tool in the shed. I don't know much about his dossier, but apart from the petition, it can't have amounted to much. Even then, what's a petition worth at the end of the day? It wasn't just me he had a problem with, you know. He was looking for a passenger, too."

A passenger. Handy that, thought Rosière, refusing to be taken for a turkey.

Lebreton and Rosière left the interview a few minutes later feeling fairly despondent. There was no doubt the public inquiry had punctured Jallateau's potential motive: the shipbuilder was hardly likely to take out a man who was threatening to sue him when officials from several different states were lining up to scupper his company. The widow's unfailing support for her heroic husband had clouded their logical interpretation of the events. But there was still reason to suspect Jallateau, Rosière was sure of it. The close interval between Guénan's visit and his murder rendered the shipbuilder's innocence highly unlikely. All they had otherwise was this mystery passenger, about whom Jallateau had been unable to provide any details whatsoever.

At the end of their long day, the officers settled in to their hotel, where they had adjoining rooms linked by a small balcony. Earlier they had updated the *commissariat* before deciding to stay on for the evening to enjoy some ocean air and make the journey feel more worthwhile. As they ambled along the beach, the dense sand had resisted their weight. They didn't speak much, preferring to savor the rhythm of the waves and the backwash. The dog, on the other hand, zigzagged around for miles on end, honoring each ruined sandcastle with a delighted jet of urine, barking at the seagulls as they flew languidly away, and digging hole after hole before rubbing his sandy face against their trousers. Then they had retired to their hotel and its seafood restaurant. The ocean had gone back to sleep, all stillness and silence.

In the middle of the night, Lebreton woke with a start. *I don't know much about his dossier*: Jallateau's words had waited for this moment of calm to return to the surface. If Guénan and the shipbuilder had barely broached the dossier, then what had they spoken about?

Perhaps the mystery passenger that they had assumed was just a red herring did exist after all.

The *commandant* drew his sheet aside and crossed the room to get his overnight bag, a retro leather affair with fashionably shabby straps. He took out the dossier that Maëlle had given them and started rereading the pages for the third time, skimming through for the list of signatories to Guénan's petition. The sailor's delicate, tight handwriting was virtually illegible, but in the middle of the dozens of names, one caught his attention.

It was so unthinkable that he had to pull the sheet of paper closer to check he had read it correctly. No doubt about it. Lebreton put down the list and paused to think about what this discovery might imply.

Extraordinary.

Rosière was going to be over the moon. Lebreton was about to go and knock on her door, but the digital clock on his bedside table showed it was 4:00 a.m. It would have to wait until breakfast.

He went out to the balcony and sat down in the white plastic chair that was covered with a slick layer of sea spray. He lit a cigarette in the cool night air and looked out across the moonlit sea. He would try to sleep a little more before dawn.

Rosière was enjoying a cup of tea and some *tartines* on the terrace at Café des Sauniers, a small blue building where someone had gone to the effort of creating a mural showing a flock of seagulls. Pilou was licking his bowl thoroughly clean, pushing it right up against the table leg. The *capitaine*, never underprepared, kept a bag of dog biscuits and a bowl in the trunk of her car. She waved at Lebreton as he came out of the hotel. Pilou ran over to meet him, and the *commandant* tickled him behind the ears before heading to Rosière with his gentle stride. He had slicked back his thick hair after his shower without drying it. He grabbed the back of his chair with one hand, while the other scratched his five o'clock shadow.

"Did you shave with a stale *baguette*?"

Lebreton ordered a coffee and a *croissant* then sat down.

"I brought my razor, but I forgot the blades. *Mea culpa.*"

For months Lebreton had not forgotten a thing, purely because he had all the time in the world to get himself organized. Perhaps the joy of leaving had upset the pattern.

"*Tea forgivea,*" the *capitaine* answered, lifting her elbow impatiently to brush off some stray crumbs, but the jam was making them stick.

"Right, off we go, I suppose," she continued. "Jallateau won't take too kindly to being bothered again. It's weird that no one has managed to find a scrap of evidence against him."

"Maybe because it's not all so simple," Lebreton answered, sliding a document across the table.

With his index finger, he drew Rosière's attention to one line in particular. She picked up her cup and leaned over the sheet of paper. She frowned as her memory whirred into action.

"That name does ring a bell . . ."

Suddenly it registered, and she stared at Lebreton incredulously. The *commandant* tore his *croissant* in half and nodded, smiling in triumph.

The springs creaked as Gabriel leapt onto his bed. He had just gotten back from the births, marriages, and deaths registrar at the town hall, where he'd battled for hours to obtain duplicates. He was one of those kids who was forever checking the wrong box on official forms. It turned out that marrying the girl you love was an arduous process in this country.

The old cat sloped in and did a tour of the room, sniffing all the furniture as it went. Then he jumped onto his master's bed, got comfortable on the pillow, and fell asleep with a purr. Gabriel stroked him for a moment, then took a list out of the side pocket of his Bermuda shorts. Instinctively he flattened the crumpled piece of paper against his thigh. All the names had been crossed out, with one exception. He unlocked his cell phone. He had spoken to all the survivors without learning a thing: no one remembered any details about his mother or his father. The only person left was Yann Guénan, the onboard quartermaster. The last telephone call. After this, he would stop.

27

Capestan had summoned all her troops to a morning meeting. Or, more precisely, she had taken advantage of the unlikely presence of a decent number of officers to engage the squad in an overdue powwow.

Lebreton and Rosière were still on the road, but they wouldn't be long. They had promised some mind-blowing news. Capestan had reserved two prime seats for them on the old plaid sofa, Orsini's contribution to the communal refurbishment effort. The *capitaine* had specified that it was in fact a sofa bed, which had immediately prompted Capestan to ban anyone from unfolding it. The furniture was beginning to mount up, but the living room was big enough to handle it. They had somewhat reshuffled the desks, and the sofa—a comfortable three-seater—was now positioned in front of the fireplace.

The wallpaper process had commenced. Two days before, Évrard and Orsini had primed the walls, with Merlot—glass in hand—issuing advice throughout. Capestan and Torrez had then fitted the wallpaper in half the living room. A paint-covered drop cloth was folded up in a corner of the room by the door next to a bucket of water, a brush, a jar of paste, and three leftover rolls of wallpaper. On the telephone, Lebreton had said he would finish the job this evening after the meeting.

Everyone was in their seat, thinking caps at the ready. Merlot had his back to the window, and next to him Évrard was humming as she fidgeted with her euro coin. She was forever mumbling bits of songs, the odd note that would break off as she picked up a pen and then resume just as quickly. She would keep the rhythm by bobbing her head or tapping her foot. Only the prospect of some sort of wager would get her to sit still. Orsini was sitting, too, ankles and hands crossed, on an orange plastic chair. The door leading to the corridor was open, and through it you could catch a glimpse of Torrez perched on a stool, following the discussion from a deliberate distance.

Two officers were making their first proper appearance. A good five weeks after the official start date and with only a few fleeting visits to check out the décor, they were finally reporting for duty. Finding that the atmosphere wasn't so bad after all, they had stayed put to do some work.

The first was Dax, a young boxer who had shed as many brain cells in the ring as he had drops of sweat. With his flattened nose and cheerful smile, he had the same enthusiasm for life as a sea lion splashing around in the waves. Before the uppercuts caught up with his coconut, Dax had been one of the sharpest lieutenants in *cybercrim*. Apparently he was still capable of the odd flash of inspiration, but the team had yet to see any direct evidence of this.

Next to him was his pal Lewitz, the crazy motorhead that the higher-ups had insisted on transferring to Capestan, having failed in their attempts to fire him outright. Brigadier Lewitz loved cars, and half his career in the police force had been spent with the siren blaring. He was a hopeless driver, but he refused to admit it. Cars were his mistresses, Fernando Alonso was his idol, and his hands did not find peace unless they were gripping a steering wheel.

The state had generously allocated the squad a whiteboard and three marker pens, one of which had not dried up. Torrez had also brought along a blackboard mounted on red metal legs, as well as a box of crayons and a little sponge. His girls had grown out of it, so he was happy it would have a new home. Capestan had used it to recap the Sauzelle case, while the Guénan case was drawn up on the whiteboard. Everything was set for the brainstorming session. Capestan decided to kick off without waiting for Rosière and Lebreton—a warm-up exercise of sorts.

"Right," she said in an upbeat voice. "Where are we?"

There was a brief clinking of glasses and mugs, then everyone's attention centered on the two boards.

"At a dead end," Orsini said to himself.

"Stuck in the mud," Évrard added, holding her euro coin tight.

"In a jam!" Merlot bellowed, delighted with his contribution.

"In the shit!" Dax and Lewitz screeched, as if they'd just figured out the rules to some game.

Capestan cut them short.

"Good, so we've grasped the idea of brainstorming, but can we please try to keep it constructive."

Not another word after that. To avoid total shutdown, Capestan decided to summarize the state of play. Every lead in both cases had resulted in an impasse. After so many years, the files were like scorched earth. They had taken a closer look at Naulin and André Sauzelle, but nothing new had come up. Capestan surveyed her troops: they looked like wretched bystanders. Defeatism was rife and their enthusiasm was dwindling. If they didn't manage a breakthrough in either of these inquiries, the squad would be no different from the spent force Buron had envisaged.

Merlot, always happy to hear the sound of his own voice, took the floor:

"The motive, children, the motive! We are taking as our point of departure the presumption that Marie Sauzelle is an innocent old lady, but who knows how debauched a life she might have led? What if she had kept a gigolo for company, some tango devotee with a voracious sexual appetite? What if her wanderlust had hurled her into the clutches of drug abuse, placing her at the mercy of Naulin, her dealer? The fundamental question, dear friends, is this—who was Marie Sauzelle? Who was she?"

Dax nodded in full agreement. The leather of his jacket creaked as he leaned over to Lewitz's ear.

"Got any chewing gum?" he whispered loudly.

Lewitz took a package out of the back pocket of his jeans and offered a piece to Dax, who devoted the remainder of the meeting to mastication.

"And do we have anything on the boy described by the neighbor?" Orsini asked.

"No," Capestan acknowledged.

Their research into the green helmet had yielded nothing. It was too flimsy a starting point. In any case, Naulin had almost certainly made it up on the spot.

For the hundredth time, Capestan scanned the blackboard. Burglary, dead bolt, blinds, position of the body, neighbor, cat, flowers, brother, mail . . . She was struggling to work out where the elements of this case ended. Her head felt like a snow globe, her thoughts floating and fluttering in every direction. She had to wait for the flakes to settle before she could see anything clearly.

The team was now considering Yann Guénan's board.

"There's no point looking into a man taken out by a pro," Lewitz said to Dax, disrupting the calm atmosphere with a surprisingly lucid point. "Twenty years later, we're not going to find a thing."

"We're not trying to find anyone, we're just trying to pass the time," Dax told him, not seeming in the least concerned by it.

Orsini nodded in agreement as he picked a bit of lint off his trousers. He was patently of the opinion that, as things currently stood, this case would lead nowhere. As icy as ever, he delivered his verdict:

"What we need is fresh blood."

A shiver ran through the gathering, followed by a few childish snickers before Évrard piped up timidly, her blue eyes wide open:

"It's true, we need some new lines of inquiry to flesh out the files. We don't have anything. We don't have the resources to carry out an investigation. It's taking an age to hear back from the archives, not to mention the aborted interrogations . . ."

The *lieutenant* still had not come to terms with her Riverni experience.

"Indeed," Merlot said, adding his two cents' worth. "Here it is less 'cold case' and more 'basket case.' Back when we were in the police proper—"

"Enough! Enough."

Capestan had not raised her voice, but the room still fell silent. This meeting was fast descending into a demotivational session and she needed to put a stop to it. The *commissaire* looked around the group without focusing on anyone in particular, and for once she addressed them with a blank expression:

"In war movies, the guy who says 'We're all gonna die!' is never helping anyone. So let's stop this right now. No more talk of 'before this, before that.' Before we landed up here, all of us were done for anyway. All of us. There's no point going on about the glory days at the Orfèvres—your sentence didn't start here."

Heads dropped and eyes darted around sheepishly. But Capestan did not want the team to dwell on this, so she stood up from the corner of her desk and continued:

"No more spending 70 percent of your time doing paperwork. No more night rounds or graveyard shifts. No more junkies redecorating the toilets at the station. We're free to do the job we dreamt of doing when we signed up. We investigate without any pressure, without adhering to protocols or procedures, and without having to file reports. So let's make the most of it instead of sitting around whining like teenagers who've been barred from throwing a party. We're still part of the *police judiciaire*, just in our own branch. You don't get a chance like this twice."

Capestan could see that this had lifted their spirits. Shoulders were less droopy. An almost imperceptible ripple ran through the group, a collective movement that seemed to bind together the officers dotted around the room. The team was uniting.

This budding solidarity was greeted with a sharp *yap*. Pilou had arrived and seemed to approve of the atmosphere. Rosière and Lebreton followed close behind, leaving their bags at the door and offering a general "hello" as they approached the boards.

Rosière glanced at Lebreton, who smiled faintly and offered her the role of spokeswoman that she so clearly craved. The *capitaine* plumped up her hair, stroked her charms, and—sensing that the tension was at breaking point—began her announcement with a stern voice:

"Yann Guénan, the murdered sailor that Louis-Baptiste and I have been investigating for the last few weeks, knew plenty of people. Including some people who are of interest to us. He compiled a dossier the size of a brick, in which he noted down hundreds of names in his god-awful handwriting. Lebreton, the great *commandant* you see before you, the most thorough officer that ever lived, got busy and read the whole thing. And then, in the middle of the night, as the ocean swelled outside, one name suddenly jumped out . . ."

Lebreton raised his eyebrows, urging her to cut her long speech short. Rosière reluctantly came to the point:

"It was the name of Marie Sauzelle, the old lady strangled in Issy-les-Moulineaux. Our two cases are linked."

"What?!?" came the team's stupefied chorus, after which they sat stock-still, desperate to hear the rest. Rosière lapped up the rapt silence she had managed to provoke from her audience, then continued:

"She's on the list of passengers that Yann visited, and one of the ones who testified. The two of them were in the same boat."

Mind-blowing indeed, Capestan thought. The old lady and the sailor had gone to sea together, suffered the trauma of a shipwreck, then met up again afterward. Only to end up murdered. All of a sudden, the threads of this investigation had become interwoven.

"This changes everything," the *commissaire* said, deep in thought.

"Everything," Lebreton confirmed.

28

Capestan grabbed a piece of paper and, after checking there was nothing important on the back, started using it as a notepad. She had to note down as quickly as possible all the questions that emerged from this revelation. Inevitably her black ballpoint was yet again refusing to work, so—without even bothering to try her luck with the blue—she went for the green. Never any trouble with the greens and reds.

"Did Sauzelle and Guénan meet on the boat or did they know each other from before and take the trip together? Had André Sauzelle or Naulin ever seen the sailor before? If Marie Sauzelle is linked to the shipwreck, does that let Jallateau off the hook, or does it incriminate him further?"

Looking up for a second, Capestan realized that all the other officers were scrambling around with their stationery in search of a miracle pen. Only Orsini with his Montblanc and Lebreton with his smartphone were managing to keep up with the *commissaire*'s quick-fire dictation. Capestan sat up straight.

"We need a third board."

Lewitz obliged, pulling on his jacket and offering to go to the store. The *commissaire* gave him her wallet and added dry-erase markers and fifty ballpoints to her order. Then she paused for a second and looked at her team. She needed to allocate roles.

"Capitaine Orsini, can I leave you to dig through the press archives for anything on the shipwreck? Might be worth trying online, but—"

"No, my guess is it's too old to have been digitized. I'll contact my pals instead."

"Perfect."

Capestan went to the corridor and found Torrez:

"Can you call André Sauzelle down in Marsac, and Naulin, too? Ask them if the name Guénan means anything to them. The brother never mentioned the shipwreck to us, but that's to be expected—it was ten years before Marie's death."

Torrez scratched his beard, which sounded like a brand-new doormat.

"Yes, he won't have put two and two together. I'll see whether Marie mentioned anything in particular at the time."

Lebreton was sitting on the sofa, his feet resting on a box of solved cases that he had repurposed as a footstool. Until that point, he and Rosière had only skimmed the surface of the Sauzelle case, so he was studying the blackboard to familiarize himself with all the various aspects. One of Torrez and Capestan's problems was easy enough to resolve. Lebreton could have mentioned it out loud, but he was worried Capestan might see it as an attempt to undermine her in public. Being banished was already bad enough—the last thing they needed was to start lashing out at one another. Lebreton was observing his commander at the helm. She had a natural grace about her: gentle without being soft, firm without being hard. Authoritative, but empathetic, too. If she weren't so hot headed, she could have been a topflight negotiator. But she was incapable of putting up with provocation. Whether it was inquiries, interrogations, or even darts, Capestan never played in defense—she was always on the attack. Lebreton tapped his knee with his thumb. He wavered. He would wait for the right moment.

* * *

The *commissaire* was now making her way over to Dax. As she passed the sofa, she glanced quizzically at Rosière, who was perched comfortably between two cushions with her dog snoozing at her feet. She held up her superfluous cell phone:

"Maëlle's not answering. I'll try her again later to see if she knew the old lady."

Capestan nodded and continued over to the IT specialist. She wanted him to look into Jallateau's activities at the time of Marie Sauzelle's murder. The squad was about as likely to obtain a warrant as a toad was to win the Nobel Prize, so they were having to cut some administrative corners. On paper at least, Dax was the man for the job.

As she approached the *lieutenant*, Capestan realized he was drawing a Bart Simpson on Lewitz's freshly erected board, and she started to have her doubts. By the time he had stuck his chewing gum on the cartoon character's nose, she had given up hope entirely. She gave it a try all the same:

"*Lieutenant*, you used to be in *cybercrim* . . . Can you still get around firewalls, break through security, that sort of thing?"

Dax stood bolt upright and wrung his hands with pride.

"Muscle memory! What are we looking for?"

"Anything relating to Jallateau between April and August 2005: bank statements, telephone records, movements, his business, any henchmen . . . whatever you can find."

Dax nodded vigorously several times and cracked his knuckles. He was getting ready for his big comeback.

Capestan smiled at the *lieutenant* and went back to her swivel chair. It was time for the *commissaire* to pick her way through the Guénan file with a renewed focus. This case had just become her own.

A line was emerging. Lebreton and Rosière had been so focused on Jallateau that they had failed to consider the victim's temperament. A sailor with that much perseverance, who gathers together hundreds of documents and puts the whole thing in writing, must have kept some sort of journal, almost like a ship's logbook. If so, it would surely contain some vital clues. Capestan wanted to avoid broadcasting this oversight to the group, especially since relations between her and Lebreton were still frosty—better not make it more awkward. But she promised to tackle the issue the moment they were one-on-one.

The studious atmosphere that had settled on the room was interrupted by the screech of Torrez's chair on the floor. He crossed the room, his sheepskin jacket already on his back. The silence continued until the front door clicked shut.

Midday, Capestan thought. Lunchtime. They would all make better progress with some food in their bellies.

29

Lebreton and Évrard had taken the whole squad's order and gone to fetch burgers and fries. Back on the overcrowded terrace, the brown paper bags were distributed and each officer buried their nose inside to check that everything was present and correct. Pilote trotted from one to the other, desperately searching for the biggest pushover.

Merlot set upon his cheeseburger with the expression of an intrepid explorer. He was discovering the virgin terrain of junk food, devouring the flabby bun with gusto and sending a jet of ketchup into the distance. His round pickle slice slid down the red sauce like a shaky surfer and landed on the *capitaine*'s already stained tie. Nonchalant as ever, he took a paper napkin and flicked the offending condiment onto the floor tiles of the terrace. The dog went over to inspect the spoils but seemed unconvinced, preferring to wait for something a little meatier to fall. Lewitz pointed at the animal, then swallowed and directed a question at Rosière:

"Did you name him after a particular pilot?"

"Yes. The first of a series."

This surprised Dax, who stopped chewing:

"So you want more than one dog?"

"No, series as in television series," she said.

Évrard closed the plastic lid on her barely touched salad and tore open a packet of *petit-beurre* cookies from the shopping bag, offering them around as she nibbled at the corners of her own. Dax held out an interested hand.

"I bet you ten euros you can't eat three in under a minute," Évrard whispered.

"No money!" Capestan said straightaway. "How many in a minute?"

"Three," Évrard repeated, nodding to suggest the odds were stacked in her favor.

"Is that all?!" Dax blurted.

He leapt to his feet, ready for action, shaking his arms and rotating his head to loosen his neck.

"Let's do this," he said.

A crowd rapidly formed around the contender. This foolish challenge reminded Capestan of something, maybe a YouTube clip or a scene from a film. Three cookies in under a minute. Good, clean fun among colleagues. Dax stuffed in all three at once, his jaw going into overdrive as he tried to mash them up and get them down.

Sitting with her back to the window, Capestan watched from a distance, deep in thought as she picked at her fries. Lebreton took this as his opportunity to have a quiet word with her:

"I'm with you on the missing cat: it's bizarre. If we want peace of mind, we have to look for the carrier."

Capestan sat up straight to show he had her attention. Lebreton continued in the same tone:

"If we call Marie Sauzelle's local vet, we should get a date for their last visit and a summary of the cat's health. And the vet will know whether the animal had some sort of carrier. If the carrier is missing, then it means the murderer took it with him."

"Marie might have thrown it out when the cat died," Capestan said.

"You don't throw that sort of thing out so quickly. Plus the vet can tell us if the cat had died a long time before."

"You're right. The vet, the carrier. Good idea. I'll look into it this afternoon. Thank you, *commandant*."

Dax was staring at the stopwatch. One minute, thirty seconds. He had failed. He was refusing to believe it. Lewitz picked up the baton, opting for a diametrically opposite technique: he nibbled each cookie in turn, biting continuously, like Bugs Bunny on a carrot.

Capestan could have made the most of her talk with Lebreton to flag up her views on Guénan, but she was worried about coming across as overly competitive ("Think you can teach me a lesson? Have a listen to this . . ."). The *commissaire* did not like to use that sort of tone. Lebreton could sense she was holding something back.

"And the Guénan case?" he asked. "Any thoughts after looking at it with fresh eyes?"

"Yes, in fact. I figure that a sailor like Guénan would instinctively have kept a journal to log his thoughts. Our mystery passenger must have gotten his hands on it."

"A journal. Of course," Lebreton said. "The widow told us that he spoke about the shipwreck all the time. Maybe he wrote things down for comfort."

Lebreton was annoyed with himself for overlooking this possibility. They hadn't varied their questions enough when they interviewed Maëlle. He would have to go and see her again as soon as possible. The *commandant* thanked Capestan with a nod, then went over to join Rosière. It was her turn, and she was guzzling down her third cookie under the watchful eye of Évrard and her digital watch.

"One minute, ten! A new record!" the referee announced. "But no one's broken the one-minute mark yet."

"More training required," Rosière said with a splutter. "We'll get there . . ."

A few hours later, as Merlot indulged in a diligent siesta on the sofa, his colleagues' research was progressing.

Away in his den, Torrez had called André Sauzelle and they had had a long conversation. The brother did remember Guénan. He had never met the sailor, but Marie had spoken about him after the accident. Apparently they had spent several evenings together, weeping as they tried to describe their trauma, and—more important—to overcome it. One day the sailor had disappeared and André never heard anything more of him. Marie had not known him before the trip, so either they met on board or during their stay in Florida. Torrez had also contacted Naulin, but the neighbor had never even heard of Guénan.

Orsini had been faxed a series of articles about the shipwreck. They showed the incident in a different light, one that was both more emotionally charged than the Wikipedia entry Lebreton had printed off and better synthesized than the sailor's dossier. But none of the cuttings contained the smallest clue for them to hang on to. Orsini was going to deepen his research at the public library.

At their end, Rosière and Lebreton still hadn't managed to reach Maëlle Guénan, though they had had better luck with Jallateau. The name Sauzelle "rang a vague bell," and "yes, it might have been from the petition," but the main point to emerge was that they should "just get lost for once." Rosière was filling in Capestan, who was writing all the information up on the board, when Dax called out to them from his PC:

"I've got it!"

In a split second the officers swooped on the *lieutenant* and his pal Lewitz, who was already congratulating him with a shake of the shoulder. With his fingers on the keyboard and wearing a gleeful expression, Dax jabbed his chin at the screen:

"Jallateau's criminal record! It took me ages to crack the *préfecture*'s security system, but I got it in the end. Jallateau: blank folder."

Capestan was so incredulous that it took a moment for her to pull herself together. For the last few hours, she had watched him thrash his mouse around and hammer at his keyboard like a jazz pianist on speed. His forehead glistening with sweat, Dax had paused just once, and only then for as long as it takes to siphon off three pints of tap water. All that energy and determination for him to come up with a document that was present in the original file they had received from the *brigade criminelle*. Capestan smiled to mask her dismay:

"Fine effort, *lieutenant*. But we already had that folder. Rosière's put in a call to have it updated. I mentioned it to you earlier on . . ."

"Ah," Dax said, then gnawed the inside of his cheek for a moment. "Right, I suppose I heard 'folder' and then just started looking."

Capestan nodded, as if this explanation justified his actions in full, then headed to the kitchen. She needed a coffee.

* * *

The *commissaire* unfolded a paper filter and slipped it into the machine. Rosière's giggling could be heard drifting in from the terrace, where she was smoking with Lebreton.

"'Muscle memory'—that's a good one! Shame he hasn't been to the gym for a while! The guy knows how to run a search, he just doesn't know what for. Did you see him in there?" she said, turning to Lebreton for approval. No reaction, but she carried on in the same vein anyway:

"Most teams get an IT whizz. Not us—we get an IT cretin."

She exhaled wearily:

"We've got a long way to go, I'm telling you. A long way to go."

Lebreton made no comment beside her. Capestan could not tell whether his silence was due to indifference or a stubborn refusal to bad-mouth anyone. It was too close to call, but her intuition was leaning toward the latter option.

She joined them outside, soon followed by Évrard and Lewitz. As she stirred the sugar into her coffee, she shared the latest cause for surprise with her colleagues:

"I didn't find the passenger list in the file from *crim*. There's the one from Guénan's dossier with the names of the petition signatories, but nothing about who was on board."

Rosière and Lebreton shook their heads to indicate that they had not tracked it down either.

"Leave it to me. I'll sort that out with the US ferry company," said Évrard, checking her watch to calculate the time difference. "I'll call them this evening."

"Are you bilingual?" Lewitz asked, clearly impressed.

"Vacations in Vegas. Didn't always work out for the best, but at least I picked up some English."

All they had to do now was touch base with the elusive Maëlle Guénan.

Lebreton was sitting at the back of a Vietnamese restaurant on rue Volta. A television perched next to some fluorescent tubes was playing video clips with the sound turned off. The *commandant* was watching it without taking anything in, mixing his *bo bun* with *nem* sauce. With the big bowl in his hand, he was shaking the broth off the noodles on his chopsticks when his iPhone rang on the Formica table. Maëlle Guénan. He set down the bowl and the chopsticks and wiped his fingers on his paper napkin before answering.

"Hello?"

"Hello, I'm sorry to be calling you so late. I've spent the whole day in the countryside with my son for his birthday. It was wonderful but there wasn't any signal."

"No problem."

"We can meet up tomorrow, if you like? I'm not sure what's going on—everyone seems to want to talk to me right now."

30

Lebreton locked his mailbox with a half turn of the key, then walked out into rue du Faubourg-Saint-Martin. That morning, a pale gray sky was sucking all the color out of the city. Paris was suffocating, floundering helplessly beneath the grubby canvas of this parachute. Lebreton took a right toward rue de l'Échiquier. The journal, the link with Sauzelle, the passengers, and anything the widow had forgotten or kept hidden. The *commandant* had spent the whole night attempting to collate all of Maëlle Guénan's stories: the salt shaker, the glasses, the feet trampling on faces, the wives drowning their husbands . . . The panic had made those human souls seethe, provoking any number of unforgivable acts, and the bubbles must have carried on popping in people's heads for months afterward. Maybe one of them drove someone to murder.

As he turned on to rue Mazagran, Lebreton saw three police cars. The lights were flashing in silence. Uniformed officers were darting this way and that as they set up a security perimeter around Maëlle Guénan's building. Orders were issued in tinny voices that crackled through the walkie-talkies. A vanload of forensics officers from *identité judiciaire* came to a halt a few yards from the entrance, the team slamming the doors shut before filling the lobby.

It was the same building, but surely this commotion had nothing to do with Maëlle, Lebreton thought, refusing to believe it for a second.

He took his POLICE band out of his pocket and slipped it onto his arm. He flashed his ID at one of the officers at the door, then took the stairs four at a time.

The widow's gentle face embedded itself in his mind. They should never have reopened the inquiry.

He met two agents on the second-floor landing going door-to-door to question the neighbors. This early in the morning, the man who opened up had his hair all over the place and still looked half-asleep. Lebreton hurried past them. The worn-out tablecloth, the chewed fingernails, the frayed sweater. A day in the countryside for her son's birthday. The details of a life rushed by and filled his heart with remorse.

Up on the fourth floor, the widow's door was wide open, and the familiar sounds of police activity reached Lebreton's ears. He took one step into the apartment and saw a running shoe on the foot of a corpse. A silver star gleamed on the lace. The *commandant* walked farther into the hallway and recognized Maëlle Guénan without even seeing her face. The body had fallen in a heap on the carpet. Bloodstains had transformed the embroidered butterflies on her jeans into scarlet swabs. The handle of a kitchen knife protruded from her abdomen.

The room was thick with the coppery smell of blood. Forensics officers in their white paper pajamas were dusting the surroundings and putting down yellow markers, while the photographer's violent flash operated on shy Maëlle. Lebreton still could not see the full scene, and he was about to make his way through to the living room when a black suit, immaculate and buttoned up, stood in his way. On top of it was a face like a blade, with a dark complexion and watchful eyes. Lebreton immediately recognized Divisionnaire Valincourt, the head of *brigades centrales*.

"Who are you?" he snapped.

The crime scene was inexorably luring Lebreton in, and he could not stop himself from making furtive glances over the *division-naire*'s shoulder, despite the urgent need to answer the question. His information radically shifted the perspective on Maëlle's murder, and *crim* needed it to get their investigation under way. Lebreton stated his name, rank, and department.

"Yes, okay. And what are you doing here, *commandant*?"

Lebreton outlined the bulk of what they had on Yann Guénan, all the while observing Valincourt's body language. The *divisionnaire* was swaying gently from side to side; haughty, distracted, eager to get this over with. He was listening to Lebreton, but not attaching any real importance to the words. He was still giving out instructions, responding to one or another of his officers, or browsing any paperwork he was presented with. The *commandant* fell silent when he was done, obliging the man to display a modicum of courtesy, the sudden pause forcing the senior officer to pay Lebreton more attention.

"Good, very good. And it dates from when, your case?"

"July 1993."

"I see."

A half smile crept across the *divisionnaire*'s face. It would have made Capestan livid.

"*Commandant*," he said in an insincere voice, "this is all extremely interesting, and we'll be sure to look into it . . ."

He took Lebreton by the elbow and ushered him toward the door. A polite yet firm way of ejecting him from the crime scene. The *commandant* pretended to be heavy footed and uncertain, hampering Valincourt's maneuver so he could buy himself some time to examine the living room. He wanted to know if someone had searched the room. He spotted a large red notebook next to the telephone on a side table. It looked like a directory of some sort. One thing was for sure: it had not been there on their previous visit. After years at RAID, when he would often have only a few seconds to take mental pictures of a room, Lebreton's memory was fail-safe.

Maëlle must have put the notebook aside after their telephone call the night before.

Having led Lebreton to the door, Valincourt reiterated just how little importance he was attributing to the squad's information:

"Do send an overview to me at the Orfèvres. In the meantime, you know the drill. We'll take it from here. Thank you, *commandant*, you may leave now."

The *divisionnaire* signaled to a policeman to escort the intruder downstairs, and the *commandant* had no choice but to leave the premises without any further intelligence, dismissed like the lowliest, most untrustworthy of witnesses.

Lebreton mulled everything over on his way downstairs. He waited until he was at the junction with boulevard de Bonne-Nouvelle before calling Rosière, who picked up immediately:

"Hi, Louis-Baptiste . . . Pilote, down! Sit! No more jumping around now."

"She's been murdered," Lebreton announced, his spirits all the more dampened by repeating the news.

They had met her barely a week before. They had told her that they would find her husband's murderer. Now this. She had left behind a son. And to cap it all off, they had been blocked from the inquiry.

But they still had control of the Yann Guénan case. This murder could still be considered a fresh lead. The *police judiciaire* would have to relay the information to them. In the meantime, they had to make sure nothing got past them.

"*Crim* has taken control of it, and of course they don't want us getting in the way. But it's imperative that we retrieve the information. Give Capestan the heads-up. I'll wait for you in the *brasserie* on the corner with the *boulevard*, opposite the post office. I'll keep an eye on things. See you shortly."

31

In the *brasserie*, intermittent blasts from the coffee machine rose above the hum of conversation, while the radio was tuned to a station that bombarded the clientele with frenetic ads. Lebreton couldn't hear himself think. At the far end of the bar, the smoking area accommodated a line of people puffing away obediently. Just next to the till, the owner, damp cloth on shoulder, was pulling half-pints with the solemn expression of a judge. The *commandant* was slightly removed at a table in a bow window with an unrestricted view of rue Mazagran and its Stalinist post office.

Through the glass, he saw the black Lexus slide alongside the pavement and come to a smooth halt. Capestan jumped out of the passenger seat and made for the café, quickly followed by Orsini, Rosière, and Pilote. Lebreton stood up as they came in.

"Torrez is on his way," Capestan announced. "He had an idea and needed to stop home first."

As always, everyone battened down their hatches at the mere mention of Lieutenant Malchance: it was as though the *commissaire* had not said anything at all. She was carrying on regardless, though, determined to play it down as much as possible. She shrugged off her coat with an elegant movement and folded it over the back of her chair.

"So?" she said, looking back at Lebreton.

"I introduced myself and I was shown the door. Valincourt was in charge: do you know who I mean?"

"I know who you mean. Did he play the 'overview' card?"

"Precisely," Lebreton said.

Capestan shook her head, more furious than offended. That welcome hardly surprised her. Lebreton stayed on his feet while Capestan sat down at the table. Merlot burst into the café and went directly to the bar to shake hands with the owner. Évrard and Dax followed soon after and joined them at the table.

"They can have their overview. We'll wind up their inquiry before they can even get it off the ground. That will settle it," the *commissaire* said.

"To do that we'll need the preliminary findings, the time of death, the autopsy report . . . Can you go through Buron?"

Capestan thought about it for a moment. So far her calls to the decision makers at 36 had taught her one lesson. If the squad was about to launch a competing investigation into Maëlle's death, then they'd be better off keeping it under their hats to avoid being slapped with an official injunction. On the other hand, the widow's murder constituted a development in the Yann Guénan case, and by extension the Sauzelle case. If they were simply pursuing the investigations they had already started, then there was no need for authorization. Setting all good faith to one side, they were not step-ping on the *brigade criminelle*'s toes; rather, they would be working in parallel. It was a blatantly underhand approach, and no doubt Buron would give her a dressing-down for it, but it did avoid the risk of being directly disobedient. No contravention meant no pun-ishment. There was one drawback, however: they could not ask for anything.

"No. For now, we're staying on our own. Low profile," Capestan said.

Lebreton made a face. He would have preferred to keep his supe-riors in the loop. Even though his love for protocol had started to wane in recent weeks, he still was not a fan of all these roundabout routes in the outer fringes of the law. He frowned and leaned back against the window, his hands in his trouser pockets. Nevertheless, he nodded his agreement:

"Maëlle had set the journal aside for me; I saw it next to her telephone."

"Did you show it to the others?" Capestan said with a smile.

"No," Lebreton said. "Let's just say that something about Valincourt's patronizing tone made me reconsider."

"We have to get that journal."

"We can't exactly steal it, though."

Capestan hesitated for a moment before deciding to skirt around the issue:

"Anything else?"

"When we were there the first time, she had a blue filing cabinet in her living room that contained the dossier and other bits of paperwork. It was lockable. I couldn't get close enough to see if it had been forced, but if it was, then the killer was looking for documents, just like us."

"We have to get back in there," Capestan said. "*Crim* are inside, along with officers from the *commissariat* in the tenth and the forensics guys . . . It'll be tricky for anyone to distinguish between us and the officers working on the investigations. As soon as Valincourt leaves, we can try to get ourselves onto the premises."

"Even if we can take a peek, we'll never manage to stay and take notes without being spotted," Rosière objected. "If we want a proper look, we'll have to ask."

"No deal," Capestan said, still smiling.

"What then? Snatch the details right out of their hands?"

"No, not that. If anyone has any other ideas . . ."

All of them looked at each other in silence. They had identified a problem but not a solution. They didn't even know the time of death. At present their hopes of a parallel investigation seemed like a long shot.

Capestan looked out the window to see a breathless Torrez arriving with a paper bag under his arm. He waved at her and she went to join him out on the street.

"We'll be able to listen in on what they're saying," he said.

"Listen? Lieutenant, please tell me you're not suggesting we go and plant microphones in a crime scene."

Capestan quickly filed this notion away in the folder marked PRISON. She was desperate to solve this case before the *brigade criminelle* did, but she was less than willing to sacrifice her freedom in the process.

"Hidden mics are illegal. But these should do the job!" Torrez said excitedly.

He pulled a box out of the bag and waved it in Capestan's face:

"Baby monitors! Look at these beauties: three-hundred-yard range plus a no-signal indicator, three different alarm settings, night-light, low electromagnetic radiation . . . these are the ultimate in baby surveillance. They've worked for my two youngest," he said with satisfaction.

Capestan looked at the lieutenant: he really was resourceful. He was beaming with paternal pride. Baby monitors in an old woman's apartment. The world's least discreet spying tool, and yet no policeman would ever notice their presence.

32

Évrard stealthily worked her way up the tired wooden steps, involuntarily stroking the baby monitor in her pocket. It was as round and smooth as a lucky pebble.

The key was putting it in a good spot. If Évrard nailed this task, they had a chance of solving both Guénan murders and being recognized as legitimate police officers rather than a bunch of has-beens. But if she failed, she would be done for attempting to engage in illegal tapping. Double or quits.

Discretion, going unnoticed, passing like a shadow . . . Évrard knew how to do all this and more. Not quite a blonde or a redhead or a brunette, she had always slipped under the radar. Over time, this tactic proved to be her undoing. No one saw her anymore. Soon she grew tired of duping her dull, insipid opponents and went off to get her fix in increasingly seedy spots.

At first she had taken to gambling for the thrill of victory, but then, like any addict, she had started playing to lose. For the thrill of standing at the roulette table with your whole life in your hands, gobbling up savings, sinking deeper into debt, breaking up families. The lure of the abyss. Not often you get to look chance in the face and see it waver.

She had never had much to lose, but right now she was happy in her new squad. Évrard felt like she was closer to the surface. She was walking along the ridge of a mountain, slightly off-balance, but advancing nonetheless. And now she had to plant the baby monitor.

The timer suddenly cut out and Évrard was plunged into darkness. She froze instinctively, then groped around for a light switch. She heard Merlot stumble and swear heartily as he clattered onto the landing. The light returned with a *click* and Évrard saw a young agent rushing downstairs, his hand sliding down the banister. She automatically dropped her eyes and pressed herself against the wall, and the man brushed past without noticing her. Merlot's voice rang out a few yards below: "Whoa there! Easy does it!" The agent apologized and reduced his speed before disappearing from sight. The gift of Merlot's gab was going to torpedo any attempt at subtlety. He caught up with her, desperately trying to regain his breath, and held his hand aloft:

"Allow me to lead the way, dear girl."

Against her better judgment, Évrard nodded: he was going to ruin everything.

Eventually they arrived at the fourth floor. Through the half-open door they could make out the sounds of various teams at work. A square-jawed detective from the *police judiciaire* in a hoodie left the Guénans' apartment. Évrard saw an officer from the organized crime division she had come across back in her gambling task force days. She felt a sudden cold sweat: if he recognized her, they were screwed. Évrard's hand trembled in her pocket and she renewed her grip on the device. The officer's first glance passed over her, but something told her it would linger for longer the next time. Of all the times for someone to remember her, it had to be now.

Just as the officer was about to click, Merlot bellowed at him like a *bon vivant* fresh from his country estate:

"What a delight to see you again, *mon vieux*! It's been an age since the Canal de l'Ourcq!"

As square-jaw stopped to say hello to this jovial colleague, racking his brains for any canal-related memories, Évrard seized her chance to slip into the apartment.

In the chaotic living room, the crime scene investigator was switching on his dictating machine to record the preliminary findings; around him, the forensics team was finishing collecting fingerprints. Évrard let out one of those greetings that sound more normal than silence, quiet enough not to draw anyone's full attention. The officers returned the *lieutenant*'s hello, while barely registering her presence. Évrard was like an ultrasonic pulse: she was there, but nobody heard her. A phantom bird call.

She tightened her grip on the baby monitor in her pocket and placed her thumb on the power button. She switched it on and a faint crackle snuck into the room. Heads shot up.

Évrard stopped herself from swinging around suddenly. One of the technicians examining the carpet stood up and turned off his walkie-talkie, which was lying on a chair, before going back to work. Évrard walked over to a toy basket in a corner of the living room and set the monitor down in the middle of some rubber blocks. A bit of adhesive tape covered the "on" light.

Now all she needed to do was grab the journal. "Slide it up your sleeve," Rosière had teased her. That was exactly what Évrard was planning. She spotted the telephone, walked over and swiped the journal using her best sleight of hand.

Mission accomplished.

Before leaving, she glanced at the filing cabinet.

There was no doubt about it. Someone had forced it.

33

The group had ordered coffee while they waited for the spies to return. Lunchtime was approaching and the *brasserie* was livening up with the background clink of cutlery. Capestan was watching Lebreton, who still had his back to the window. An anxious furrow had appeared above his right eyebrow that ran perpendicular to the line running down his cheek. He seemed to be mulling over the recent turn of events. For the first time in his career, he was directly engaging in illegal activity. It was for a just cause, but the methods employed were like a stain on his immaculate shirtfront. He must have had enough of skipping so many steps. Capestan was surprised to find herself sympathizing, despite her long history of not so much skipping steps as kicking down whole stairways. The *commandant* checked his pack of cigarettes—only four left—then went out to smoke one with Rosière.

Capestan had followed Lebreton's advice and called the vet. He had confirmed that Tunafix, a young cat in full health at the time of the crime, did indeed have a carrier, which he happened to remember was a gray and dark-red model with a plaid rug covered in cat hair. Earlier that morning, the *commissaire* had returned to check the house. The carrier was nowhere to be seen: the murderer had indeed taken the cat with him. So that it wouldn't die? So that it wouldn't alert the neighbors with its meowing?

Capestan was still thinking this through as she removed the baby monitor from its box. A moment later, Lewitz arrived and parked his car—a yellow Chevrolet Laguna with spoilers and four rows of brake lights—on the pedestrian crossing. Lebreton waved his cigarette at the windshield, ordering the *brigadier* to move along: he was blocking the way for strollers and wheelchairs. Lewitz obliged. Maneuvering his Renault as if it were a Smart car, he boldly parked at right angles with the curb, swinging his two rear wheels onto the pavement and presenting his exhaust pipe to the unfortunate patrons of the terrace. Lebreton admitted defeat with a sigh.

Torrez was sitting to one side, keeping an eye on things from a bench pushed up against a defunct old pinball machine. In addition to his childcare equipment, the *lieutenant* had shared some news from his research into Marie Sauzelle's timetable. Through calling various clubs to identify the infamous get-together she was supposed to be attending, he had hit on several dates: on the evening of May 30, she had attended—and even participated vigorously in, as far as the instructor recalled—an end-of-term tango show. On June 4, however, she had missed the summer raffle at her tarot club, despite having expressed an interest in one of the prizes (a leg of lamb, the chairman had specified). Marie must have died between the two. That tightened the net, but they still did not have the key date. Torrez had called Marie's brother back about the dance show, but André was adamant that she had spoken at length about a "reunion." So it couldn't have been the tango.

Capestan switched on the power button on the receiver. The squad huddled together on the window seat like a gaggle of teenagers around a single can of beer. On the table, the crackling baby monitor took center stage among the coffee cups, saucers, and crumpled sugar packets. Suddenly it emitted a clearer sound, followed by the tinny timbre of an amplified voice. Success! Évrard had managed to plant the other monitor in the living room. The officers all leaned closer to the speaker.

"...—*iminary forensics . . . occurred this morning between six and eight . . .*"

The whole team nodded: they had the time of death. The speaking was dotted with lots of pauses, no doubt for the purpose of note taking.

"That'll be the crime scene investigator," Rosière said.

"*. . . no sexual assault . . . no sign of self-defense . . .*"

"The murderer was either quick or the victim knew her attacker," Capestan said.

"*. . . knife wound . . . no money or jewels left . . . no computer . . .*"

Behind the distorted voice, they could make out the scraping of furniture, the rustling of plastic sheets, the sound of a zipper, and some more distant conversations that were barely audible.

"*. . . five knives identical to the murder weapon in the kitchen . . . burglary . . .*"

"Of course," Lebreton said with a frustrated pout.

The *commandant* was right: the burglary had only been intended as a decoy. That said, the computer had been stolen.

"*. . . one son, Cédric Guénan, twenty-four years old, resident of Malakoff . . .*"

Valincourt would already be over there telling him the sad news. Capestan felt a knot in her stomach.

Other than these basic elements, the squad did not learn a great deal, apart from that Commandant Servier—a quai des Orfèvres thoroughbred—was heading up the inquiry. Capestan and Rosière knew him fleetingly, but he was hardly someone they could ask for inside information for old times' sake.

Merlot and Évrard marched in a few minutes later like triumphant heroes.

"Leave it to the professionals!" Merlot shouted, holding up his arms with a self-satisfied gurgle.

After warmly accepting his colleagues' congratulations, Merlot cleaved through the crowd toward the bar, his belly jutting out like the prow of a ship, to claim his just reward. Évrard stayed by the table, a few strands of hair still clinging to her clammy forehead.

"So?" she said. "Where are we? Are we ahead of the game?"

Rosière answered as she untangled Pilou's leash from around her chair:

"We've got a small head start thanks to the husband's case, but nothing substantial: there are more of them and they have more resources, plus every officer in the neighborhood is chomping at the bit to help out *crim.*"

"It's an inquiry, not a competition," Lebreton said.

"Tut-tut-tut!" Rosière shot back. "Of course it's a competition, my chicken! How do you think we'll earn our stripes? By wrapping up the case and handing it to them with a nice little ribbon on top? Why not throw in your bank card and PIN number while we're at it?"

"Let's just say that it's not a competition, but we're eager to cross the finish line first," Capestan intervened lightheartedly.

"So what are we going to do, then?" Évrard said.

"We stay here until they back away, just in case they find something new."

Capestan stood up and went to find Merlot before he made too big a dent in the bar stocks.

"Capitaine . . ."

"The governor!" he proclaimed, hoisting his glass of *pastis.* "How might I be of service?"

"I asked you to check if there was any history between Buron and Riverni—did you find anything out in the end?"

"Indeed you did! I had forgotten."

Merlot protectively returned his glass to the bar, patted his jacket to locate his glasses, and slid them on to read a tattered scrap of paper he had pulled from his trouser pocket.

"2009. Buron was all set to take the helm at the *police judiciaire,* but Riverni was minister of the interior at the time, and he blocked it. Something about a friend of a friend and returning a favor. Anyhow, it would appear that Buron took it philosophically enough at the time. And that's that," Merlot said, folding up the piece of paper and removing his glasses. "Do my findings meet with your approval, *commissaire*?"

"Absolutely, *capitaine*, thank you very much."

Capestan still wasn't sure whether it was good news or bad, but it was definitely news. She decided to think over the various theories by herself before informing the troops. She had a trump card, she just wasn't sure about the rest of her hand.

Two hours later, the *brigade criminelle* still hadn't moved and the squad was still lounging in the *brasserie*. Évrard, Dax, and Lewitz were standing at the bar arguing over a game of dice and studiously ignoring Merlot, who was narrating the more elaborate version of his recent exploits. Orsini was still sitting beside Capestan in the window, but without participating in the discussion, choosing instead to admire his slender hands. Rosière had commandeered the table behind theirs and was digging into a plate of *confit de canard* with *pommes salardaises*. Catching the rays coming through the glass, her red mane was shining like a halo. Capestan spoke to Lebreton, who was perched between the two tables on a chair he had tipped back against the window.

"Any suspects for Maëlle Guénan?"

The *commandant* nodded slowly as he gazed into the bottom of his cup.

"I was just wondering that myself. Yesterday on the telephone, Maëlle hinted that some other people wanted to see her. She may have had a meeting this morning."

"Jallateau?"

"No, I don't think so. There was nothing hostile about her tone, but there was no sign of closeness either. My guess is that it was someone she vaguely knew," Lebreton said, shrugging uncertainly as he looked up at Capestan. "Or there could just as well be no link at all."

He wasn't convinced either way.

Capestan turned to Rosière:

"What do you think?"

Rosière finished her mouthful before answering with a wave of her knife:

"Jallateau's still my favorite. He has links with Yann Guénan and Sauzelle, and soon after our trip to Sables-d'Olonne, the widow gets bumped off. It's too much of a coincidence for us to ignore. Maybe we said something that panicked him and made him want to clear the ground. He seemed to be the sort of guy who likes to be in control. In any case: the violent killing of a wife twenty years after her husband's murder, right in the middle of our investigation . . . that's no accident."

Rosière grinned between forkloads of duck, then said:

"I say we head back to Sables and give him a good going-over."

Capestan was struggling to make up her mind on the shipbuilder from the Vendée. She had never seen him or heard his voice. She tapped her chin with her index finger and turned to look down the street. On the far pavement, a young man in Bermuda shorts was getting off his bike. Funny-looking kid, Capestan thought to herself before she had even noticed the green flash of his helmet.

Suddenly it dawned on her: the helmet, the shorts, the sneakers . . . She couldn't make out the mutilated ear, but the profile matched Naulin's visitor perfectly. What was he doing there?

The boy, drenched with sweat, unzipped his hoodie and laid it on the saddle while he chained his bike to the traffic light. He straightened up and poked at the bits of hair sticking through his helmet. That was when he saw the police cars. He stopped dead.

Why that reaction? Capestan leapt up from her chair and called out to Torrez across the room:

"Torrez! Outside, Naulin's squirrel! I'm going."

34

The young man cautiously approached the crowd that had gathered around the security perimeter. A couple of busybodies standing there talking must have said something that alarmed the Squirrel, because he made a half turn, the color drained from his face. Capestan waited for him to get back to the junction with the boulevard so that she could intercept him without attracting the attention of the officers on duty.

He came up alongside her, tugging nervously at the strap of his green helmet still on his head. He was about to put his hoodie back on and set off when Capestan took a step toward him and showed him her police badge. The *commissaire* watched as his brown eyes bulged. The young man froze for a second before shooting down the boulevard like a dart, abandoning both hoodie and bike.

Caught by surprise, Capestan shoved her ID back in her coat pocket and took off after him. As she passed the *brasserie*, she sensed Torrez fall in at her left flank.

The boy was young, swift, and nimble. He ran down the slope of the boulevard and reached the crossroads with rue Saint-Denis in a matter of seconds. At the pedestrian crossing, the traffic lights changed from red to green. Just as the cars were about to move off, the Squirrel flung himself across the road, causing a screech of tires and a chorus of car horns. The drivers lurched forward, revving their engines angrily and preventing Capestan from crossing. She was blocked on the wrong side, hopping from foot to foot as she desperately scanned for a gap in the traffic, but there was no way through. Beyond the rush of cars, she saw the boy cutting across rue Saint-Denis. A group of four teenagers appeared at the same instant, obscuring her view for a second. By the time they were gone, the boy had disappeared.

Capestan jumped on the spot to try and make him out in the crowd. He couldn't just vanish like that. Naulin had seen him at Marie Sauzelle's place, and now they had run into him outside Maëlle Guénan's building. Along with the sailor's petition, this boy was a link. The squad had a new thread to bind the two cases together. So long as he was good to talk, all they had to do was ask a few questions to get an explanation. And yet somehow he had already managed to cut and run.

The lights were refusing to change. Capestan attempted to take one step, but a Chevrolet skimmed past her and sent her flying back onto the pavement. The Squirrel must have been making good headway. As the next car sped past, Capestan made a spontaneous dash for it.

Behind she could hear Torrez's panic-stricken voice shouting "No!!" at the top of his lungs, but by then she had made it to the middle of the boulevard. Holding up her hand to slow down the oncoming traffic, she crossed the last section of the road and leapt onto the pavement. A hundred yards ahead she could make out the green helmet disappearing into the distance. She upped her pace.

Without slowing down for a second, the boy glanced back to see Capestan fast approaching. He wove his way through the pedestrians and veered left down passage Lemoine. The *commissaire* lost him and started really sprinting, reaching the passage just in time to see him take a right onto boulevard de Sébastopol. She hurtled after him, knocking into two men smoking on the pavement outside a jeans shop.

Who was this boy? What was he doing there?

He'd crossed boulevard de Sébastopol and was level with rue de Tracy when a woman suddenly moved her bicycle forward, sending him completely off-balance as he bore down on her. Capestan was afraid he might jump onto the bike and lose her once and for all, but no, he swerved abruptly to avoid the woman, buying the *commissaire* a few precious yards. Her lungs were starting to burn and she wondered how long she'd be able to keep this pace up. Ahead, her target—twenty years her junior and with fewer miles on the clock—was still charging along, showing no sign of slowing down. Capestan needed to find a way of catching him fast: if it came down to stamina, she didn't stand a chance.

How did he know Marie and Maëlle? What did he want from them?

He turned past the railings of square Émile-Chautemps and erupted onto rue Saint-Martin, barging into someone leaving the post office and sending his parcel flying onto the street. The man was unleashing a volley of furious obscenities as Capestan tore past him. She spotted the green helmet cutting diagonally across the junction with rue Réaumur, and was summoning her final reserves of energy when a screech of brakes made her turn sideways. A bus was heading right for her. She could make out the driver's horrified expression through the windshield. Capestan had just enough time to raise her arm to protect herself.

She felt an impact, but it wasn't the bus: a pair of hands had shoved her in the back and propelled her forward onto the far pavement. As she landed, her hip slammed onto the concrete and she let out a cry of pain. Capestan heard the dull thud of a collision behind her and people screaming all around. She looked back and saw Torrez stretched out on the ground, blood gushing from his head. Clutching her side, she crawled toward him, calling out to him, praying he wasn't dead. Slowly he lifted his head and looked at her and, with a lopsided smile, reassured her with a weak voice:

"I'm fine. I'm happy."

He was still smiling when he passed out.

The wail of an ambulance drew nearer. Capestan sat next to the lieutenant and waited.

35

A long-haired medic had just taken over from the on-call doctor. Torrez had a broken collarbone and extensive bruising, including one that covered the whole of his right thigh. He had been severely shaken up, but his days were no longer numbered. He was sleeping.

Rosière swung open the double doors separating the intensive care unit from the main lobby, quickly followed by Lebreton.

"He's going to be fine," Capestan said.

The two officers heaved a sigh of relief.

"They're going to transfer him to his own room. His wife is on her way, but we'll have to do shifts, too, to make sure someone from the squad is always here."

"Of course," Lebreton said, then held out an item of clothing. "We recovered the hoodie."

Capestan noticed cat hair on the sleeves. It would need to go in for some tests. She asked Lebreton to take care of it, and also to arrange for a lookout to keep tabs on the boy's bike.

What a waste letting him get away like that.

"The kid matches Naulin's description, right?" Rosière said.

"Yes. We absolutely have to identify him. He's linked to both victims—we need to find out how. We need to question him, but first we need to find him."

"Bearing in mind his age, he could be anyone: a son, a nephew, a student, someone's younger brother . . . ," Lebreton said, trailing off.

Capestan's face suddenly lit up:

"The Guénan boy?"

"No. They had a framed photo: it's not him."

The *commissaire* shook her head slowly and stared down the corridor, thinking for a few seconds as she rubbed the scar on her finger.

"We need Naulin to remember the exact words of his conversation with the boy, and we need to call everyone again: Jallateau, André Sauzelle, the victims' friends, even that property developer . . . If possible, we'll need to talk to Maëlle Guénan's son. They're roughly the same age. Maybe our Squirrel was looking for him?"

Capestan stood up straight and turned to Lebreton.

"*Commandant*, I'm going to leave this research in your hands. I'm off to see Buron. Our information is becoming too important to keep them in the cold. I'm going to request that we join forces for the investigation."

Rosière looked unsure.

"He'll never agree," she warned the *commissaire*. "At least not without something to cushion those butt cheeks of his."

Before braving the headquarters of the *police judiciaire* and meeting with the big cheese himself, Capestan decided to take a breather along the Seine, strolling gently down the embankment. After Notre-Dame, the riverside momentarily lost its touristy charm, with the occasional lampposts lighting up nothing but loose paving stones spattered with bird droppings and pigeon feathers. As she walked through the dingy underpass beneath Pont Saint-Michel, she could hear the brackish water lapping at the river wall. The smell of this mire added to the city's fetid stench. Her footsteps echoed in the archway, then suddenly the embankment widened again and she was back in the hubbub of normal Paris. As a reflex action, Capestan sat down on the bench where she used to escape to think during her days in the *brigade de répression du banditisme*. She shivered at the touch of the cold stone. She was trying hard to clear her head when she was disturbed by the shrill laugh of a man talking to a friend. That laugh, that frame: for a split-second Capestan thought it was her ex-husband, and a profound sadness weighed down on her shoulders. She dismissed the image hurriedly and stood up. It was time to see Buron.

36

Buron's lair was now filled top to bottom with old glass cabinets displaying exhibits of every description: medals, pipes, antique pill boxes, leather-bound anthologies of French poetry, and, within easy reach, the pearls of his spectacles collection, which he alternated depending on whether he was in a mood for flirtation or manipulation. Dusk was falling over the river, and the gloomy room was lit only by the faint glow of an emerald-green lamp. As Capestan came in, the chief remained seated and simply gestured toward the chair opposite his. He left his paperwork where it was on his desk and put the top back on his pen, laying it on the documents for later.

"Good evening, Capestan. I don't have an awful lot of time. What brings you here?"

"I want our squad attached to the *brigade criminelle* for the rue Mazagran investigation."

"Out of the question," Buron said, lining up the edges of his pile of paper.

"We have complementary information from investigating the husband's murder and—"

"No. I said no."

Buron had decided to play obtuse. Capestan shifted her weight and leaned forward. She could not understand why he was putting up such a resistance. It made no sense.

"So what exactly are we supposed to do? Why create our unit if we can't even offer our help?"

"As I've told you already, it's to bundle all of you together. Don't make me spell it out for you again . . . ," he said, waving his hand exaggeratedly.

"No, I'd like you to."

"Capestan . . . We put you all in the same pound because we had to isolate you. You are all unmanageable. More to the point, you are all un-de-sir-able. I don't want you anywhere near an official investigation."

"You can't tar us all with that brush. We're not so terrible," Capestan protested, before the memory of her own track record forced her to change tack. "Fine, perhaps not in my case, but the others are—"

"The only reason you're all there is because we can't fire you!" Buron snapped, hammering each syllable home. "Can't you get that into your head? We're paying you to play dominoes or do some knitting. Get Évrard to teach you baccarat! Anything, *commissaire*, but just leave me in peace."

Buron was hopping mad. Capestan was exhausted: she was done in by the chase, Torrez was out for the count, the boy was still at large, and her hip was killing her. She had come to offer valuable information and instead she found herself on the receiving end of an unfair tirade. Her head was in a mush. She felt completely at sea.

"They're not all completely nuts. I don't understand—"

"Not all completely nuts? Get a life, Capestan! Dax and Lewitz are hyperactive cretins, then there's that grape-brain Merlot, Rosière and her wretched soap opera, Torrez—"

"Actually Torrez is in the hospital . . ."

"Why won't he just resign and stop plaguing us with his bad luck! And don't get me started on Orsini . . ."

Capestan had had her fill. Buron was going overboard and there was no way she'd be able to talk him down. She opted for an abrupt change of strategy.

"Does your catalog of flawed character traits happen to include 'underhandedness'?"

"Capestan, that's quite enough . . . ," the chief said, leaning back in his chair and unfolding the arms of his metal-rimmed glasses.

"Don't take this the wrong way, but I've done a little digging. Riverni—now that wouldn't be the same Riverni who stonewalled you back in 2009, by any chance? And also, while I think of it, what's with these cases we keep picking up? Are we the only people who know there's a link, or not? *Crim* throws out cases just like that and you don't seem to see anything wrong with it? The *brigade criminelle* ignoring criminal activity? Seriously, what's going on?"

Buron twisted his glasses pensively, not answering. His basset hound's eyes were watering slightly as usual. If it weren't for his gray crew cut, he wouldn't have looked like a police officer at all. He scratched the side of his head with the end of his glasses. The two of them sat there in silence.

Capestan shifted her gaze outside the window. The plane tree on the embankment had shed its last leaves. The prickly seedballs were covered in petrified bugs, clinging on for dear life, lending them the appearance of baubles on some macabre Christmas tree. Capestan sighed and turned back to Buron.

"The fact is, I know you've stowed us away over there on purpose. You want us to answer the questions you're asking yourself. You know exactly which buttons to press to get me going, but I know you, too, Monsieur le Directeur. I'm not sure why yet, but you have some cases that you want handled in secret. That's why you set up our squad. That's the only reason. So give me the resources I need. We'll investigate on the down-low if that's how it has to be, but I want the Maëlle Guénan file."

A faint, sporting smile of defeat snuck across Buron's face, and again Capestan was left with the unpleasant feeling that she had been led exactly where he wanted her.

"I'll get you a copy of the file," he said.

"And a siren," Capestan said. "For Torrez. He misses his siren."

37

The smell of frying onions was wafting down the stairs, hitting Capestan with a sudden and powerful urge to eat. Tucked under her arm was the copy of the Maëlle Guénan file that Buron had eventually managed to secure for her. She wiped her feet on the doormat and walked into the *commissariat*.

It was 9:00 p.m. and the flat was pitch black apart from a strip of light under the door into the kitchen—no doubt the source of the appetizing aroma, however unlikely it was for a police station. Capestan was starting to feel comfortable in this squad. Life was rolling along happily, and a budding solidarity was forming. The job seemed less serious here.

She put the file on her desk and stood in the darkness, looking out at the square through the windowpane. The street lamps were casting a yellow glow onto the rain-streaked pavement below. What with the colorful neon signs of its multiple sex shops, rue Saint-Denis seemed to be boasting a bit of Belle Époque swagger. Attic windows interrupted the zinc roofs across the square. For a moment it was hard to work out whether they were in the Paris of Toulouse-Lautrec or *Ratatouille*.

In the building to the right, a large, curtainless window revealed an average-size room that must have been a studio apartment. A young man in a T-shirt was sitting at a table, staring at his laptop as he tore the plastic blister off a package of processed ham. He rolled up a slice and guzzled it in two bites. After consigning two further slices to the same fate, he scratched at the bottom of the package to dislodge a bright-red sticker, probably some sort of coupon. He rocked to one side to get his wallet out of the back pocket of his jeans, opened the flap, and carefully placed the coupon into one of the slits reserved for credit cards.

Coupons. Capestan felt a pang of nostalgia as she remembered her grandmother. Every morning, swathed in her brown-and-gold-patterned kimono, she would sit at the head of her huge oak monastery table in the kitchen. She would pour hot water onto her chicory coffee granules, light a cigarette, and then attack the previous day's stack of brochures and leaflets. She turned each page meticulously and, whenever she hit upon a suitably attractive offer, she would balance her cigarette on the ashtray, pluck the pair of scissors from beside her on the table, and cut out the precious token. She would then file it away in one of three categories: food, hardware, services. It was like piling up banknotes, only with more color, more variety—a glimpse of a world where everything should be sampled. None of the grandchildren at the table would ever dare disturb a task of such importance. They simply watched in fascination.

Capestan took a step back from the window and was about to join her colleagues in the kitchen when a thought came to her with an electrifying jolt: the box of coupons on Marie Sauzelle's shelf and the sticker saying NO JUNK MAIL PLEASE on her mailbox. The two were completely incompatible. If Sauzelle collected coupons, she was hardly going to block off her principal supply. The sticker must have been put there by someone else. If Marie had not gotten rid of it, that was because she hadn't seen it. And if she had not seen it, that was because she was dead when it was put there.

The killer had brought it with him.

But why? No doubt to avoid the full-mailbox effect, which is a surefire indicator that either someone is away or something is amiss. The neighbors would have become worried sooner, and the murderer had wanted to delay the discovery of the body.

Why else? The sticker had not served to complicate the autopsy: the cause of death, by strangling, was clear enough. Capestan concentrated for a moment. The delay it caused, however, had made it impossible to establish the time of death with any certainty, thereby allowing the murderer time to come up with an alibi.

He had acted alone and he did not associate with anyone trustworthy enough to cover for him.

If the killer had come with the sticker on his person, then the murder was not opportunistic: it was premeditated. They were no longer dealing with a hothead who couldn't keep his emotions in check, but a calculating assassin. Capestan's thoughts returned to the old lady and her dignified posture, then to the spared cat. A calculating criminal with some degree of moral awareness, but who, if the link with the Guénans turned out to be rock solid, had without hesitation killed three people.

The *commissaire* nudged open the kitchen door to find Rosière standing before the old gas stove, stirring a vast copper saucepan with a wooden spoon. She could hear some onions sweating in olive oil. Pilou was glued to his mistress's heel, on the lookout as ever for any scraps to blot the pristine floor. Lebreton was smoking on a chair in the open doorway onto the terrace. They had opened a bottle and were sipping their wine. Capestan noticed the pile of mysterious planks that Lewitz had left at the foot of the bay window. He obviously rated his carpentry skills highly and had vowed to create a fully fitted-out kitchen. The brand-new toolbox might have suggested that he was really a novice, although a plastic container of hinges and a bag of assorted handles implied that the squad was at the mercy of a DIY enthusiast. The kitchen was to be installed with determination rather than ability.

"What are you still doing here?" Capestan exclaimed chirpily, more to announce her presence than anything else. "Don't you have homes to go to?"

Lebreton turned to the terrace with a minuscule frown and blew out a plume of smoke. There was a tinge of sadness in Rosière's grin, so Capestan hastily added:

"Me neither, as you can see. Smells good."

"Spaghetti with onions, olives, and Parmesan. One of my own rec-ipes. If you'd like some, I've made enough for a whole squadron . . ."

"Lovely, thanks," Capestan said, securing her hair with the black tie she kept around her wrist. "How's Torrez?"

"Fine, the doc's optimistic. Although his colleagues aren't exactly lining up to be at his bedside . . . They like the guy, but—"

"Fine, I get it. I'll go tomorrow. And the boy—"

"Uh-uh," Rosière cut in with a smile. "Eat. Drink. Stop working. Later."

"True. They can't take away our downtime, too."

Lebreton went off in search of a *baguette*, while Rosière attended to her saucepan and Capestan kept half an eye on the pasta jiggling in the boiling water. The fridge was purring in the corner.

"What about you, then? Single?" Rosière asked with her usual self-assurance, all the more direct now she was on her second glass of wine.

"Yup."

"For long?"

Capestan took a deep breath, as if to suggest she didn't know the date.

"Since the last time I fired my gun."

"You killed your ex?!"

Capestan burst out laughing.

"No, definitely not! Let's just say it didn't take long . . . The shot was the pretext."

Capestan's husband had thought that there was no coming back from it; that something had flipped inside her. The feeling that he might have been right did occur to the *commissaire*, but she blinked it aside and gave the spaghetti another stir.

"Basically, he asked for a divorce, and I let him have one," Capestan said, setting her wooden spoon down on one of the unused hobs. "The pasta's good to go."

She had changed the subject, but her mind was now transfixed with the image of a back and some suitcases walking out of her door.

Her future, her strength, and her happiness had disappeared, as if they'd been sucked down the plughole. The door seemed to reverberate after it had shut. Capestan had sat down on the sofa and stared into the emptiness for several hours before resolving to do something else. She leaned forward to pick up the TV remote from the coffee table and selected the video-on-demand menu. *The Magnificent Seven* was available for 2.99 euros. She pressed the button.

The following day they took away her service weapon.

Both losses had been a struggle, but once the emotional pain had passed, Capestan was astonished to find that she enjoyed her solitary existence. She liked living in the comfort of an inner world that was designed for her and her alone, under the watchful, silent eye of her affectionate cat. Perhaps this would only be a passing pleasure, but she wasn't so sure.

Capestan distractedly carried the pan of spaghetti over to the sink and drained it carefully, making sure not to scald herself. She stood there in disbelief as the tangle of spaghetti spread across the sink.

"You have to be kidding me . . . I forgot the colander," Capestan said, rushing off to fetch it before rinsing the pasta.

"And you, Eva. Any family?"

"Yes. A dog and a son. But of the two, the dog probably gets in touch more often," Rosière said, with a long-suffering shrug.

They washed down their pasta with Côtes-du-Rhône, old stories from the beat, on-screen adventures, and tales about dogs. Afterward, Rosière and Lebreton went for a cigarette while Capestan lit a fire under the watchful nose of Pilote, who didn't seem remotely worried about frazzling his coat.

The smokers returned a few minutes later, carrying their glasses and the remainder of the bottle. Capestan brought the three investigation boards over to the fireplace, where she joined Rosière on the enormous sofa she was hogging. Lebreton was sitting in one of the shabby armchairs.

The *commissaire* summed up her thoughts on the sticker and the idea that it was premeditated, then finished with a watered-down version of her talk with Buron. She had strongly considered telling them about the strange role the chief was apparently assigning the team, but felt that the boundaries of their responsibilities were still too blurred. She was afraid that it was simply a matter of settling grudges, and that this ill-fated assignment would shower neither the squad nor Buron in glory. A blend of loyalty and optimism was persuading Capestan to keep it quiet until she knew more. The main thing was that the chief had handed over Maëlle Guénan's file, which Capestan had now fanned out on the coffee table.

On the whole, it did not tell them much more than the preliminary findings they had snatched thanks to the baby monitors, especially because the autopsy was still under way. The current thinking at the *brigade criminelle* was that it was an assault carried out during a burglary.

"That doesn't make any sense," Lebreton said, his legs stretched out in front of him and his balloon glass rotating slowly in his palm. "First things first, it was in the morning—if the burglar didn't want to be disturbed, he could have buzzed to make sure the apartment was empty. Then he would either come in through a window, which couldn't have been the case here, or he'd break in, which wasn't the case either," he said, pointing to a line in the report with the base of his wineglass. "As for the murder weapon, I'm certain it was brought onto the premises."

"Why do you say that?" Capestan said. "They found the rest of the knife set in the kitchen."

"Maëlle couldn't have afforded a high-end set like that. Even if she could, she'd have chosen a less designer-brand—something daintier and more colorful, or wooden. The knives jar with her apartment."

"Maybe they were a present?"

"I don't think so. The way I see it, the murderer came with the intention of killing her, then made it look like a burglary, or like an unplanned crime in which the weapon was grabbed in the heat of the moment."

"Same drill as with Marie Sauzelle," Capestan said. "Double insurance: the murderer conceals his crime, but if he gets unlucky and it does come back to him, he can still deny premeditation and aggravating circumstances."

"There's a different MO with the sailor, though," Rosière pointed out as she slid a cushion behind her back.

"That was the first murder—he hadn't developed a strategy. Or maybe the two crimes are linked, but we're dealing with different killers."

"Your boy who's shown up both times . . . Do we think he might fit the profile of the killer who returns to the crime scene?"

"He would have been two or three years old at the time of the first murder," Capestan replied with a wry smile.

"What's that Corneille quote? 'For souls nobly born, valor does not await the passing of years,'" Rosière recited, tapping her nose knowingly.

"By the way, did you take the cat hair in for analysis?" Capestan asked Lebreton.

"Yes. We'll get the results in six or seven months . . . ," he said with a grim smile.

"Well, that's perfect."

Capestan frowned irritably. She looked at the boards, shifting her attention from one to the next before adjusting her position on the sofa, as if trying to recalibrate her brain in its cranial cavity.

"Right, let's recap: three connected cases; three premeditated murders. The first, the sailor, happens twenty years ago with minimal staging. The second, the old lady, happens eight years ago. The third happens today. Why the big gaps? An anniversary? An impulse? A deadline?"

"The sailor and the old lady were both killed in virtually the same month," Lebreton said. "Not the widow, though. Maybe the first two were genuinely linked, whereas Maëlle was more like a repercussion?"

"Yes. Maëlle, like the Squirrel, binds the case to the present. The murderer is still around; he still has a reason to act. I'm positive the kid can lead us to him. We haven't gotten any further on that front, have we? Any friends or suspects recognize the description? Maëlle's son?"

"So far his description hasn't triggered anything, not even with Cédric Guénan," Lebreton said. "But Naulin did remember an extra detail: the boy wanted to see Marie Sauzelle 'about a boat that sank.'"

"Back to that again."

A log spat in the fire, causing Pilote to lift a vigilant ear, then resumed its soft crackle. Capestan gazed into the phosphorescent, gray-edged embers, her cheeks reddening in the heat of the flames. She was trying to gather her thoughts.

"The boat. The boat is what all the cases have in common . . ."

"And us!" Rosière exclaimed, staring at her two colleagues in turn, her green eyes still piercing despite her tipsiness.

"Us?"

"The sailor and the old lady," Rosière said, sitting bolt upright and making her saint medallions jangle. "It's weird, isn't it? We stumble on two cases in two different boxes, and they're linked. That's one heck of a coincidence."

"You're right," Lebreton said. "Did anyone else in the squad find a murder in the files?"

"No," Capestan said. "We went through all the boxes and these were the only murders."

"So there was a very good chance that these would be the cases we'd end up investigating."

"They really were put there for us," Capestan murmured.

"They must have been burned by the same guy—he ditched them there thinking he was trashing them," Rosière said, hammering the table with her podgy fist. "I'm getting a whiff of something crooked . . . I'm telling you, there's something crooked here . . ."

A nasty shiver ran down Capestan's spine. Rosière was right. A police officer was involved—corrupt at best, criminal at worst. A second later, Capestan's mind was racing through all the various probabilities, like the flicking letters on a departures board at the airport. One by one they stopped and spelled out a name. No. No, that had to be wrong; it couldn't be him. He couldn't have trapped her like that, not after all these years. He wouldn't have dared. Her eyes met Lebreton's, and he was intrigued to see how pale she had gone. Capestan stood up and went to gather the files from the various desks, trying desperately to restore her calm. She sat back down on the sofa and opened the folders on the coffee table. Her eyes darted across the different sheets, and just as easily as picking out a red marble in the middle of some gravel, she pinpointed the same name one, two, three times: Buron.

Buron. Her mentor, her sponsor, her chief. Her friend. So, this was the aim of the squad. But why entrust them, and more to the point *her*, with these cases? Was he testing her intelligence? Her dedication? Or was he playing a game of Russian roulette to assuage his remorse? Suddenly the questions were banking up on all sides, overwhelming the *commissaire* with so many thoughts she feared she might suffocate. Buron. She needed to dunk her head in cold water; she needed to concentrate. Lebreton and Rosière waited. They had read the name, too.

"Right," Capestan said abruptly. "Buron features in each file. He was section *commissaire* at *criminelle* in '93—he led the first Guénan inquiry. In 2005, before joining the antigang squad, he became head of *crim*. It was his group who took care of the Sauzelle case. He stayed put for Maëlle yesterday but sent Valincourt, his second-in-command."

"Buron has been an officer at 36, quai des Orfèvres for thirty years. It's perfectly normal for his name to appear on all the files," Lebreton pointed out.

True, Capestan thought, relieved to feel a slight return to sanity after the emotional shock.

"No, it's not normal at all," Rosière stated, draining her glass with a resolute swig. "Given his reputation as an officer, inquiries like these shouldn't come up short. *Crim*'s usual way of doing things is to close each and every door. Here you get the impression they haven't opened a single one."

Rosière hauled herself up from the sofa to stretch her limbs. She was concentrating hard on keeping her balance, managing to stay upright through sheer force of will. She skirted around the table and, using her scarlet fingernail as a tool, started pushing out the air bubbles from the only sheet of wallpaper that Merlot had deigned to paste. The walls were all resplendent now, creating a marked contrast with the yellowed, crumbling ceiling. No one had volunteered to repaint that—it was a job where the only guarantee was a stiff neck.

"I agree," Capestan admitted reluctantly. "There's no rigor in these files, and no persistence either."

"Going from that to suggesting he's committed the murders seems a bit hasty to me," Lebreton said.

Capestan stared at the *commandant*. He wasn't wrong; she even hoped he might be right. That said, Buron's behavior since the formation of this squad had been intriguing. Something about it didn't flow. His usual serenity seemed to be stymied. The *commissaire* couldn't hold off sharing this any longer:

"There's something else about Buron. I don't think he created our squad on a whim."

"How do you mean?" Lebreton said, his attention piqued.

Capestan gave a brief outline of the situation: Merlot's discovery of the spat between Buron and Riverni, her own misgivings, and the details of her conversations with the police chief. Two seconds of shocked silence followed her declaration. Pilou sat up, on high alert.

"And you're only telling us this now?!" Rosière spluttered.

"Yes, I didn't consider it worth discussing before," the *commissaire* answered firmly. "We only would have come up with a load of wild theories about his intentions. I wanted to let it play out on its own."

Lebreton turned to the flickering flames to absorb the information, while Rosière grumbled, still poking at her strip of wallpaper.

"Whatever, it couldn't be clearer, these cases reek of crooked cops," she concluded. "And if that's true, then Buron is the killer and he's hoping we'll serve up a nice little scapegoat so he can sit back and enjoy his retirement."

"If he's guilty, the last thing he'd want is for these files to resurface," Lebreton objected. "The cases were wrapped up happily and waiting to lapse—it was ideal."

"If that's right, then why does he just throw them our way rather than giving us a proper heads-up? He twiddles his thumbs at HQ, he doesn't give Anne any info when she goes to see him . . . He throws us some blocks and some rings and tells us to play ring throw. Does that sound like an innocent man to you?"

Rosière came and sat back down, pulling a rolled-up tissue from her sleeve and rubbing her nose irritably. The *commissaire* was deep in thought. Yet again, she was finding it impossible to tease out a theory about the chief—his fondness for manipulation meant that no theory was off-limits.

The smell of wood smoke was now masking the onions, bringing with it a different kind of comfort. Capestan felt the tough cotton of the sofa's armrest softening under her hand. This investigation required a delicate approach, come what may.

The *commissaire* took a deep breath before airing her thoughts:

"The fact is, one way or another, Buron is involved. He knows something we don't, and he doesn't want to share it with us. We can't question him, but we can put him under twenty-four-hour surveillance and see where he leads us."

Buron, in his slightly tight-fitting black Lanvin suit, presented his ticket to the usher without forgetting to give her a smile. The young woman guided him to the third row of the boxes and pointed to the fourth seat in. As always, Buron's features contorted in a brief grimace as he contemplated how narrow the gap was. Damn these Italian-style theaters, he thought to himself. The hum of the audience in the Salle Richelieu began to swell, and heady gusts of perfume wafted across the walkways. The *divisionnaire* was already reveling in the spectacle. *Don Giovanni* in French—absolutely unmissable. The customary three claps sounded as he wedged himself into the red-velvet seat. He was feeling marvelously at ease that evening, safe in the knowledge that Capestan would do what was necessary.

38

The neon lights were buzzing in the hospital's lackluster corridor, and the air was thick with the unmistakable smell of bleach. Capestan's shoes squeaked on the blue-black marble-effect linoleum as she followed the numbers on the patient room doors. One of them was ajar, revealing a bed-bound patient in a crumpled hospital gown wriggling up toward her dinner tray. Capestan knocked when she reached number 413.

Wearing a pair of yellow flannel pajamas with brown bears on them, Torrez was sitting up in bed, propped against a white pillow. He had a bandage double-wrapped around his head and a splint was preventing his shoulder and elbow from moving. His right hand was attached to a drip via a plastic cannula, and the bag was filled with a thick, transparent liquid. He was gripping the remote in his right hand even though the TV was off. His face lit up when he saw Capestan. The *commissaire* had brought along a portable stereo and a CD of French classics, which she placed on his bedside table.

"How are we this evening?" she said, adopting the tone of a nurse about to empty a bedpan.

"We're fine, we're happy. We'd quite like to pee."

"Oh! Do you want me to call someone?" Capestan asked.

"No, I'm only joking."

Torrez smiled broadly, causing his bandages to crinkle. Capestan wasn't sure she had seen that expression on his face before. He winced as he sat up a bit higher. The monitor next to his bed emitted some beeps that sounded like a game of Breakout on an old Atari Arcade. Capestan didn't know how to express her thoughts, so she kept things simple for lack of a better option:

"Thank you. If it weren't for you I would have been a goner."

"Don't you realize?" Torrez said, seeming genuinely happy. "You're not dead. I took the hit."

She felt terrible, but Torrez was in high spirits:

"The spell's over. It's been reversed, even. I didn't just avoid cursing you, I actually kept you alive, too."

"I was certain nothing would happen to me. I don't believe in bad luck. I'm all about good luck."

A shadow fell over the *lieutenant*'s swollen face:

"You think it'll only work on you?" he said.

"No! No, not at all," Capestan said, backpedaling furiously. "It's superstition, that's all it is—you've just proved that."

Capestan sat down and filled him in on the developments before explaining the plan of action: a couple of officers staking out the bicycle; some of the others busily looking into the Squirrel and the boat; and the last few doing tag teams to keep an eye on Buron (who, incidentally, had dropped a strong hint about a certain siren for Lieutenant Torrez).

"At last!" he exclaimed, as if collecting a long-overdue distinction.

They chatted for a bit longer about life at the Commissariat des Innocents. The wallpaper was up, they had hung some curtains to make the living room feel cozier and had brought in a few cooking utensils. Évrard was insisting they needed to wrap the shrubs against the winter, Dax had torn up the parquet floor after catching his foot on a nail, and Merlot had broken the photocopier by sitting on it. Lewitz was putting the finishing touches on their new-look kitchen, which protruded a bit into the bay window but was otherwise fine. That morning, Orsini had made a joke. The team was so stunned they forgot to laugh. He was a good sport about it, acknowledging that it wasn't the first time he had had that effect.

Torrez gave a running commentary, including a promise to donate a dessert set they no longer needed in their kitchen at home. The conversation gradually petered out and a peaceful silence fell on the room. Like police officers at a stakeout, the two of them let their thoughts drift around the room, neither of them wanting to disturb the other. Then Torrez cleared his throat and Capestan knew he was about to ask the question he had not dared to ask until now.

"The guy you . . . What happened?"

Capestan sank back in her chair. She was not really in the mood for discussing that episode from her past.

"As stories go, it's not a barrel of laughs. Are you sure?"

Torrez looked down, not wanting to push her. The *commissaire* could tell that he now considered her a proper partner, and that he wouldn't mind keeping it hazy if need be. He could handle the uncertainty. But the man had just body-checked a bus for her—they were beyond hiding from their pasts. She sighed, folded her arms, and prepared to answer the lieutenant's questions.

"Three years ago, I was with the BRB."

"The antigang squad?" Torrez said in amazement.

This squad was legendary, the high point of any career. Yet now she had been relegated. The *lieutenant* tried to fathom such a fall from grace.

"Yup, antigang," Capestan replied with a hint of nostalgia. "I was doing well there. Then one day I was reassigned to the *brigade de protection de mineurs* at quai des Gesvres. Big pay raise—I couldn't say no."

"But you should have?"

"Yes," she said, unfolding her arms.

Children, kidnappings, distressed families, abuse . . . Always the most poignant and tragic events. And it was relentless. Every evening, Capestan was confronted by her own powerlessness, by the feeling that she was buried in the battlefield. She barely lasted a year before having to admit to herself that she was not up to it. She had never been calm by instinct; she could not keep her emotions at arm's length. On her previous postings, she could always recover between one ghastly case and the next. Not there; not once. Her ability to detach vanished in the space of a few months. She had drained her reserves of cool-headedness; now it was only hot, ready to boil over for the smallest reason. She put in a transfer request. Buron refused, saying she had to do another year. So she stayed.

"A brother and a sister, aged twelve and eight, had disappeared," Capestan started. "We prayed they had run away, but obviously we feared it was a nutjob. The search wasn't going anywhere—we were floundering. Weeks went by, then months."

Months. The thought devastated her all over again.

"They had been kidnapped. Eventually we found a lead and tracked the guy down to some godforsaken place near Melun. While my colleagues searched the house, I went to check the hut around the back. I smashed the padlock. The two children were in there, emaciated and black with grime. At first I stood there in the doorway, knocked senseless. They stayed there holding each other on a straw mattress on the ground. Next to them was an old man, also showing signs of malnourishment. But he was dead, had been for a day, maybe more. When I arrived, the kids didn't make a sound—silent as the grave. Eventually I tried to reassure them, then I heard a sound behind me. The man was standing there in the doorway. The sun was behind him, so I could make out his profile perfectly, but I couldn't discern his facial features or what he had in his hands. There was a pad of paper in one of them, for sure, but in the other I couldn't tell if it was a pen or a knife. When he saw me he didn't try to flee. Quite the opposite—he asked me what I was doing on his property. I saw the little girl's hand grasp the earth next to me. I stood up and positioned myself between the man and the children so they wouldn't see. And then I shot him."

"Sexual abuse?"

"Not sexual, no. He was a megalomaniac. He'd been studying the Great Famine from the time of the Ancien Régime. The bastard wanted to get to the truth. He was carrying out a clinical study of the effects of hunger on the most vulnerable segments of society: children and the elderly. Not on thirty-year-old rugby players, of course. In his view, science justified making sacrifices, like doctors who run tests on monkeys."

Capestan couldn't help thinking that, in her current state, she would not be averse to putting a bullet in those doctors, either. Torrez smoothed out his sheet with his hand. The father in him approved of the shot; the policeman wanted her arrested. He scratched the remote control distractedly.

"Do you regret it?" he said after a while.

That old question. Three lives ruined versus one dead son of a bitch? Capestan was too respectful of math to have any regrets. But she also knew that made her seem like a sociopath.

"I'm undecided," she lied.

Torrez appeared to take it as a yes.

"Was it a knife?" he asked.

"What?"

"Was he holding a knife?"

"It was a pen."

"And did your colleagues cover for you?"

"Even better," she replied. "My boss did. Buron was first on the scene. His version of events was categorical: self-defense. If Buron said so . . ."

If it had not been for him, she would not only have been dismissed—she would have ended up in jail. His word had saved her, and his invoice had just arrived.

Was that what this was? Was he making her pay? Had he set up the squad with Capestan, his debtor, in charge so that she would find him a nice scapegoat? She could feel the threat lurking beneath the surface: Buron was expecting her to protect him; otherwise their pact was off. Was she supposed to rig the investigations, hide the evidence, and ultimately betray the victims? This was out of the question.

But betraying Buron was not something she could do lightly.

Capestan's mind was in disarray from the chief's machinations. Could her mentor really do something so cynical? Capestan refused to believe it. She refused with such certainty, in fact, that she obliterated the thought entirely. She needed to analyze the facts, to recover her ability to examine each aspect with complete objectivity.

As for Torrez, he was still caught up with the *commissaire*'s debt:

"If Buron got you off the hook, I don't see why he would have assigned you to this squad. You made a big mistake, but it was isolated."

Isolated. Nothing could have been further from the truth. In the months leading up to the incident, she had already let off a few stray bullets into the kneecaps of certain thugs. She had been involved in a couple of questionable hit-and-runs, which would never have fooled Buron at police HQ, let alone Lebreton at the IGS. The truth was, the shot she fired in that hut had brought her dark spiral to a close. Capestan had earned her dismissal twenty times over.

The sound of heels clicking down the corridor was followed by a knock on Torrez's door. He told whoever it was to come in, and after a few seconds of hesitation, Rosière poked her head around the door, then flung it wide open. Lebreton followed her into the room. They greeted Torrez with outstretched palms, displaying a blend of caution and camaraderie. Lebreton then tugged at his shirt cuff before slinking off to lean against the wall opposite the bed. Rosière stayed by his side, furiously fiddling with her saint medallions.

"How are things going with the passenger list?" Capestan wanted to know, still by the bedside of the semi-mummified lieutenant.

"So far, so good. The company's based in Miami. They're sending it to Évrard so we should have it in two or three days."

"Perfect. How about the tailing?"

"That's been a bit more problematic," Lebreton admitted, shifting his weight to the other leg.

"In what way?"

"Buron's a canny policeman. It's hard to follow him without being spotted, especially because he knows most of us. At a distance, out in the street, we can stay undercover—"

"The old boy's not a fucking gazelle," Rosière cut in with a chuckle. "He's not going to leave us in the dust."

Various sounds were creeping into the room from the corridor: a cart rolling past, trays being cleared, and the singsong voices of the nurses doing their rounds.

"The trouble is we can't stake him out at number 36," Lebreton continued. "What with the cameras and the windows that look out on the embankment, it's impossible to go unnoticed. Cars can't park, tourists just walk straight past. I wondered if we should forget about direct surveillance and post teams on the side roads leading up to the building, but there's not enough of us—"

"Or we focus on his out-of-office movements and drop number 36 completely. But then that's hardly a tail," said Rosière, who was wearing a dazzling white-vinyl raincoat.

No, if they were going to keep Buron under surveillance, then they certainly were not going to skip around his work-related activity. But number 36 was hard to pin down—they needed to find a solution.

"What about some binoculars on the opposite bank?" Capestan suggested.

Lebreton dismissed the idea with a shake of the head.

"Visible from the floors higher up, plus very suspect. We thought about renting an apartment . . ."

". . . but cheap studios with views of the Seine are hard to come by," Rosière chimed in. "And the well-to-do aren't really the sort to lend you a window for a couple of euros . . ."

"We could try and requisition one . . . ," Capestan ventured.

". . . but they'd complain to high heaven," Rosière said, joining the *commissaire* with a sardonic grin.

The *capitaine* was getting hot in her shiny raincoat, especially because Torrez had cranked up the radiators. She flapped both sides to try and get some ventilation before shrugging it off and folding it over her arm.

"There's construction going on at the moment, isn't there?"

"Affirmative," the *commandant* said. "Some scaffolding up to the top floor and part of the roof. But we can't just plunk ourselves there, not even in construction gear. We're talking about spying on the *police judiciaire*, not some bunch of ruffians. The construction company would never agree to it. And I've checked, there isn't room for a construction trailer at street level. Trust me, it's impossible: there's no way to plant someone on the sly at number 36."

"We've run dry," Rosière agreed.

Torrez turned the remote control over in his fingers, running his nail across the rubber buttons. The *commissaire* racked her memory of quai des Orfèvres and the surrounding area, picturing the massive barred windows, the entrance, the walkway above the Seine's embankment, the horse chestnuts, the handful of parking spaces beyond the automatic barrier. Nowhere to hide. They needed to find another option. An idea was starting to form.

"Well, if we can't be discreet, let's do it in full view," Capestan declared.

Key West Island, South Florida
May 2, 1993

The air was extremely humid and heavy with the scent of salt and flowers. Two emerald-green parakeets were fluttering around the banyan tree, whose roots were mangling the road surface. The colors, the warmth, the silence. Alexandre never wanted to go back to France.

He was going to have to, though, to tend to Attila.

Attila. The nickname spoke volumes. The little boy was exploring the bottom part of the garden under Alexandre's watchful eye. He was wielding a spade that was normally reserved for building sand castles, slamming it into one trunk after the next. He had never used that spade to build anything. Alexandre sighed and mopped his sweaty forehead with his handkerchief.

The young man who owned the bike rental shack waved to him as he walked down the street. His trusty, dignified pirate's parrot was perched on his shoulder, swaying from side to side. They swaggered into Sloppy Joe's on Duval Street. What Alexandre would have done for a nice glass of bourbon. France. No more diving; no more days draped in linen and cotton. Back to work, which meant wool and uniforms. The brief dalliance had run its course.

A rooster appeared on the opposite roadside. There were never many cars on these broad, tree-lined streets, and if there were they went at a gentle pace. The unperturbed rooster was in no hurry itself as it made its way toward Alexandre's open gate. He tried to scare it away with a whistle, but the fowl was stubborn as well as stupid. It was normal for the roosters there to roam wild, since the locals trained them to hunt and eat scorpions. The roosters respected their side of the bargain, and in return they expected to be left in peace. With its comb held high and its chest puffed out, the rooster came farther into the garden. Attila spotted it straightaway and tore toward it, brandishing the spade and yelling at the top of his lungs. Alexandre abruptly shot out his hand to intercept the child and clung onto him. Red-faced and furious, Attila thrashed his limbs in every direction, but soon he tired himself out and succumbed to Alexandre's viselike grip.

"He's got the blood of a *guerrillero*," the boy's mother said, with a twinkle of Cuban pride in her eye.

"*Guerrilleros* are only for times of revolution, Rosa" came the reply.

His wife had just pulled up in her mud-spattered white jeep. She put the hand brake on and got out of the car, then headed around to the passenger side. She unfastened the seat belt and carefully took little Gabriel in her arms. The tears had long since dried on the child's cheeks, and in his hand he had one of those colorful lollipops the doctor lets you have. The bandage around his little finger made it hard to hold. Alexandre felt a tightness in his chest and looked searchingly at Rosa. She waited until she was by his side before pointing to the Band-Aid on Gabriel's ear.

"They couldn't sew it back: the lobe was torn off."

39

"Do you think that if number 36 had been at number 38, they still would have called it 36?" Dax said.

Évrard pretended to think it through before giving her answer: "No."

Sitting on the stone wall of the quai des Orfèvres embankment, opposite the entrance to the headquarters of the Parisian section of the *police judiciaire*, she was observing the windows on the third floor, which is where the management had their offices.

"Yeah, number 38 sounds bad," Dax went on. "Could be worse, though. Could have been number 132, flat B. Can you imagine? 'Open up! Number 132, Flat B here.' They'd have to find another name, I'm telling you."

Évrard smiled and let her gaze drift down the Seine. A boatman was steering his barge with a steady hand behind the thick glass of his wheelhouse, enjoying his morning coffee with careful, deliberate sips as the early autumn sunshine broke through the trees, bridges, and apartment buildings. Évrard envied the traveler's freedom. She kicked her legs alternately to get some kind of rhythm and keep herself awake in the monotony of the surveillance. The grainy stone scratched her through the fabric of her jeans.

Today she had been paired up with Dax for Buron's surveillance, and she was hoping that the saying about sticks and stones and words would ring true. On top of her windbreaker she was sporting a T-shirt that Orsini, ever the man of letters, had decorated with the slogan COMMISSARIAT ON STRIKE. Capestan's idea. Since undercover surveillance was not an option, they were pretending to be pickets—the ideal excuse to be both stationary and conspicuous. Plus, with no equipment and even fewer rights, the *commissaire* reminded them that their relegated squad had plenty to complain about. Évrard had not been convinced by this strategy, objecting that Buron wouldn't risk going anywhere if he knew they were outside. Capestan had insisted: "He'll never suspect we're tailing him, he'll think it's a genuine strike. He thinks we're a bunch of idiots. And anyway, that's not the point—we still don't know what we're looking for, but we do know there's a link with number 36, so best we keep an eye on what happens there. Let's see who does respond to our presence."

Dax, sitting on the wall next to her, had also daubed his T-shirt in fat, slightly smudged block capitals saying THE FORCE IS NOT WITH US. Helpful as ever, he and Lewitz had come up with A PIECE 4 THE POLICE; CASH, NOT TRASH; and a variety of football-related slogans. Capestan felt apprehensive about this bombardment and ended up going for the least moronic suggestion. She did, however, decide it was best to split up the two friends on this mission.

And so Dax and Évrard had arrived at 8:00 a.m., and barely a minute into their surveillance of Buron, the duty guard at the entrance—a young, stocky guy with a pale complexion and short arms—was squinting at them curiously. He smiled mockingly and phoned up a superior to ask what was to be done with this "picket line" made up of "two very quiet people." The answer must have been "Clear them away," since he came up and asked if they wouldn't mind moving along. Évrard had refused outright. The orderly went off to get some further instructions, returning with two other similarly bewildered guards.

They kicked off the evacuation by grabbing Dax's elbow. The *lieutenant* had howled as if they were beating him to a pulp: "Police brutality! Police brutality!" Passersby turned to stare and some tourists started taking photographs, and in the end the lackey's walkie-talkie spluttered into action. One of the bosses upstairs must have ordered them to let the striking dogs lie, in case the general public started taking an interest.

After that, Évrard and Dax observed the comings and goings without interference, always keeping one eye on Chief Buron's window.

Évrard, throwing herself into the mission and her disguise, was trying to maintain the solemn air of the unjustly treated, dispossessed police officer, even though Dax and his constant look of enthusiasm were not making her job any easier. The upper branches of the horse chestnut on the embankment below, which tickled the top of her head at the slightest breeze, were also making it hard to concentrate. But despite these various obstacles, nothing escaped the notice of the indifferent, bluffing *lieutenant*. She was using her cell phone's hands-free kit to communicate with Capestan, who was positioned out of sight on a bench in place Dauphine. She had put headphones over the earpiece to make it look like she was listening to music, and the *commissaire's* free minutes meant they could stay in constant contact.

Dax clamped the post of his HUNGER STRIKE placard between his knees to free up his hands, then fished out a sandwich the size of an encyclopedia from his yellow-and-gray knapsack. When he unwrapped the silver foil, a strong waft of cold meat filled the fresh autumn air.

"Want a bite?" the young *lieutenant* offered his partner for the day. "It's got ham, chicken, bacon, and pastrami. My mother made it for me. She really knows how to make a good snack. A little dollop of mustard, and no lettuce at all. That way the bread doesn't get soggy. Then she puts a layer of paper towels beneath the foil to stop it tasting all metallic. Want some?"

Évrard declined with a smile, and Dax started in on the beast with visible glee. The guard came up to him, plainly irritated.

"I thought you were on a hunger strike?"

Dax nodded vigorously, his mouth full, and tried to reply when a stream of crumbs dropped from his sizable maw. He gathered them up promptly, damned if he was going to let such a good meal go to waste. Évrard picked up the placard in embarrassment:

"I'm taking over for a couple of hours. He's on a break."

"You're doing shifts? You're taking a lunch break during a hunger strike?" the officer asked snidely.

"That's right," Évrard confirmed, with the tight-lipped Dax nodding in agreement.

"Do you take us for idiots?"

There was only one thing for it: if they were to keep their credibility and avoid losing their observation post, they had to turn this accusation on its head. Évrard summoned as much bitterness as she could and played the passive-aggressive card:

"No. *You* are taking *us* for idiots. So we're falling in line. And we're taking a disciplined approach. Isn't that the key to good police work? That way the bosses up there will reinstate us—a normal squad for normal officers."

She didn't want to lay into the guard too much, but she said her piece to stay in character. During her little speech, Évrard had taken out one of her earphones, to make it more realistic. In the other, she was aware that Capestan was listening in the distance, following the exchange with amusement.

A small flash of light from the chief's window caught Évrard's attention. Buron was pacing back and forth at his window, eventually stopping for a few minutes and giving the *lieutenant* an exaggerated wave. She waited for the guard to go away before informing Capestan:

"Buron says hi."

She heard the *commissaire*'s voice in her left ear:

"Do you get the feeling he's greeting you, surprised to see you, or trying to irritate you?"

Évrard thought for a moment before facing the facts:

"I think he's trying to irritate me."

A hundred yards away, Capestan wondered yet again what Buron was after, and whether he knew he was being watched. Sitting on her bench by the *pétanque* area that dominated place Dauphine—that delightful, leafy haven in the shadow of the Palais de Justice—the *commissaire* was soaking up the view at the same time as organizing the rotation schedule for her teams. As she kept one ear on Dax and Évrard, with the other she enjoyed the sounds of the game of *pétanque* that was under way: the dull thud of the steel *boules*, the muted rolls on the sand and gravel surface, the curses, the jibes, and the issuing of urgent advice. They were having fun, but they wanted to win, too. One game after another, whatever the weather.

Capestan never stopped scouring the surrounding area from her vantage point. A man crossed the square. He had dreadlocks that made him look like an octopus taking a nap. Another young man cycled past a bit farther away. He had a green helmet and Bermuda shorts.

The *commissaire* sat bolt upright. It was the Squirrel. He was perched on a bicycle, the very same one that Merlot was supposedly staking out. It didn't matter. They had found him, and this time they could not let him get away. He was heading toward the entrance of the *police judiciaire*. Capestan grabbed the mic for her hands-free and warned Évrard:

"The kid I chased with Torrez is coming up on your left. Green helmet. Tail him, too. He's our primary target."

The bike had barely left her sight when Capestan's second telephone rang. She picked up. It was Rosière:

"Hi, Anne? You'll never guess!"

"Buron's on the passenger list?"

"No. At least we're not sure—it hasn't arrived yet. But we have something better: on June 2, 2005, a court in Miami made the ferry company pay damages to the survivors. To celebrate, the French chapter of the Shipwreck Survivors Association organized a party in Boulogne. And we have a video. We checked the event against Torrez's time line and found that it coincides with the date of Marie Sauzelle's murder."

"We need to watch that. We don't have a video player at the Innocents, where might—"

"Oh yes we do," Rosière said with delight. "We've got a video recorder, DVD player, Blu-ray, flat-screen . . . I've even called up CanalSat to get cable. Shall we wait for you?"

"Yes. Let me contact Orsini to get him to relieve me here, then I'll be with you."

Capestan hung up and raced through her contacts for Orsini's number. She couldn't help but smile—honestly, cable TV?

Dax made the most of his break from tailing duty to swing home and take a shower. Once he'd put on a fresh set of clothes, he sank his fingers up to the second knuckle in a pot of ultrastrong hair wax, then rubbed the substance across his palms and applied it evenly to his wet locks. He combed his short hair to one side and topped off his handiwork with a quiff. Pleased with the result, he smiled at his reflection in the wardrobe mirror and then washed his hands thoroughly. "If you want a nice girl, you need to wash your hands like a nice boy," his mother would often say. Dax's hands were always gleaming: the day that nice girl came his way, he would not need to find a sink. He dried them carefully on the spotless white hand towel, then put the finishing touch to his toilette by dousing himself in cologne. Dax liked to smell good. He could never understand guys like the ones they'd been following. Biking makes you sweat. Anyway, that kid must have relations in high places. He sauntered into number 36 without having to show his papers. HQ was like home to him.

40

The answer would be in the video. Capestan pressed PLAY. A few black streaks wiggled across the snowy-white screen, then the color appeared and the picture eventually settled down. Rosière and Lebreton fell silent over on the sofa. They could hear the tape whirring in the video player.

The commemoration was an open-air event. On a wide, raised area of ground someone had erected a wooden stage with a giant screen on top. Long trestle tables ran down each side. The ones on the right were lined with benches, while those on the left served as a kind of buffet, with cardboard trays of neatly arranged *petits fours*. One end of each table had towers of plastic cups surrounded by jugs of wine, bottles of soda, and cartons of fruit juice. It was hardly a chic garden party at the Élysée, but it was late afternoon and the sky was still blue, and the guests were greeting each warmly.

A man in a suit stood up on the stage and tapped the microphone. He mouthed a few words as he looked searchingly at the sound guy. Some loud feedback cut through the atmosphere, causing the scattered groups of the congregation to turn to the stage as one.

The static video camera was facing the raised area and had the stage and the screen in its shot. The man in the suit blushed and, hunched over the microphone, started speaking, the speakers only kicking in after the third or fourth word: ". . . My dear friends, may this year be about remembering . . ."

"There!" Rosière exclaimed. "Bottom left—the old lady with the curly hair!"

It was indeed Marie Sauzelle. But still no Buron, which put Capestan's mind to rest. She did not want to see the chief's tall, slightly droopy figure. She was scanning the crowd feverishly, hoping against hope not to find anything. Suddenly another figure, more upright than the one she was looking for, caught her eye. She pointed at the screen to alert Rosière and Lebreton. They waited for the man to turn around to confirm it. There was no doubt.

"Valincourt," Lebreton said.

"What's he doing there?" Rosière added. "Look . . ."

Marie Sauzelle went up to Valincourt, greeted him, and stood next to him. They exchanged a few words, all the while watching the man on the stage. "After months of research, the committee I represent has managed to produce a film that pays homage to the victims of the shipwreck . . ."

Valincourt straightened. He was no longer listening to his neighbor.

". . . and as we play the slideshow of photographs, could I please ask you to pay your respects in absolute silence . . ."

The opening notes of the "*Étoiles du cinéma*" theme rang out and a series of people's faces started crossfading on the screen while the man read out their names.

"So cheesy . . . ," Rosière muttered.

Lebreton shook his head, while Capestan's attention shifted back to the bottom left of the screen. Valincourt was as tense as a tightrope. Marie took out a hankie and started dabbing her eyes, then all of a sudden she froze and stared at the big screen. Then at Valincourt, then back at the screen, and finally Valincourt again. The tribute reel lasted a few more seconds before the last picture faded into a black background.

Marie turned square-on to the *divisionnaire* and began speaking to him animatedly. He made a gesture of denial and placed a hand on the old lady's shoulder, appeasing but authoritative, too. She nodded, but she did not look wholly convinced. All the same, she let herself be ushered toward the buffet, and they disappeared offscreen. Shortly after, the video cut out.

"I wonder what Sauzelle said to him that made him react like that," Capestan said as she switched off the TV.

She ejected the cassette and returned it to its plastic box. With the help of this one video, they could now be certain about several things. The *commissaire* listed them: Valincourt, like Marie Sauzelle, was part of the Association, which meant they had both traveled on the *Key Line Express*, the boat on which Yann Guénan had been a crew member. All three of them had definitely crossed paths. Most important, Sauzelle had met the *divisionnaire* just before her death.

"I think we can drop Buron," Rosière said. "We've got ourselves another crooked officer . . ."

Capestan nodded vigorously, not afraid to show her relief. With a newfound optimism, she darted toward the stack of folders on her desk. She came back to the sofa and spread copies of the Guénan file across the coffee table. The three of them almost bumped heads as they scoured the list of signatures. No mention of Valincourt.

"But he was there for Marie Sauzelle, and as for Maëlle Guénan, there's no doubt whatsoever—we saw him at the scene," Capestan said.

"We've found our culprit!" Rosière crowed.

"No, no, hold on," Lebreton said, trying to calm everyone down. "He was carrying out an investigation and he happened to know at least one of the victims. To go from there to concluding he committed the murders . . ."

"Wait, Louis-Baptiste," Capestan said. "He knew the victim but, more important, he never mentioned that fact. Not in the case notes at the time, nor when I visited him. He explicitly said that the first time he'd met her was when she was dead. There's forgetful, and then there's . . ."

Lebreton leaned back heavily in his armchair and crossed his legs. The *commandant* was never one to rush to hasty conclusions.

"Perhaps. We need to establish the reason for his silence. On top of—"

"Oh, all your official IGS nonsense is getting on my nerves!" Rosière shouted. "Come on, the guy's guilty as sin!"

"All right, all right, don't lose your temper, Eva. What do we do now?" Lebreton asked, smiling in spite of himself.

"We shift our tail to Valincourt. Same profile, same approach," Capestan said.

"We've got enough on him to pay a courtesy call, surely?" Rosière said greedily.

"No, it's too early," the *commissaire* said, applying the brakes. "We don't have enough incriminating evidence to bring him in."

"Are you joking?"

"No. We've got no formal evidence, no DNA, no fingerprints . . . Just a few coincidences."

"That hasn't stopped us in the past . . ."

"Yes, but this is Valincourt we're talking about. The man's got more stripes than a zebra. If we go for him head-on, we'll only get a bloody nose, like with Riverni. We need a motive and we need to be prepared. We need to know everything about the *divisionnaire* before we attack."

Finding the murderer was one thing; catching him would be another.

41

There was a palpable enthusiasm in the Commissariat des Innocents. The investigation was gathering momentum.

Merlot, feet up on his desk, had wedged his considerable girth between the arms of a swivel chair, which was putting up a noble but short-term resistance. With the receiver in one hand and a glass of whisky in the other, he was doing his best gentrified-Marlowe impression as he wrangled with every HR manager the *police judiciaire* could throw at him.

"Indeed, *mon ami*, the very same Valincourt as he who commands the *brigades centrales*! I would not be chivying you if this were a matter of meager importance. Ah, the usual little snapshot if you will: parents, marriage, children, qualifications, previous postings, what he has for breakfast, and his favorite brand of underwear. Mum's the word, eh?" he guffawed, like a Freemason bumping into an old pal at the lodge. "How does a bottle of Napoléon cognac sound for a little 'incentive'?"

Lebreton pinned a sheet to the wall with details of the surveillance rotation schedule. Évrard was still keeping an eye on the Squirrel while Orsini was in charge of Divisionnaire Valincourt. The *commandant* then untangled the headphones of his hands-free kit so he could call up everyone from the inquiry to ask the all-important question: "Did you know this man outside his role as a detective?" Midconversation he made his way calmly to the terrace, where he stood gazing across the rooftops of Paris in the direction of the voice in the distance.

Lewitz had gone down to the parking garage along with Rosière, who had made arrangements for a vehicle that was more suitable for stakeouts than the *brigadier*'s bright-yellow Laguna. The *capitaine* had then returned to the apartment without Lewitz, giving him a bit of time to break in his new toy. Dax, fresh from his shower, was back at his computer screen, fingers on keyboard, gaping at her like a schoolboy waiting to take dictation. The *commissaire* knew it was in her interest to choose her words wisely.

"Merlot's in charge of Valincourt's civil status and general bio. So I'd like you to dig up his telephone records: landline and cell phone. We're looking for a call to one of these," she said, handing him a Post-it with Maëlle Guénan's numbers. "I'd also like details of credit card transactions, in particular for the purchase of a set of knives."

"More likely to buy a murder weapon with cash," Rosière pointed out, walking toward the *commissaire* with the journal in her hand.

"True, but you never know."

"Shall I check out his online identity, too?" Dax said.

"Do you really think old Geronimo's on Facebook? Maybe he's got a Twitter account to share his latest gags, too?"

Capestan ignored Rosière and her typical sarcasm.

"Yes, I'd be interested in his digital footprint, too. Do whatever you think is necessary, Dax, but remember we don't have much time."

The *lieutenant* gave Capestan a salute and revved up his computer with a toothy grin.

Two hours later, dripping with sweat, he summoned the troops.

"I've got everything!"

Capestan, Lebreton, and Rosière flocked to his station. A carefully stacked pile of printed sheets was looming in front of the hacker. He grabbed the top one and handed it to Capestan, then doled out the rest:

"Statements for his IKEA card, Fnac card, Bizzbee card, Sephora card . . ."

The *commissaire* became increasingly disconcerted as she took delivery of these documents and scanned their contents, each one more breathtakingly useless than the last. Rosière, too miffed this time to tease him, turned to the *lieutenant*:

"Dax, do you honestly see the *divisionnaire* going around with a Sephora card? They sell cosmetics!"

"Yeah, why not—I've got a Sephora card."

"Capestan asked for credit cards, not loyalty cards."

"Ah. Must have missed the 'credit' part. Still, I've got plenty of info on Valincourt," Dax protested.

"Although apparently not the right Valincourt, unless the *divisionnaire* goes by the name 'Charlotte'?"

Dax sulkily carried on handing the sheets to Capestan, who carried on glancing down at them. Suddenly she put her hand out and touched Rosière's arm.

"Wait, wait," she said. "There on the telephone record—that's Maëlle's number . . . Valincourt, first name 'Gabriel.' Same as on that Decathlon card . . . It's the son, not the father! Dax, did you look for a Facebook account in the name Valincourt?"

The *lieutenant* jogged his mouse and clicked to maximize the page.

"Bingo!" Capestan said, pumping her fist. "Look at the profile pic."

"Oh yeah, you're right," Dax said. "I didn't recognize him without the helmet—it's the kid from number 36!"

Finally they had an ID on him. The Squirrel was named Gabriel Valincourt, son of Divisionnaire Alexandre Valincourt, head of the *brigades centrales de la police judiciaire*, and a triple-murder suspect. The son had called Maëlle Guénan the day before her death.

"Super work, Dax," Capestan congratulated him, beaming ear to ear.

For a few minutes they stayed like that next to the computer, in stunned, contented silence as Pilou wagged his tale earnestly. However eccentric his methods, Dax had just made a major breakthrough.

* * *

The day was drawing to a close. Orsini was tailing the *divisionnaire* and Lewitz had gone home, but the rest of the team was still hanging around the *commissariat*, enjoying a well-earned rest. Before taking over surveillance duty on the son, Merlot had heard back from HR: Valincourt, widower and father to an only child, had spent two years training in Miami at the start of his career, and later on had taken leave in Florida with his family. The ferry must have sunk on his return journey to France.

As for Torrez, he had called to let them know that he was out of the hospital. Capestan had not managed to talk him out of joining the surveillance operation. He was technically on sick leave, but enforcing that rule in this squad was verging on the ridiculous, as was any talk of insurance with Torrez. As such, he would be teaming up with the *commissaire* for the following day's stakeout on boulevard Beaumarchais, just up from the *divisionnaire*'s apartment building. Torrez promised to bring some Spanish tortilla for sustenance.

Leaning against one of the new kitchen cabinets, Anne Capestan observed her officers, who had been drawn to the terrace by the last glimmer of sunlight. Évrard and Dax were propping up the wall, having a peaceful chat over a package of Haribo. Rosière, sitting at the round wrought-iron table, was scribbling page after page, then stacking them carelessly on top of her handbag. By her feet, Pilou checked each dispatch with a discreet sniff. Over in his deck chair, Lebreton seemed to be at odds with a midge that had landed on his jacket lapel. Just as he was about to shoo it away with a flick, he decided against it. Capestan's initial thought was that he didn't want to stain his clothing, but Lebreton chose not to blow it off either— he didn't want to harm the insect. Capestan saw the *commandant* slide a cautious hand under his jacket and tap the material from inside to encourage a reaction. The midge took off and Lebreton, with an air of satisfaction, sat back in the deck chair and stretched his legs far out in front of him. His preference for peaceful solutions was without compromise, and even extended to insects. With every passing day, Capestan was appreciating her team more and more.

The ones who had turned up, that is: her budget still way exceeded the ten or so officers who had reported for duty.

Lebreton glanced at his watch. It was 8:00 p.m. He straightened his limbs and somehow managed to extract himself from the deck chair with elegance before suggesting they order pizza. They all agreed, opting for two *Napoletanas,* one *La Reine,* one *Quattro Stagioni,* and three containers of vanilla and macadamia ice cream.

Once they had finished their feast, empty pizza boxes lay strewn across the coffee table. A roll of paper towels, which they had been using as plates, had escaped across the floor. Dax scooped it up before going to fetch the ice cream from the freezer. Capestan suddenly remembered that it was Thursday. Not only that, but they had a TV.

"*Laura Flames,* season 3!" the *commissaire* exclaimed joyfully, grabbing the remote control.

Rosière gave her a sideways glance from her armchair, where she was gracefully administering her pizza crusts to the dog. She was not sure whether Capestan was teasing or not. But the *commissaire* was already sitting cross-legged on the sofa, giving the screen her full attention. She turned momentarily toward Rosière:

"I'm not just saying it, but I love your series. I can't have missed more than two or three episodes ever."

For once, Rosière was speechless. For as long as she could recall, her series had only sparked a handful of scathing reviews; never a word of appreciation, just plenty of fault finding. This was the first time any colleague had acknowledged, in such an unaffected way, that they watched *Laura Flames.* Bit by bit, the others pulled up their seats, armchairs, or footstools and gathered around the screen. Rosière, still dumbstruck, held her dog a little more tightly on her lap.

As the theme song started up, Pilou yelped with joy like the well-trained fan he was. The moment Eva Rosière's name appeared in the opening credits, Dax turned to her with a whisper that drowned out the music:

"Will you talk about us in the next one, huh?"

Capestan felt her cell phone vibrating. She disappeared to answer it and was back in her seat two seconds later. The show still hadn't begun.

"Any news?" Lebreton asked.

"Merlot lost the Squirrel."

"That's not too serious. We know where to find him now. Although we could do with a word with him, couldn't we?"

The *commissaire* nodded slowly. A plan of sorts was forming.

"Yes. In fact, I think we should even arrest him."

Standing on the freshly polished concrete floor of his garage, Lewitz pulled his mechanic's overalls on top of his clothes. He zipped them up, then plucked a torque wrench from the set of tools lined up on his workbench. He approached the vehicle lift and gazed lovingly at the beauty that was mounted on it: hydraulic front-wheel assist, twin steering axles, and a 3.5-meter turning radius. Bound to handle like a dream. Lewitz felt a joyous tingle of anticipation down his spine. Sure, the engine—a 2800 cc VM HR 494 Turbo Diesel—did strike him as a little modest. All it would need was a little opening up.

42

The radio crackled and belched, filling the car with the occasional flurry of voices. Torrez's right arm was still in a sling, though his head was now free of its bandages. Perched at the edge of his seat, he was trying to adjust the tuning with his left hand. With her index finger resting against the bottom of the steering wheel, Capestan did her best to ignore the racket as she surveyed the entrance to Valincourt's building on the opposite side of boulevard Beaumarchais. The accident had drawn a line under Torrez's bad luck and filled him with a renewed sense of purpose, a point illustrated loud and clear by this radio, which he had added to his demands for a siren and a flashing light. He was doing everything in his power to find the police frequency.

A constant swirl of pedestrians paraded back and forth in front of their windshield, one mass of people immediately replaced by the next. The passersby kept obstructing their view of the entrance, causing Capestan to refocus at various intervals. This busy street was a nightmare for a stakeout.

The stale cigarette smoke in the 306 had been erased by the delicious smell of tortilla and peppers, but their day of surveillance had thus far yielded nothing new on the *divisionnaire*, and the Squirrel still had not been around to see his father. They would have to exercise some real patience as they waited for Valincourt to make a significant blunder. Aside from the video, they did not have anything substantive enough to collar him. They would need something more to lever a confession out of him.

In the DNA era, scientific proof was sacrosanct, but Capestan still swore by good, old-fashioned testimonial evidence: the detailed confession. Cross-checking information, a bit of remorse, words start tumbling out with relief, and then the final word in the story. The suspect relaxes his shoulders, the culprit finds peace again, and the police officer can savor the sweet scratch of pen on paper. But with someone of Valincourt's caliber, it was no foregone conclusion. They would need something concrete.

On Capestan's lap, the sailor's journal was lying open at some blank pages near the end. Her initial analysis had been extremely attentive, then she had skimmed it a second time. The journal charted the wanderings of a traumatized man trying to find peace. Various scenes from the shipwreck would pop up from time to time in the course of a long, introspective passage, but nothing in these ramblings ever corresponded with Valincourt: not a single name or detail seemed to relate to him. They were going to have to look elsewhere for the sequence of events.

"The reception's terrible, but I think this is it. Something going on in the twentieth," Torrez said, still fussing with the CB.

"Yes, an airport run. That's the taxi frequency."

Torrez let out a groan and hurled himself back into the search. As he bent down, Capestan suddenly noticed that the *lieutenant*'s thick, black hair was cut in a very unusual way—it was about an inch shorter on the right, with a slight wedge at the back. The *commissaire* was reminded of his head bandage in the hospital.

"Did they clip you up top?" she asked.

Without looking up from the radio, he ran one of his bearlike mitts around the back of his skull.

"No, it was my son. He wants to be a hairdresser, so I let him do mine. I give him two euros and—just like that—he's happy and he's learning."

Capestan was touched by this fatherly sacrifice to his *coiffure*.

"How old is your son?"

"Nine. I know it's not perfect, but I don't mind. The poor kid's got to make do with rounded scissors."

Capestan gazed at the lieutenant's hairdo for a few more seconds, then returned her focus to the surveillance. It would be a big help if Valincourt decided to leave his house. According to Orsini's summary, the previous evening had involved a bit of shopping at the supermarket, a trip to the dry cleaner's to pick up a uniform, then back to his apartment for the rest of the night. It was late afternoon now, and the light was still on in the window to his apartment.

Capestan's cell phone vibrated. It was Lewitz.

"Yes, *brigadier*?"

"I've just spotted the boy. He's on the *boulevard*, around Bastille, and he's headed your way. Shall we nab him?"

Capestan hesitated for a moment. All they had on the young man was the offense of fleeing the scene at Maëlle Guénan's and a telephone record that they'd obtained illegally. Not exactly a winning hand.

"Yes, arrest him, but go easy on him. Wait until he's tying up his bike—that way he'll have his hands full."

She hung up and turned to Torrez. He stared at her, wide eyed with disbelief:

"Did you just ask Lewitz to make an arrest?"

"Yes."

In an effort to mask her slight apprehension, Capestan had answered a bit abruptly. She turned to look down the street. The *commissaire* was always keen to put reputations to one side and promote a policy of trust, but at the moment of truth, some risks were more prevalent than others. Behind the wheel, Lewitz was capable of wreaking havoc. As the Squirrel aimed his green helmet down the street, Capestan was beginning to have her doubts.

The bicycle was weaving in and out of the traffic. At the lights, he veered right and came off at the pedestrian crossing, bringing his wheels deftly onto the pavement. He was moving fast and the *commissaire* feared he would reach his father's door before they had time to intercept him. There was still no sign of Lewitz—the boy was going to escape from under their noses yet again. Capestan was about to open her door to race after him when the *brigadier* burst into view on the corner of rue du Pasteur-Wagner.

A bright-green street sweeper roared past the lights, all horns blaring, and joined the flow of traffic. In the glass operator's cab, Lewitz was virtually standing up behind the wheel. He spotted the bicycle and sped after it with a tremendous rev of the engine. Cars swerved in every direction, drivers honking furiously, and a jam started to form in the wake of the mad runaway cleaning vehicle. Capestan saw Torrez jump up in his seat.

"Is that one of those pooper-scooper things?" Torrez said.

"No, it's not a Motocrotte, I think it's an Aquazura . . ."

"How on earth did he get one of those?"

"Rosière found it online. Apparently local authorities sell off their equipment when it goes out of date."

Capestan's nerves were on edge. A vehicle that was not too powerful and that would melt into the background: on paper, it seemed the perfect fit for a stakeout, especially given the driver's past history. When it was going at full tilt, however, it lost marks on discretion, nor did it carry quite the same sense of danger.

Lewitz slalomed between the cars until he saw a pedestrian crossing that was wide enough to let him mount the pavement. He flung it around at 90 degrees, causing the sweeper's tires to screech on the asphalt. After an almighty yaw from clipping the curb, he managed to steady his trajectory and continue full steam ahead. Bewildered pedestrians flattened themselves against the walls to avoid the brushes that were skimming the ground: thanks to this particular police effort, the pavements were gleaming. Lewitz, his face lit up by a combination of giddy happiness and stern concentration, was making good ground. He stepped on it again before having to make an abrupt swerve to steer clear of a bus shelter. The cleaning mechanism at the back of the vehicle came flying off with the momentum. Like a snake being held by its tail, it started flailing around in the air at the end of its hose, blindly whacking into posts and windows. A man dropped flat against the floor to avoid being decapitated. On the roof of the cab, beside the usual orange flashing light, the blue two-tone of the *police judiciaire* kept any would-be heroes at bay. The bike was now just a few yards away.

"Hey, that's my siren!" Torrez said indignantly.

"Yes, but sometimes it's nice to share . . . ," Capestan said, trying to appease her partner without letting her eyes off Lewitz.

A hundred or so yards up the pavement, the glass exterior of a *café* jutted halfway across the pavement. Lewitz would never have room to get through. For a moment, Capestan was afraid he might try to smash straight through it, but he turned at the last second and hurled the vehicle into the bus lane, his left wheels biting into the tarmac while the right ones stayed on the pavement.

The sweeper careened like a speedboat doing a stunt, the brushes turning in midair and water splashing all around. In his helicopter-style cockpit, Lewitz tilted sideways, too, as if he were a superbike rider dragging his knee. He dodged a parking meter before righting himself with a clean turn that brought the vehicle back onto the pavement. Lewitz had not let the bike out of his sight for a second. He was bearing down on him, guzzling the last few yards between them.

The boy, alerted by the racket behind, skidded neatly to a halt. Lewitz slowed down as he made his approach, and the cleaning device slumped to the ground, dragging behind the vehicle like a defunct kitchen utensil. The *brigadier* stopped alongside the bike and leapt from the cabin. Contact with *terra firma* brought him rapidly back to his senses. He advanced toward the boy and took him by the biceps with a gentleness that surprised Capestan.

Mission accomplished. No injuries. No damage. The *commissaire* could breathe at last.

43

Gabriel was wondering what he had done to end up in the back seat of the 306. The lead weights he had felt knocking together in his stomach for weeks had disappeared. Now that he was under arrest, he did not feel uneasy anymore; he just felt scared.

It was because he had run away. He felt so ashamed. After hiding at Manon's for three days, he had decided to go home to fess up and ask his father for advice. And now he was being questioned. His father could have helped him, told him how to behave, and explained what his rights were. Alone in the back seat, Gabriel felt lost.

He looked through the window at the people going about their normal lives. They walked briskly, looked at shop fronts, or stopped in the middle of the pavement to read a text. As for Gabriel, he was in the back of a police car. He tried to calm down, but his father returned. Doubts were forming, timidly at first, then more insistent, like crows pecking at roof tiles. He felt the weights return to his stomach, solidifying into a dense mass.

His father.

Gabriel Valincourt did indeed have the squirrelly physique described by Naulin: good looking, nimble, and lively, with a reddish-brown complexion that matched his hair and eyes. He had a gentle expression, although that day it was swinging between alarm and despondency. Capestan decided it was best to avoid any strong-arm tactics with this young cub. That said, she needed to extract as much information as possible if she wanted to piece together any more of this story.

She ushered him toward the armchair by the fireplace. Despite the boy's meager frame, they heard the pop of a spring. Évrard handed Gabriel a cup of tea, which he accepted with a polite smile. Lebreton spent a few minutes getting the fire going, then went and sat in the second armchair. Gabriel, who was familiar with his father's place of work at number 36, stared at the freshly pasted wallpaper, the antique mirror, and Rosière's golden slippers. He seemed to be wondering where on earth he had ended up.

Without any animosity, Capestan started questioning him about what he was doing at Marie Sauzelle's and, more important, why he had fled the scene of a crime. Gabriel started apologizing profusely.

"I know, I never should have run away like that, I'm sorry, I really am, I made a mistake. It's because . . . I was doing some personal research. My mother died when a ferry sank in the Gulf of Mexico in 1993. I was only two at the time and I don't have any memories of her. All I have left is this photo," he said, bringing out the laminated photograph of a woman. "Everything disappeared in the shipwreck."

After showing it to Capestan, he carefully returned it to his inside pocket. He then smoothed it with the palm of his hand through the material of his jacket to make sure it didn't get more crumpled.

So Valincourt's wife had perished in the shipwreck. Capestan wondered how, as Gabriel continued, not looking any of the police officers in the eye.

"My father never talks to me about her anymore. It makes him sad, and I don't want to force him. So I asked for the names of the survivors from the Association, then went to meet them with this photograph . . ."

Évrard pushed the sugar bowl across the table toward the boy, who vacantly fished out four lumps before continuing:

". . . to ask . . . I don't know. If anyone had met her. Remembered something about her, anything. If they had made friends on board. That's why I went to Issy-les-Moulineaux . . . Madame Sauzelle was at the top of the list. I also wanted to meet the sailor, Monsieur Gué-nan, who was the only French crew member."

Gabriel, with his hair flopping over his eyes, gazed deep into his mug. To avoid frightening him, the four officers tried not to make too much noise—the only sound was their breathing and the crackle of the fire.

"I saw on the list that Monsieur Guénan had died not long after his return. So I called his wife. The day before . . . well, you know."

The son had planned to question the victims. The father had not let him. Gradually, the gist of the matter started forming in Capestan's mind.

"You and your father managed to escape, but not your mother? Were they separated during the accident?" Rosière said, trying not to let her voice grate too much.

"Yes. At least, my father told my mother not to move while he went to get me from the cabin, and when he came back, she wasn't there anymore. He thought she might have already boarded a lifeboat."

"Your parents left you in the cabin by yourself? When you were two?" Évrard said in disbelief.

She had hit on a sore point, and Gabriel seemed upset.

"Yes. I don't know, that's what Papa always said, but maybe I misunderstood him . . ."

A man as cautious as Valincourt would never have left a toddler unsupervised on a ferry, Capestan thought to herself. The father had lied to his son. Gabriel sat deeper in his armchair, gripping his mug in both hands. He was reaching his limit, but Capestan got the feeling that his day was far from over.

"You know we're going to have to call your father?" she said.

"Yes."

"Would you rather do it yourself?"

"Yes, I would."

Rosière went to her desk and scooped up her beige handset, a standard-issue France Télécom model from the nineties, and stretched the cord until it reached the young man.

"Are you ever separated from your cell phone?" Capestan said. "Sometimes leave it on your bed when you go to the bathroom, or on the table in the living room before you go to the kitchen?"

Gabriel pulled on the drawstrings of his hoodie and his feet knocked quietly against the wooden floor.

"Yes. Sometimes."

The boy did his best to ignore the *commissaire*'s insinuation. He took Rosière's telephone set, placed it on his lap, and looked at it for a long while before dialing the number.

44

The sound of the doorbell announced the arrival of Alexandre Valincourt. He was on his way back from a ceremony where the *préfet de police* had awarded him the *Légion d'Honneur*. The squad had been waiting for him, closed ranks, for over an hour. The nerves in the main room were palpable. Each person ran through their role scrupulously. Capestan had laid out her plan: a two-stage relay race followed by a sprint finish. Failure was not an option. If they botched it with Valincourt, they would all end up in some hellhole of a dungeon, having kissed good-bye to any prospect of a pension. They were well aware that they were punching above their weight.

After a final glance around her troops, Capestan stood up and went to answer it. The *divisionnaire*, in full ceremonial garb, stood in the doorway and sized her up without saying a word. His hooked nose and big brown eyes dominated his aquiline face, which sat on top of his long, hardened, marathon-runner's frame. Capestan adopted a colder tone for the father than she had for the son.

"*Bonjour*, Monsieur le Divisionnaire," she said.

Valincourt merely lifted his chin and stepped into the room, with his officer's cap under his arm, then took in the surroundings with a haughty look.

"They're original, your premises. What is it exactly that you do here? Admin, sorting through the archives, revisiting old reports?"

The *divisionnaire* was playing the role of the grandee deigning to rub shoulders with his lowly subjects. Capestan decided to get in there early with a frostiness of her own:

"Sorting through the archives. Your archives, as it happens . . ."

Valincourt ignored her. He was happy to nonchalantly inspect the lay of the land, but refused to rise to a jab that he deemed to be beneath him. Capestan had counted on him reacting like this: their relay tactic was really a war of attrition. To crack someone as distinguished as Valincourt, they were going to attempt the classic "carpet trick": grill the suspect in one room, then transfer him somewhere with a slightly different, slicker tone and décor, where another officer would elicit a confession. A slowly-slowly psychological method that had stood the test of time at number 36. Today they faced a tough adversary who was well versed in those tactics. They would need to embellish their approach. But the squad did have one sneaky weapon up their sleeve, one that was perfect for unsettling their suspect: Malchance, the unlucky charm. They had Torrez.

"Lieutenant Torrez will look after you while I wrap up the paperwork with your son."

Valincourt blinked slightly, but not enough to lose face. The man was more than impressive. Without moving a muscle, hemmed in by the members of the squad, he still dominated the room. The officers seemed like a set of small, ramshackle buildings in the shadow of Notre-Dame. To nip this sense of supremacy in the bud, Capestan gave Torrez the nod to come in.

An exaggerated shudder went around the room and the squad parted in silence, forming a sort of guard of horror as Malchance prowled forward. He was wearing a dark brown corduroy jacket over his sling. His beard was starting to show again, darkening his cheeks, and his black eye completed the macabre sinister look. The *lieutenant*, more serious than ever, walked up to Valincourt and stopped a little too close to him, deliberately intruding into his senior officer's personal space.

"If you'd care to follow me, Monsieur le Divisionnaire."

Still ramrod straight, Valincourt hesitated for a moment. He was visibly conflicted. If he followed the *lieutenant*, he was capitulating to the demands of this pitiful squad. But if he refused, it would look as though he were flinching in the face of superstition and fear. Either outcome would damage his credibility. He was trapped. In the long term, cowardice must have struck him as the more harmful option since, with a nod at Capestan, he made up his mind to accompany Torrez to his office.

Torrez opened the door and invited the *divisionnaire* to go in ahead of him.

"Please, take a seat," he said, not gesturing toward any chair in particular.

Valincourt, hands behind his back and gripping the visor of his cap, studied the room, doing his best not to touch anything. He believes the stories about me, Torrez thought to himself. This proximity was frightening him.

There were two chairs facing the desk. Valincourt chose the less accessible one and sat down as calmly as possible.

"That one's mine, in fact," Torrez said, feigning embarrassment. "No, no, stay there, please. It'll be fine."

The *divisionnaire* could not prevent his backside from lifting up an inch or so.

"Commissaire Capestan won't be much longer, I don't think," Torrez said, moving to the other side of his desk.

Then he simply waited, drawing out the moment to exacerbate any mounting paranoia. Torrez had that effect on people. Others officers shied away in his presence like arachnophobes from a basket of tarantulas. The more audacious simply avoided running into him. Occasionally some hothead or other might play the toreador and approach him, body tensed and ready, but just one look would send them packing. Crazy people dice with death, but they do not fool around with someone cursed with bad luck. Bad luck carries the threat of terrible things: disease, ruin, an accident for you or a loved one. It lurks just below the surface, festering and unexpected.

Valincourt stayed where he was, perfectly motionless. He had already come into contact with various elements—nothing he could do about that—but he was reluctant to add to the haul. Torrez worried that his powers of intimidation were waning. Around Capestan, Malchance had become less resolute: the façade was cracking and he was breathing more easily. He now had a colleague he could have coffee with or talk to about the weekend, something he had spent twenty years of his career dreaming about. Capestan was prouder than a band of Corsicans, but she always had a smile and a kind word at the ready for her team. Capestan was no toreador, not with him at least. And she had trusted him with the first leg of the relay.

Valincourt cleared his throat. He was eager to regain the upper hand.

"Alright. Where's my son?"

"In an office down the corridor, with Commissaire Capestan and Lieutenant Évrard. They're looking after him; you have nothing to worry about."

"That's not what I asked," the *divisionnaire* said, sweeping aside any suggestion that he was being overprotective. "What's he doing here? What are you accusing him of?"

"I have no idea, I'm not working on that case," Torrez said, pulling a file out of one of his drawers.

He placed it on his desk and crossed his hands on top of it. Valincourt wriggled slightly with a mixture of impatience and discomfort. These irritants were nibbling at his defenses.

"No, I'm working on a different case . . . ," Torrez continued.

"I don't give a damn about your little cases! It's not as though I'm planning on moving in. I've had enough. If you think I have the time to entertain your . . . Take me to Gabriel, let's be done with this."

Valincourt considered himself far too important to be kept waiting like this, and Torrez's presence was only increasing his sense of urgency.

"I'm dealing with a different case," the lieutenant repeated, unfazed. "It dates back to 2005, but we have a new lead."

A hint of surprise flashed across the *divisionnaire*'s face. Curiosity was taking hold of him. For several years, Valincourt had been sitting on a handful of murders that had gone unpunished. He wanted to know what they knew. Torrez slowly removed the elastic ties from the corners of the file, pulled out a color photograph, and slid it toward the *divisionnaire*. It was of Marie Sauzelle.

"Do you know her?"

Valincourt barely even looked at him.

"Of course, I headed up the case."

Torrez nodded gravely, pulled an afflicted expression, and took out a second picture, this one of a mailbox. He turned it toward the *divisionnaire* and poked one of his thick fingers onto the print to indicate the NO JUNK MAIL PLEASE sticker.

"You see stickers like this on the doors of eco-minded folk, or people away on vacation," Torrez said, nodding as though approving of such sensible measures. "But do you know where you never find them?"

Valincourt avoided meeting his eye, so Torrez answered his own question:

"On the doors of old ladies who collect discount coupons."

Torrez mulled over his words before coming to the natural conclusion:

"But a sticker like that isn't a spur-of-the-moment thing. He must have brought it with him. In a murder case, that means premeditation."

The *lieutenant* enunciated each syllable of that last word. Valincourt pursed his lips for a moment, but must have considered it wiser not to comment. After all, he had not been overtly accused. He arched his eyebrows and looked at Torrez scornfully. The *divisionnaire* was good at controlling his facial expressions, but he could not avoid turning pale. They had him. It was time to pass on the baton. Torrez held out a hand and gently tapped the *divisionnaire*'s arm. His own special *coup de grâce*.

"Follow me."

Torrez led Valincourt, shaken but still standing, down the corridor to the main room, where Lebreton was waiting next to his perfectly tidy desk. Rosière and Orsini were in the background, each holding a thick notebook.

The *divisionnaire* had just looked Destiny in the eye. Now Torrez was delivering him to the instruments of Law and Opinion: Lebreton and the IGS; Orsini and the press; Rosière and the mob. Valincourt was standing firm, but his brow was starting to glisten from the pressure of this ordeal. Nevertheless, he managed to recover all his outward dignity, and, still not seeing his son, protested with a strident voice:

"Look, where is he? I'm ordering you to release him. Right away."

Lebreton moved closer to the wastepaper basket at the foot of his desk, then took a step back.

"No."

"Excuse me? Do you have any idea who you're talking to? You can start by telling me on what grounds you're holding my son."

Lebreton tucked a stray propeller pencil away in its container before eventually going to stand impassively behind his chair.

"Fleeing the scene of a crime, as he said on the telephone earlier."

"Don't make me laugh, *capitaine*—"

"*Commandant . . .*"

"He was walking down a street, correct? He ran off when Capestan confronted him? She's a good-looking lady—you know how shy young men can be. She's wrong to take it so personally."

Lebreton grinned with amusement. Valincourt was attempting to sound lighthearted, but the effects of his fifteen minutes with Torrez were clear: sarcasm is harder to pull off when your voice is trembling. The *divisionnaire* was aware of the slight stammer, too, and his face was overcome with irritation.

"He happened to be walking down the street of a murder victim," Lebreton said, gesturing toward one of the armchairs.

Valincourt grabbed hold of the arm and paused for a moment before deciding to sit down.

"He was coming to see me. Listen, you do realize this counts as an arbitrary arrest. You can't charge my son with anything—you've got nothing."

"Absolutely."

"You're not even entitled to place him in custody," he said with a disdainful, sweeping motion that took in the room and the squad.

"No, I'm not sure we are," Lebreton conceded blankly.

He studied the body language of the *divisionnaire*, who still had a stiff, almost military bearing. He had deliberately not changed before arriving, choosing to present himself in ceremonial uniform. Nothing incidental about that: he was trying to reassert his status and remind them of his rank.

"Fine, then," Valincourt said. "Let him go."

"Of course," Lebreton said.

Valincourt made as if to stand up without any further comment, but the *commandant* cut him off to clarify what he meant:

"I'll let him go. He hasn't murdered anyone, after all. You, on the other hand . . ."

The *divisionnaire* bristled, but he checked himself immediately, regaining the necessary composure.

"How dare you, you shitty little officers? What right do you have to make such accusations?"

"My own. Are you making any progress on the Maëlle Guénan case? Because . . . well, we've got the culprit," Lebreton said.

"Stop with your theatrics. I was staying out of courtesy, but this time . . ."

Valincourt stood up and put on his police cap. He was about to set off down the corridor to fetch Gabriel.

"What were you doing on Thursday, September 20, between 8:00 a.m. and 10:00 a.m.?" Lebreton said.

"I'm not answering your questions."

"Then I'll answer them myself. On September 20, you went to rue Mazagran with a set of kitchen knives, you rang Maëlle Guénan's doorbell, then you stabbed her to death before searching the apartment for any documents belonging to her husband."

As he delivered that last point, Lebreton was watching for any sign of confirmation: Valincourt flinched, and the *commandant* knew he had found his target.

"You killed her, just as you killed Yann Guénan and Marie Sauzelle. You knew the victims and you deliberately hid that fact from us. Don't bother with any unnecessary objections, we have it on video. Does the memorial of a shipwreck sound at all familiar?"

Lebreton pointed the remote at the TV and revealed the paused picture of Valincourt with Sauzelle. This time there was no doubt whatsoever about his aim. All means of escape had been sealed. A look of panic shot across Valincourt's face, but his survival instincts quickly chased it away.

"You're making it sound as though I should be calling my lawyer."

Lebreton turned to Orsini and Rosière behind him, who had been scribbling away in their notebooks nonstop, punctuating the interview with satisfied nods.

"Note down that, during a courtesy call, Divisionnaire Valincourt requested a lawyer to be present."

Lebreton looked back at the *divisionnaire* before politely asking:

"Would you like to contact your lawyer?"

Valincourt batted the question away with a look of disgust, and Lebreton stared at him for a moment, his smile gone. Bad luck, links, premeditation . . . He let the *divisionnaire* fully digest the implications of the previous half-hour's exchanges.

The greasy smell of reheated panini wafted in from the street through the half-open windows. From around the Fontaine des Innocents came the sound of mooing boys and chirruping girls; the local teenage fauna were patrolling Les Halles as the Indian summer finally drew to its close. The *commandant* looked Valincourt up and down. He was a paragon of self-denial, authority in motion. A slight feverishness in his movements was the only evidence that his armor had been breached. He waited for the gap to widen a little before delivering his closing speech:

"Yann Guénan was a proper job. Professional. But with Marie Sauzelle, you acted hastily. The muted TV, the dead bolt, flowers despite the fact she hated them: everything pointed toward a visitor, not a burglar. You didn't know her well enough for your presence to fade into the furnishings. You removed the mail so no one would find the invitation to the reunion, without leaving a single other envelope behind. Maybe pity clouded your judgment, too. The cat, for example. Why take the cat? So that it wouldn't alert the neighbors? Capestan thinks you're an animal lover: that the cat's death wasn't justifiable, and that you only killed out of necessity. But I'm not so sure."

With that final sentence, Lebreton made out as though the question of the *divisionnaire*'s temperament was still in the balance, whereas the question of murder was already absolutely settled. He tightened his grip one more notch:

"We've taken a sample of cat hair from your son's sweater. Forensics are checking for a match as we speak."

The *divisionnaire*'s lips parted in a faint grimace, and the *commandant* made a prearranged signal to Orsini, who went off to find Capestan. Valincourt was all hers now.

Capestan had thought long and hard about the motive. Only one theory held water: Valincourt had murdered Marie Sauzelle, Yann Guénan, and his wife, Maëlle Guénan, because the three of them knew something that Valincourt wanted to keep hidden. She just needed to find out what.

But whatever the original error, to go to such lengths Valincourt must have wanted to shield it from someone very important. His son, of course. Gabriel was the key to finding the truth.

As she emerged from the corridor that led to Gabriel, Capestan signaled to the squad to slip away. She walked up to Valincourt with a deadpan expression and took hold of the chair that Lebreton had just vacated. Before she had even sat down, she started speaking in a sharp tone.

"Your son's not in great shape, Monsieur le Divisionnaire. And mercifully for him, he still hasn't read this," she said, throwing the sailor's journal onto the desk.

Valincourt had gone to Maëlle Guénan's house to silence her before Gabriel got there, but also to look for any compromising documents, as was obvious from the forced filing cabinet. The journal contained nothing incriminating, but Valincourt did not know that. He had a nasty story to cover up, the sort that seems written on every wall and in every book the moment you stand accused. The *divisionnaire* clearly felt plenty of remorse. He had saved the cat. He had fixed Marie's hair. This was a man with a conscience: that was where she had to hit him.

"Do you recognize this notebook? You killed a forty-three-year-old woman to secure it. In doing so, you made her son an orphan. First his father, then his mother."

Capestan woke up the buzzing computer, turned the screen toward Valincourt, and placed the keyboard in front of him. He recoiled at the movement, then reached out to touch one of the keys before choosing to ignore it. But the temptation to type up a confession had left its mark. Capestan rammed home the advantage.

"You screwed up, Valincourt, and I can see you haven't cut any corners to cover that up," she said, resting her hand on the journal. "Now, you know that my colleagues are civilized people. But you also know that I am capable of anything. I'm going to give this notebook to Gabriel. He'll suffer the shock and he'll have nothing to dull the pain. And if you insist on refusing to surrender, you will leave your son with the moral obligation to denounce you."

Capestan would never have stooped so low, but she knew how to make the most of her reputation, which had in no small part been upheld by big shots like the one in front of her.

Valincourt swallowed hard. Was she bluffing or not? His grip was weakening fast. He was witnessing the prosecution's closing statement before he had had any time to analyze the situation. Having first pushed the image of his son into the foreground, Capestan was now advancing at breakneck speed. So long as his emotions had the upper hand, the need to justify his actions would inevitably follow.

"You're really not sparing him anything," Capestan said, withdrawing the journal.

She stood up. Valincourt glanced at the journal and sighed. His shoulders slumped a little and his face seemed to slacken with an immense fatigue. He was coming to terms with his surrender.

"That's not true," he said calmly. "I did spare him, in fact . . ."

"Prove it by signing a confession. And talk to him in person, without shirking behind a third party. Or worse, the press."

Capestan was hammering it home, eager to clinch the moment. She jabbed her chin at the keyboard.

"Take responsibility for what you did," she said. "In return, I'll let you have two hours one-on-one with your son. I won't contact Buron till afterward; then it'll be up to him to contact the public prosecutor. Two hours."

Capestan left a pause, enough to make Valincourt aware of the stakes, then brought their talk to a close, the harshness gone from her voice:

"It's over for you. But not for him. He's only just beginning."

Valincourt pulled the keyboard toward him in silence. Before typing, he simply said:

"He has a fiancée. Manon. I'll give you her number. I'd be grateful if you called and asked her to be here in two hours' time. Gabriel will need her."

45

It was time. Alexandre Valincourt had spent the last twenty years of his life dreading this moment. A moment that every single decision in the last twenty years had sought to delay, to avoid. All those murders just for twenty measly years wrenched from the truth. And now here he was, on a wobbly armchair in this degenerate *commissariat*, typing out his confession on a worn-out keyboard. In two minutes he'll have to see his son and tell him, tell him . . . How was he supposed to tell his son?

The situation was looking very bleak for him. Valincourt pushed the keyboard back toward Capestan, who printed off the document. She waited over by the printer, then handed the sheets to him without reading them. He took a pen from his suit jacket and scrawled his signature. He stood up, put his pen back in his pocket, and followed Capestan to the office where Gabriel was being held. She knocked and signaled to the two lieutenants to leave before stepping aside to let the *divisionnaire* in.

He now felt a tremendous calm, a sort of infinite peace that must have been like death, or something similar to death. Capestan closed the door behind him.

"Hello, Gabriel," Valincourt said, without moving too close to his son. "They're going to let you go."

He was reaching for his next words, but nothing at all convincing came to him, so he had to make do with the raw facts.

"I, however . . . I have to stay. I'm giving myself up. I have killed some people. I had no choice. It was . . . It was the only way for you to grow up in peace."

There was no need for him to ask Gabriel to let him speak, to not interrupt him: his son was sitting bolt upright, not even daring to tremble. One of the braids on the armrest had come loose, and the young man was tugging at it vacantly with his right hand. His feet were planted on the ground. He looked sprightly, ready to pounce. Valincourt took a breath, grabbed a chair from against the wall, sat down at the edge of it, and continued:

"I can explain—"

"It's the boat, isn't it? Something happened?" Gabriel cut in, desperate to be wrong.

"Yes," Valincourt said.

He rubbed his eyes. He was struggling to concentrate. The memory of the shipwreck came flooding back and made his head throb. Alexandre Valincourt was assailed by cries that got louder and louder, the useless blast of a foghorn, and passengers barging their way past him. He shook his head roughly to wake himself up and confront his son, who was staring right at him, but he could not hold his gaze.

"You fled without waiting for Maman?"

"No," Valincourt murmured.

For her last few hours in Florida, Rosa had chosen to wear a light, turquoise cotton dress over her slim body. She had gone ahead to the boarding deck with the children, pointing Alexandre in the direction of the ticket inspector. Alexandre was looking at her as he handed their booking details to the man, an enormous American in a sweat-soaked T-shirt. He could read the sadness etched across his wife's melancholy face. She resented him for uprooting her all over again. It was the only possible option, but she still resented him for it. When she turned to gaze across the sea, her son Antonio yet again took the chance to escape her watchful eye. He snuck off toward a parrot that had been caged up by its owners for the journey. The boy hit the bars with his palms, causing the poor animal to flap its wings and squawk in terror.

That child was poisonous. Not only poisonous, but pampered by his mother, who utterly adored him and forgave him everything because he had grown up without his father. A father who was surely no better himself, but who Rosa continued to revere for obscure political reasons. He was just another *guerrillero* who reveled in his courageous deeds in battle yet ignored any responsibility toward his family. He had abandoned Antonio, leaving the miniature Attila to be raised by Alexandre, who had to watch the little tyrant like a hawk the moment he went near Gabriel, his beloved son, the apple of his eye, the wonderful embodiment of his love for Rosa. Gabriel was sweet, charming, and smiley. He wasn't even two years old, but already he had nothing in common with his stupid, barbaric half brother, the beast who had bitten off his ear lobe.

From a distance, Alexandre saw Attila grab Gabriel's hand and shove it against the cage, then try to slip it between the bars so the parrot could bite him. Alexandre dropped the luggage and sprinted toward the children. He lifted Attila up with one hand and with the other he gave him an almighty smack. Rosa let out a scream. Seconds later she was standing in front of Alexandre, berating him furiously. As had happened so many times before, in spite of their boundless love for each other, Rosa and Alexandre were flung into a violent argument sparked by the child rolling around at their feet. Attila would always lie between them, like a tick blighting their perfect happiness, a parasite whose only purpose was to hijack Rosa's love.

As she sidestepped the commotion, the old lady they had chatted with back at the terminal directed a disapproving glare at them. Such a nice-looking family, tearing itself apart like that. By that point, the ferry was casting off from the jetty and the crew members were at their posts, inviting passengers to head to the bar or the vast, blue-carpeted cabins. The skipper was putting out to sea, unconcerned by the dark, relentless winds blowing in from the ocean.

* * *

"Did you abandon her? Is that what happened? What did you do, Papa, tell me," Gabriel begged, his voice cracking.

Valincourt tried to muster his strength and return to the room where his son was imploring him. He had never spoken to him of Antonio. The boy did not share his name; he did not appear anywhere. But now Gabriel had to know.

"You had a brother."

A glimmer of joy passed over Gabriel's face. With a regretful shake of his head, Valincourt made it disappear straightaway.

"A half brother. You never liked him," he said, as if to console him.

"Where is he?"

Valincourt took another deep breath. The waters of the Gulf of Mexico were starting to lap at his heels, and a thin drizzle clung to his face, blurring his vision.

After their argument, Rosa had gone straight to the bar on the upper deck. On her own. In spite of her fury, she had entrusted both Antonio and Gabriel to Alexandre's care. Maybe it was a punishment, or perhaps she was putting his sense of duty to the test. Duty. Nobody was more attuned to this quality than Alexandre Valincourt.

The three of them were all together on the lower deck. The boys played as Alexandre sat pensively in his deck chair. A violent gust of wind suddenly set a halyard flapping against the hull of the ferry. There was a storm brewing. While the weather forecasts might not have expected the hurricane to hit for another day or two, the swell told a different story. As soon as the first drops fell, the deck became slippery and the people started heading below. Alexandre stood up: it was time to get the children inside. The waves were crashing against the rail and the ferry was starting to pitch more and more dramatically.

Seconds later thick, black clouds completely obscured the afternoon sun, and the heavens opened.

Cries of panic started spreading around the boat. Part of Alexandre's jacket had gotten stuck in the deck chair and he tugged at it impatiently, blindly resisting the sensible option of leaving it behind. On his feet but off balance, he bellowed at the children, who couldn't have been more than three yards away. Finally Alexandre managed to free the garment. He looked up to see Gabriel edging toward him uncertainly, holding out his arms to keep steady. A sudden jolt shook the boat. As Gabriel was flung forward, Attila, terrified, trampled over him to reach the safety of Alexandre's arms. Lying flat on his face, Gabriel was now sliding toward the edge of the deck, drenched by the water lashing against the boat. His eyes were round with horror and when he tried to call out, he swallowed his first mouthful of water. A shot of adrenaline coursed through Alexandre, who raced toward his son and clung on to his sweater in one hand. Attila, really panicking now, was trying to clamber up his stepfather's body. When he reached Alexandre's torso, the boy started hindering his movements, causing Gabriel's sweater to slip out of his grip. In that moment, Alexandre was overcome by a cold fury that wormed its way through his fear. An unbelievable opportunity was presenting itself: the chance to do away with the little brat once and for all, that child who took such pleasure in torturing his son. Perhaps this storm would solve everything.

In any event, if he were to strengthen his grip and secure Gabriel, Alexandre would need to get Attila off him. So he did.

In the same way you detach a crab that's pinching you, Alexandre coldly pried away the boy's arm, dislodging him in the process. The force made Antonio's hands slip apart, and the boy was sent flying overboard. He thrashed his arms and legs to find something to cling on to, but his cries were lost in the waves and he fell without an echo.

Alexandre clasped Gabriel against him, then leaned over the railing. Attila had disappeared. Alexandre blinked as the loudspeakers spat out inaudible instructions. A waterway on the poop deck had split open and the hold was being flooded by a continual flow from the sea, and a nauseating stench of diesel was choking the air. Alexandre stroked Gabriel's hair and turned toward the inside of the boat. The sight of Rosa rooted him to the spot.

She was standing at the entrance to the cabins, her face a mask of stunned, petrified distress. A split second later, the mask slipped to reveal scorn, pure hatred. She threw down her bag and sprinted for a life belt, grabbing it, and—without a moment's hesitation—hurling herself into the inky water to save her son. Alexandre could have done nothing to catch her. He heard a man's voice booming out to stop the woman, but it wasn't his own. It belonged to someone else, a sailor who was standing just behind him. The sailor had been there for a few moments already, and he would never forget what he had seen.

"During the shipwreck, your half brother fell in the water. Your mother dived in to save him, but she drowned. There was nothing I could do. I couldn't let go of you and dive in after her."

Rosa, swallowed up by the sea. Rosa, who had not known why, who had not understood. Rosa, who had taken him for a monster. Rosa, drowned. And with her drowned any hope of a happy life for Alexandre and his son. He had never managed to forgive himself. He had not been able to save Rosa. And things would never be the same. Attila had poisoned them to the very end.

"But . . . ," Gabriel started. He did not understand. "So it was an accident?"

"Yes," Valincourt said, not daring to believe he could escape so easily.

Gabriel shook his head, causing his curly hair to flop onto his forehead.

"So why kill the Guénans?"

Why indeed? This version was not going to be enough. He was going to have to let the truth out—just hopefully not the whole truth.

"The thing is, your half brother fell . . . he fell because I pushed him. He was blocking you from getting to safety and it was becoming dangerous. I shoved him aside and he slipped overboard. Yann Guénan saw everything, and when he arrived back in France, he tried to blackmail me."

Guénan had seen him get rid of the boy. But he had no idea what Valincourt's name was: he was just another passenger among hundreds of others. In the chaos that followed, the panic had concentrated the passengers into a few small groups. When the rescue operation finally began, the ferry had already keeled over, ending the lives of dozens of men and women. The boats and helicopters had a tough time evacuating the survivors, and the passengers ended up being scattered. Valincourt and his son had managed to get away and travel back to France without any further trouble.

But Valincourt was afraid there would be repercussions. He had discovered the sailor's name and tracked him down the moment he set foot in Paris. The idea of murdering Guénan disgusted him: he would only do it if it were absolutely necessary. There was a chance that, in the mayhem of the accident, the sailor might have erased the memory. For peace of mind, Valincourt kept him under close surveillance. And when Guénan started making his rounds of the French survivors, Valincourt felt he had no other choice. If Guénan came across his face on a list, he would have been tried for infanticide and sent to jail for many years; Gabriel would have been placed in a foster home, at the mercy of God knows what kind of maniac. The idea was unacceptable—Alexandre could not have run the risk of that happening. He had analyzed the situation and waited for the opportune moment. All he needed for the rest was to keep a cool head.

"Blackmail? But . . ."

Gabriel's train of thought was going faster and further than he would have liked. Valincourt could see it pull up at Sauzelle, an old lady, and more questions came rushing out. Without him even realizing, the boy's feet returned to the wooden floor, pressing down to test their steadiness. He was now holding the braid of the armchair in his clenched fist. Deep down, Gabriel was craving a way out, but with a look of determination he forced himself to carry on:

"The old lady?"

"Guénan told her."

At the time of their conversation at the commemoration, Marie Sauzelle had not made the link with the family she had met during boarding. But on seeing the photographs of Rosa and Antonio flicking past, her memories of the sailor's tale were stirred. The thought had perplexed her, and she had innocently put the question to Valincourt.

One murder always leads to another. Valincourt looked at his son again. The boy was devastated. The son he loved so much; the son who shared Rosa's blood. He was so young.

"I'm sorry," Valincourt murmured.

Gabriel did not acknowledge the apology. He was close to collapse, but still he fought on:

"Guénan's wife? Were you following me while I was on my search? Did you look at my cell phone? Did you do it to silence her? Was it my fault?"

Gabriel had all these questions, but Valincourt only gave him one answer:

"Nothing is your fault. Nothing. I did what I could, but you . . . You don't deserve a single second of what you're going through now. I'm sorry."

Valincourt's eyes were red and a few tears were starting to form. A long silence set in, and neither father nor son knew how to handle it. They stayed there like that, not moving, only half breathing. Then Gabriel stood up and shakily made his way to the door. When he opened it, he saw Manon leaning against the wall along the corridor. He walked to her slowly and fell into her arms.

Orsini was in line at the party shop. In addition to the banner, he had chosen balloons, three multicolored garlands, and several paper lanterns, two of which had a sun-and-moon pattern. His cell phone vibrated in his pocket. He looked at the name flashing on the screen: Chevalet, a journalist friend he had called on earlier in the investigation. Orsini sighed and brought the cell phone to his ear.

"Hi, Marcus," came the voice down the line. "So, this story you promised me?"

Orsini thought about Valincourt's crimes, then pictured the son, Gabriel. His own son had never had the chance to reach that age.

"Hi, Ludo. Afraid it didn't come to anything in the end. Next time."

He hung up. The shop owner smiled and handed him his items. Next to the counter was a stand displaying lots of pranks and practical jokes. Orsini picked out a packet of hot sweets. Those hot sweets always cracked him up.

Epilogue

The elevator stopped at the fifth floor. The doors opened with a grinding mechanical sound, and Capestan found herself looking at some legs. They turned out to belong to Orsini, who was wobbling precariously on a stepladder trying to hang the WELCOME banner above the door. He anxiously steadied himself by gripping the door frame, then turned to her:

"Good afternoon, *commissaire*. We've been waiting for you," he said.

"Hello, Orsini. Waiting for me for what?"

Orsini was trying to insert the thumbtack with such vigor you would have thought the frame was made of reinforced concrete.

"To get ready for the housewarming."

"The housewarming? First I've heard of it."

"Ah," Orsini said with an air of irritation, sucking his injured thumb before confessing: "Perhaps it was a surprise. I'm not sure, best to ask Rosière."

Of course it was best to ask Rosière. On entering the living room, she saw Évrard and Lewitz hard at work around a desk that they had transformed into a banquet table, covered in a paper cloth with a red-spiral pattern. The walls were adorned with garlands, and Dax was decorating the windows with a can of spray paint that, judging by the smell, would not be rubbing off anytime soon. Colorful paper lanterns dressed the lightbulbs that until then had been bare.

The *commissariat* resembled a primary school the day before a *fête*. Over in the kitchen, Capestan caught a glimpse of Torrez strapped into a cotton Knorr apron. Since his discharge from the hospital, the squad had seemed a lot more relaxed about having him around. They still weren't patting him on the back or making eye contact, but fewer hairs were standing on end when he walked past.

Armchairs, desks, sofas, tables: all the furniture was pushed up against the walls, making sure there was ample space for dancing. Lebreton had just finished rigging up some speakers. Rosière, with a green balloon in one hand and a pump in the other, was deep in conversation with Merlot, who was sitting on his ass offering moral support.

"Seaside or mountains!" Rosière spat. "Why should you have to choose one or the other? Ever heard of having the best of both? What's wrong with people! It's always A or B, Beatles or Stones—"

"Pink Floyd!" Dax hollered across the room.

". . . Hallyday or Mitchell . . ."

"Sardou!" Dax barked again, not quite grasping her point but enjoying the game nonetheless.

"Dog or cat, sweet or savory, I'm more into this, I'm more into that . . . It's bullshit! Why stop there? Are you more into tables or chairs?" Rosière said.

She tore the balloon from the pump and knotted the end with an expert maneuver. She was wearing a golden satin skirt suit that seemed to have been chosen with an after-party at the Moulin Rouge in mind. Her emerald eyeliner duplicated her green gaze, which was trained on the *capitaine*, challenging him for an answer. But it would take more than that to breach Merlot's defenses, accustomed as he was to holding forth from dawn till dusk. As for him, he was gleaming like a freshly minted coin, his bald pate buffed to perfection.

"Well, quite, my dear girl! Choice! Endless choice, just as I was saying."

Fed up, Rosière turned around to see Capestan.

"Not bad, hey?" she said with a sweeping gesture across the room and its party decorations. "Closed cases, a guilty man before the public prosecutor, new wallpaper . . . We thought—"

"We?"

Rosière smiled, pretending to be contrite before carrying on:

"'We' thought that was all worthy of a celebration—it's high time this *commissariat* popped some corks! What do you say?"

"'We' did a fantastic job. Who's invited?"

"Well, everyone from the squad. But I thought maybe you'd like to ask Buron yourself?"

"I'll call him."

Capestan retired to the window, her gaze lost on the toppling, higgledy-piggledy buildings of rue Saint-Denis. There was nothing in line about this street, which looked as if it could do with a trip to a good orthodontist. The *commissaire* chatted with Buron for a couple of minutes before hanging up.

Lebreton came and stood next to her, puffing away on a blue balloon.

"So, Valincourt?" he said between blows.

"Thanks to his signed confession, Buron was able to hand things straight to the public prosecutor's department," Capestan said. "None of our business anymore."

"Yeah," Dax shouted (Dax always shouted). "We nailed this case! Think about those goons back in the day who found zilch—in your face, *Crim*!"

"Well, it was Valincourt's case. It wasn't exactly in his interests to find the guilty party . . . ," Orsini pointed out, having wandered over to the group.

"Yeah, big deal," Dax said, still happy.

Hunched over the stereo, Lewitz put on a CD, letting the first few notes blare out before skipping to the next track with a confused look at the album cover. Évrard automatically twitched along to each note, stopping and starting with the DJ. She was making a face—something was bothering her. She came over to join in the conversation:

"I've been wondering . . . Why did Valincourt palm the Sauzelle case off on us? It was risky. He likes a gamble, that man."

"I'm going to check with Buron, but my guess is that the box marked CLOSED CASES might have taken a walk while Valincourt was away on holiday."

After another puff into his balloon, Lebreton gave it a look that indicated a clear intention to cut down on his smoking, then joined the conversation himself:

"The son?"

"Poor boy," Rosière said. "He must hate him."

"No," Capestan said in response. "Valincourt brought him up, and well, for twenty years. He thought he was acting out of a sense of duty, to keep his son safe. He plotted a course for him and stay focused on his objective, to the point of committing four murders. Gabriel can't hate him, he could never hate him. But he is in shock. This morning, he still wasn't angry or sad—just nothing. Completely stunned. Luckily for him, his fiancée hasn't once left his side."

A hint of sadness fell over the squad and each of them returned to their jobs.

Three hours later, the room was a scene of total chaos. Dax was constantly cranking up the music, with Orsini constantly cranking it down. Rosière and Merlot were sinking every bottle within reach, whereas Lebreton was carefully nurturing his beside his glass. Over in the corner, Torrez was sorting through the CDs. In the middle of a rock 'n' roll with Capestan, he had been delighted to sprain his own knee. Évrard and Lewitz were literally in a trance, having not left the dance floor for a single track, not even when Torrez insisted on playing his crooner classics. Capestan could make out Pilou in the kitchen nuzzling his water bowl manically against the wall, defying its antiskid rubber bottom and gouging a nick in the new paintwork. When he had finally had an elegant sufficiency, the dog trotted back to Rosière, water dripping from his chops as he went.

Capestan and Buron were standing side by side, propping up the buffet.

"So was it you who swiped Valincourt's file?" Capestan roared over the music.

"Yes," Buron said. "That failure was a stain on his career. I couldn't figure it out for the life of me."

"And how did you make the link with Guénan? Valincourt wasn't on that case."

"No, but he had just arrived at number 36 and he spent a lot of time hanging around there. A few years later, when he joined my team, his HR file came my way. I saw that he'd been living in Key West the same year as the accident. It was a coincidence, and a completely innocent soul would have mentioned it. On top of that, a few items from the case notes had gone missing . . ."

"Hold on, you suspected him of murder and then covered for him for twenty years?"

"No, not at all," Buron said, his tone more obsequious than necessary. "But I did think he'd been negligent. I took the creation of this squad as my chance to clear up the matter. Anyhow, Capestan, you suspected me at one point in this case . . ."

"No, not once," the *commissaire* retorted.

The force of her denial bordered on ridicule, and a broad smile played across the chief's lips. But another question was still nagging at her:

"Why didn't you bust him yourself?"

"I didn't want to bring down a fellow officer. I have a reputation to uphold."

"And you had no problem with me damaging mine?"

"Not really, no," he said, not ashamed in the least. "Tell me, Capestan. I received a speeding ticket for Brigadier Lewitz. Sixty miles per hour in a built-up area . . ."

"Yes, I'd be grateful if you could waive that for him—he doesn't have many points left."

". . . speeding on a Motocrotte?"

"No, those don't exist anymore—it was a street sweeper."

Rosière and Merlot's chatter reached them in dribs and drabs over the notes of Mika's "Relax":

". . . when it comes to the planet, animals, anything, I only buy organic, top-of-the-range . . ."

"All that's mighty costly, though . . ."

"As it should be! If rich people buy crappy stuff, too, you can't complain when that's the only thing available!"

"Indeed! But . . ."

"In our society, you vote every time you get your wallet out. Fuck the ballot box, it's the shopping cart that counts! Speaking of which," she said, holding out her glass.

As Merlot tipped a quarter of the bottle into her glass and a tenth onto the carpet, Lebreton chimed in:

"Take a trip around a couple of dictatorships and you'll see that the ballot box doesn't count for much there, either . . ."

"Still," Rosière said, with a nod to her vermilion Gigondas, "every time you drink, every time you eat, you vote!"

"Well, that makes you an exemplary citizen," Lebreton said, turning his shoulder on her.

"As for me, I . . . ," Merlot started, but he was interrupted by Lewitz, who was running all over the place yelling:

"I won, I won, I won! Three in a minute!"

With each syllable, a spray of cookie crumbs came spewing from his mouth. Rosière, incredulous, grabbed Évrard's arm as she walked past.

"He ate three *petits-beurres*?"

"No, they were sponge fingers, but he's so happy I can't face disqualifying him."

Capestan scooped up a cream cheese sandwich from the buffet, and Buron followed suit. She had to move aside to dodge a yellow balloon that was dropping to the ground from the ceiling.

"So," she said. "If I understand right, our squad was set up expressly to settle your personal scores."

The chief's basset hound eyes were heavy with sadness.

"No, this wasn't about 'scores.' Alexandre was my friend, you know. It was my duty to investigate him, but I couldn't bring myself to do it. Your squad is my halfway house, Capestan. A temporary solution. It's not as if I've created the 'Super Justice' league—you're just a third team, on the sidelines where you're beyond suspicion. Well put together, mind you," he added with a smile.

"You could have told it to me straight."

"Until now, I wasn't sure it would even work."

The balloon had found its way onto the dance floor, where it was bouncing merrily from officer to officer, each of them doing their best to spare it. Dax, stomping along to the beat, was digging into a bowl of candy. His jaw clenched as he bit into them, and he'd wince before going in again, intrigued. He offered one to Lewitz, with a shrug that suggested he found them weird but nice.

"It works, all right," Capestan confirmed. "And to keep the momentum going, I'm requesting at least one functioning car, as well as some respect and consideration."

"I'll see about the car."

"That's the most important thing," Capestan said, munching a goat cheese cracker.

Buron finished off his and wiped his hands on a paper napkin with little red hearts on it.

"I know you deserve better," he said. "But after all your misde-meanors, I had no choice. It was the only way out—"

"I couldn't be happier here, Buron," the *commissaire* said, looking at her squad.

Évrard, Dax, and Lewitz were tormenting the downstairs neigh-bors with their dance moves. Torrez was limping around, his arm still in its sling. Rosière was trying, in vain, to get Orsini drunk. And Merlot's snoring was competing with the music.

Lebreton met Capestan's eye and raised his glass toward her. She clinked him in return.

"This place suits me just fine," she said.

Lying at Rosière's feet, the edge of his lip flopped over her Louboutin, Pilou was stealthily keeping an eye on things, scoping out the surroundings with a keen muzzle. Wafts of charcuterie; tottering, happy humans . . . it was all very promising. A few scratches behind the ear and some *saucisson* were definitely in the cards.

Pilote stretched out a paw to embark on his hunt, but he felt his mistress's hand curtail his rump's upward trajectory. He sat back down, and with a flash of canine inspiration, looked up at the corpulent fellow next to Rosière on the sofa. The man grinned and handed him a *canapé* laden with *pâté*, which Pilou guzzled down in one gulp. Charity begins at home.

Thank you

My infinite thanks to all of the following for making this book possible and, in so doing, changing my life (nothing more, nothing less):

Stéfanie Delestré, my editor at Albin Michel, without whom I would not be able to say (over and over and over again) the words "my editor."

Patrick Raynal, the Grand Master of detective fiction, whose support for the squad has always been beyond incredible.

To everyone at Albin Michel, my French publishers, from the graphic designers and copy editors to the press team, reps, and big bosses, without whom my squad would be nothing more than a stack of paper for sale at my house.

My friends Marie La Fonta and Brigitte Lefebvre, for their kind and unswerving support.

Thank you to the following, without whom I would not be a professional writer, or at least not the same writer: Sylvie Overnoy, the ideal boss for the budding writer, especially as she is one herself; Sophie Bajos de Hérédia, for her belief in my (several) applications; the comic-in-chief Henri Pouradier Duteil; and Monsieur Simonet, my French teacher at Collège Jean-Marmoz.

For their good-hearted readings, rereadings, and re-rereadings, their constructive criticism, and their vigorous compliments, I could never thank the following enough: Anne-Isabelle Masfaraud (record holder for the number of readings, gold-medal winner for rooting out incoherence, pep-talk champion); Dominique Hénaff (top dog both for his unconditional support and his keen eye for detail); Patrick Hénaff, Marie-Thérèse Leclair, Pierre Hénaff, Brigitte Petit, Isabelle Alves, Chloé Szulzinger, and Marie-Ange Guillaume.

Jean-François Masfaraud, for his wonderful idea for the original French title, *Poulets grillés*.

Christophe Caupenne, former RAID *commandant*, for his help that was as kind as it was valuable; and Catherine Azzopardi, for her initiative and spontaneity in introducing us.

Antoine Caro and Lina Pinto, for their comments, encouragement, and the time they dedicated to reading my manuscript.

And finally, thank you to all the gangs of friends I've belonged to or still belong to, all of which were joyful enough to inspire me to create a whole new one. In order of appearance: my friends from Chevrollier, the people of Général-Plessier, my girlfriends from Verre à Soi, the Accessoire crew, the Coincoinche pioneers, the Lyon de Poche girls, my Cosmo colleagues, the lunchtime *pétanque* crowd, my fellow Perudo addicts, the Masfas from Marsac, and my dear family and friends from Sables-d'Olonne, who have been there from the start.

SOPHIE HÉNAFF

SOPHIE HÉNAFF is a journalist, author, and former Lyonnaise bar owner. She began her journalism career as a critic at *Lyon de Poche* before moving to Paris to write for *Cosmopolitan*, where she established her own humorous column, "La Cosmolite." *The Awkward Squad* is her first novel.

SAM GORDON is a literary translator from French and Spanish. His previous translations include works by Karim Miské, Timothée de Fombelle, and Annelise Heurtier.

About the Type

Typeset in Minion Pro Regular, 11.5/15 pt.

Minion Pro was designed for Adobe Systems by Robert Slimbach in 1990. Inspired by typefaces of the Renaissance, it is both easily readable and extremely functional without compromising its inherent beauty.

Typeset by Scribe Inc., Philadelphia, Pennsylvania.